Jailbait

Chris Albano

New Generation **Publishing**

Thank you for taking the time to read this book. I am humbled to have people read what I have written. I truly hope you enjoy it.

Chapter 1

Friday Night

As he came to and his head began to clear, Marcus Kelly lifted it and tried in vain to figure out where he was. His neck was sore from resting his chin on his chest while he was blacked out. He had no idea how long he had been sitting there. The room was spinning slightly but he was coherent enough to see that this was not a room but a cell.

A jail cell?

Then the smell hit him. The cell had a foreign but distinctive odor – it smelled like hopelessness in a port-a-potty. He turned to see that his elbow rested upon a disgusting toilet. He pulled away and his head swam just from moving. He had something in his system that was causing this buzz. What though?

He hauled himself up off the floor and grabbed the bars at the front of the cell for stability. Everything was grimy and cold. He could see very little as he scanned left and right as much as he could without getting dizzy again. This was the only cell in sight and he was the only unlucky guy occupying it. He resisted the urge to yell out and get somebody's attention because he did not know what would come his way if he did so.

He ran through the night's events that he could still remember. The hockey game, then the party, then fooling around in the car with Nicole, then driving home and feeling really screwed up. Then what? Police lights? Did I puke? His mouth certainly tasted as if he had. He looked down and saw a dark brown stain down his shirt.

Did somebody slip me something? Why did they bring me here? Did I hit somebody with the car? Do my parents know I am here? Do I need a lawyer?

He was in a total panic because he was confused, scared shitless and had no answers. As he was about to sit back down he caught a glimpse of a sign on the far wall.

What he could see in the dim light read:

YOU ARE NOW ENTERING VALLEY JAIL

Oh my God! The jail? Valley Jail? How? Why?

He gasped loudly and shuddered involuntarily like he was suddenly freezing cold. It was as if the evil that called Valley Jail its home had visibly passed into him as soon as he became aware of where he was.

Change was coming his way.

He stood staring at the sign with his mouth wide open and his eyes not blinking. He dropped his head in disbelief, resuming the position he had been in when he had awakened.

He had no clue how he got here or why. Is Nicole OK? Did I total the car? The last few hours were a blur of confusion as he tried to comprehend his current dilemma.

Why am I in jail?

He instinctively reached for his cell phone then cursed himself for being so silly to think they let him keep it in jail. There is no get-out-of-jail app, Marcus.

He did not anticipate a welcoming committee coming down to explain it all, either. This was not good. He began to pace like a caged animal. He also felt a strange stirring within his body, a feeling of a call to arms.

He was in the jail. What the fuck?

He leaned against the wall and slowly slid to the floor. He placed his head in his hands and held back an onslaught of sobs.

What did I do? Why am I here?

Chapter 2

The keys were the first sound Marcus heard as they jingled against the hip of whoever was coming around the corner. He had dozed off and was still groggy and under the influence of something. He sprung to his feet and had to fall into the bars to keep his balance as his sudden movement, coupled with the adrenaline rush from hearing the keys, almost made him fall flat on his face. He could get some answers now.

The jail guard saw the misstep from the shadows from which he had just emerged slightly and guffawed mockingly.

Marcus could not help but blurt out, "Why am I here?" It came out as a desperate plea for help.

"You are here because you fucked up bad," replied the guard as he dropped some papers on a desk that was barely visible to Marcus. "I ain't answering any more questions so don't fucking ask any. Matter of fact, I don't want to hear your fucking voice again, inmate!" He was riled up but giggling and whispering to himself, too.

Giggling?

Marcus was staring into the darkness where the voice was coming from and was in disbelief as the guard threw a jumpsuit at the bars and told Marcus to put it on. But first he had to be strip-searched. The guard laughed when he made Marcus spread his butt cheeks and Marcus almost fell headfirst into the toilet.

Marcus hurriedly put on the starched, bright orange XL jumpsuit. It was a good fit. He was now inmate #456-B5.

The guard then made Marcus stand for a photo in the cell. As Marcus tried to see his face the guard

7

snapped the picture, blinding Marcus with the flash. This guy did not want to be seen. Marcus heard the guard mumbling something about making sure it was official and by the book as he kept saying "just in case" over and over as he filled out some paperwork, sitting at the desk in the semi-darkness. He stapled the picture he had just taken to the papers.

Marcus was fighting to stay vigilant but his brain was not cooperating fully. His state of mind went from almost normal to nowhere near normal in the blink of an eye, but at least the mind-altered trips were becoming a little less intense. The downside of that was that Marcus was coming to grips with the fact that he was in a bright orange jumpsuit in Valley Jail and he had no idea why.

"Come on, Marcus Superstar. I got some people I so dearly want you to meet. One guy in particular, actually." The guard opened the cell door and stayed in the shadows as Marcus exited.

"You are going to be really popular in jail, Marcus," mocked the guard in a high-pitched, feminine voice just loud enough to be heard.

"Ready to meet the other campers, Superstar?"

Chapter 3

Jail is defined as a place where criminals are kept.

Kept. Put away. Held.

If it were really only that simple – criminals stored like books on a shelf for a pre-determined amount of time. Take them down, dust them off and send them on their way when their punishments were complete. Like a time out for a disobedient child, society hoped that a jail sentence would be all that was needed to rehabilitate the convicted.

There are many effective correctional facilities in this country. They are to be applauded as they overcome bureaucratic hurdles and work within their dwindling budgets to at least attempt to train or educate their inmates so they can reintegrate decent, able humans back into society.

Valley Jail was not one of those jails and it deserved no applause for its effort. You would boo Valley Jail lustily. Inmates exited this jail worse than when they arrived. Always. This jail and its inhabitants found the parts of inmates' brains that would accept the invitation to promote violence and dug in deep. This caused good people to do bad things and bad people to do horrendous things.

Fucking evil things.

All jails are horrible places, but Valley Jail was uniquely dreadful for a few distinct reasons.

First, any inmates from within the Massachusetts County Jail System who were not behaving and considered troublemakers were sent to Valley Jail. No trades of bad guys for bad guys. Just bad guys in, none sent out. The worst of the worst inmates housed in deplorable conditions in an overpopulated, outdated prison.

What could possibly go wrong?

Secondly, it was also the jail to which the local courts sent their scofflaws on a daily basis. Even non-violent offenders were among the vanloads of violators sent to Valley Jail from the courts. There were no alternatives in the area. Either release them or send them to Valley Jail, those were the choices.

Deadbeat Dads, small-time drug dealers, petty thieves and any other criminals who could not make bail, were all sent to Valley Jail. Judges figured that'd teach them a lesson. If they only knew the reality of what they had just done to many who did not deserve what they got once inside the jail.

Beatings. Rapes. Extortion.

Although on paper there existed a separation between the classifications of inmates within the jail, in reality that was not the case. All inmates were mixed into the same blocks due to lack of beds and funds. This provided the seasoned hunters within the inmate population with fresh victims almost every day. The lack of supervision was the last ingredient needed to really fuel this vicious fire.

New meat was a food group within the blocks and they were preyed upon without mercy – just malice.

Get somebody to put money in my canteen fund or I will kill you. Give me those cigarettes or I will fuck you up. Suck my dick, bitch.

Although the outside of the jail was frightening, you did not fully understand what made this jail so ghastly until you went inside and experienced it. It was then that the prison revealed itself to you like a doped-up flasher wearing nothing but a trench coat. Full on, unrestrained and as subtle as a sucker punch.

The putrid smell. The constant noise. The echoed shrieks. The disgusting filth. The asshole guards.

All who visited Valley Jail's inmates did so reluctantly. There were few repeat visitors. Most visitors to the jail thanked whatever God to which they prayed once they were outside the walls again and sucked in deep gulps of fresh air that had never been so sorely missed. The visitors, to whom brutality and depravity did not come naturally, felt violated by the assault the jail had made upon them – however brief their visit. The friends and relatives of the incarcerated promised they would write more letters instead of visiting if they, for some reason, were not able to ever come again.

Ever. Again. Ever.

There were many wives or mothers who visited their husbands or sons and did not recognize the men whom they had just seen. They would sit in stunned silence in their car in the jail's lot after the visit, blankly staring into space while trying to come to grips with the horrible changes happening to the man whom they had just been with but did not know any more.

The last feature that made Valley Jail unique was the feeling of the building itself having a devilish, spiritual occupancy. Most who spent time inside it believed the jail had an evil spirit living within its walls that over time had become one unified, powerful mixture of all whose souls returned to exact revenge. This spirit – this evil, if you will – was what brought out the worst in the men held there. It fed on bloodshed and violence and pushed the buttons necessary to bring it about as often as possible.

It was an angry motherfucker.

There was an undeniable presence, even to those who thought of evil spirits as hogwash. Those who chose to ignore the evil explained the change that occurred within the men held there as simply a matter of the animal instinct that exists in all men rearing its ugly head to survive.

Evil or no evil, the result was the same – carnage.

Juniper Valley, MA was a bucolic suburb of Boston with a horrible jail hidden in the woods. It was mostly ignored in the hope that it would either just go away or never be an issue. It was the place to which Valley parents threatened to send their kids when they were brats but otherwise it was mentioned very infrequently around the city. It was treated like an evil myth – they believed it existed but they didn't ever want to see it up close to prove its existence, nor taunt it by talking about it. It was referred to locally as "the jail," never worthy of being capitalized and never with Valley attached to it. The city went out of its way to detach itself from any connection with their unwanted inmate hotel.

From the outside the jail looked like a castle from a horror movie. It was a stone fortress built just after the Civil War. The material used in the making of the building did its part to add to the evil reputation, too. It was often said that the jail's walls were made of thick granite slabs so that what went on within the confines of this loathsome, scary place was contained and never noticed by society.

The location of the jail was chosen perfectly. The Juniper River surrounded it on three sides and created a formidable moat. Behind the jail was the quarry that was used when building the jail. The cliffs were steep and impossible to climb. So despite having no outside security details and only an eight-foot high fence topped with ordinary barbed wire, Valley Jail could boast of never allowing an escape to occur. That was one of the things the State Board of Corrections would point to when deciding if Valley Jail needed any attention or money. "Well, it has had no escapes." Therefore it never got updated or upgraded.

The guards who worked there were collectively considered to be a bunch of assholes by society – a society in which most of them failed or struggled. Many had been only one or two incidents away from being an inmate themselves. But within the walls life made sense for some of them, albeit in a warped way.

There was a group of Valley Corrections Officers (COs) at the jail who had worked there for twenty years or more. These old-timers were a beaten down lot counting the days to a pension. They were weary and did not give a shit. One less day to a pension was all they thought about as they entered and exited the jail mindlessly.

The most senior guys, the guys who really knew the jail and how to handle the dickhead inmates, instead were allowed to work as far away from the inmate population as they could. They sat among themselves in control rooms and offices and read newspapers while doing administrative work. They did not mentor any of the new, young guards. Seniority allowed them to coast and slack off. Their laziness and sloppiness in their jobs allowed the violence within the blocks to continue unabated. The blind eye theory had daily consequences, especially to the new arrivals from court.

The new, younger guards were eager to learn but had to do it the hard way and made many mistakes as they did so. The inmates knew they were young and nervous and took every advantage they could over the newbie COs.

Their social circle was almost exclusively their fellow guards and some local cops. They shot guns at the local ranges and then sat in shitty bars and drank and talked about the pieces of shit in the jail cells they had to put up with. Their occupation fostered high rates of divorce, alcoholism and drug use. They drank to forget. For many Valley Jail guards it was a pint of vodka on the way home, often heated by the defroster in the car being warmed up in the colder months.

It did take a different sort of guy to voluntarily report to a place where they were outnumbered five hundred to ten on a typical day. The guards at Valley were often spit upon, sworn at and threatened. Breaking up fights was a daily task. They saw horrible injuries. The risk of disease was ever-present and cigarette smoke thickly polluted the air they breathed inside.

Yet, most of these guys were perfect for this job. These were the guys to whom Jack Nicholson's character was referring when he spoke of the guys you wanted on "that wall" to protect the masses. The younger guys banded together and their bond, especially within the blocks during their shift, was strong and real. When a guard had to run into a block of over one hundred inmates to break up a fight in a cell he needed to not have to worry if the other guards were on their way, too.

You had to have some balls to show up to work in the blocks.

Their pay was not very good despite being unionized. Therefore, the temptation for a CO at the jail to turn into a "lugger" to earn more pay illegally was hard to resist for some. Lugging was the term used when a guard brought in contraband items for an inmate and was paid to do so. Drugs, phones, porn, cigarettes, pre-paid phone cards, batteries and some food items were among the most popular items lugged. A relative or friend of the inmate who provided the contraband at a hidden location outside of the jail also paid the CO. The only thing the CO had to do was get the items into the inmate's hands. It was easy to do once they overcame the guilt of the act.

These luggers were despised by the other COs and treated like lepers if discovered. The luggers could not usually stop once the money started flowing in. They ignored how badly compromised in their job this made them. The money was too good. There were only a few known luggers currently working at the jail.

That this jail was in such good structural shape despite having been built so long ago was a tribute to those who had built and designed it. It was built to last despite getting little to no maintenance or upkeep – perhaps the evil itself helped keep it standing. The spirit of the jail needed it to continue to operate so it could express itself in its most vulgar form. It had found a home and it had decorated.

The quirky, old construction gave the jail more nooks and crannies than an English muffin and the inmates knew all the places to go to be unobserved and do things that they did not want anybody to see. There was every bodily fluid imaginable on the floors of some of the most hidden places in the jail. The alleys and passageways absorbed the screams of terror from victims of beatings or sexual assaults well before they could be heard.

Fun place, huh? Ready to go inside?

Chapter 4

The jail's newest guest, Marcus Kelly, was a supremely talented high school athlete who had been written up in a story in the Boston Herald that day. He was still woozy from whatever was in his system as he walked from the holding cell with the same guard behind him. He heard none of the jail's background noise as his focus was on the pile of disgusting mattresses in the corner of the admittance area into which he had just been led.

What the fuck? Is this an elaborate prank? Are my parents in on it? Am I being Punk'd, like on MTV?

What a weird night, and it all happened so fast. He was still unsuccessfully attempting to think through what had transpired since Fish's party and he was bewildered by the situation in which he now found himself. The details were blurry because he was still buzzed but he knew he was coming down. Puking must have helped purge whatever it was from his system. He had been way more than just drunk though. How?

The chuckle of the chubby jail guard behind him startled him back to reality. Marcus had snuck a few glances at his captor and the guard looked vaguely familiar, but he could not focus on that right now.

"Pick out a mattress, inmate, this ain't the fucking Hilton Hotel." The mattress pile belonged in a town dump and should have been burned long ago.

Crusty, stained and stinky.

Since his first words to Marcus, the guard's tone had given off a hint of a guy who was thrilled to see Marcus in here. It was akin to a guy telling his wife he had just won the lottery but he was divorcing her sorry ass and she would not see a dime of his winnings.

Sick pleasure.

Why? How do I know this jerk? Are there cameras filming this? Is this going to be a funny story to tell? You got me, time to stop the game. I'll never drink again, I promise, where do I sign?

Marcus was petrified. He was nineteen, had just played a high school hockey game that evening and had gotten Nicole into his car at that party and then ... what?

What ... the ... fuck?

He almost broke down but each time he almost cried a new voice in his head held him together. This voice was nasty and meant business. Then that feeling would fade and he'd be back to almost crying again. He was not typically prone to cry but he really wanted to do just that. And suck his thumb. And scream for Mommy. He remained stoic on the outside but he was total mush on the inside.

This was real. He was in fucking jail. He had seen plenty of jail movies, he saw what went on in them – he was petrified. He had to stay silent, he kept telling himself, as he fought back tears.

"I'd pick one with fresh piss stains, probably drowned a few of the bugs," chuckled the portly but still formidable Corrections Officer. "You ain't a big hockey stud in here. Go ahead and cry, pussy," he hissed just behind Marcus's ear, getting some spit on his cheek.

What the fuck was going on? Does anybody know where I am? His waves of nausea had been replaced by waves of total, utter panic. He also occasionally felt brief moments of an unfamiliar boldness that had him momentarily welcoming the scent of violence the jail used as cologne, arousing an animal instinct in him. It felt better than being terrified but he seemed to have no

17

control over either one. His heart was hammering in his chest.

He wanted to turn around and ask what was happening but the guard behind him still gave him no hint that he was in a mood to provide Marcus with any information. Marcus also feared that if he opened his mouth he would begin bawling. Not just tears, either. He'd be doing the gasp-for-breath blubbering that chicks do in movies when they get dumped.

Marcus was listening to the new voice in his head telling him to keep his fucking mouth shut. It seemed to know what it was doing in here, much more so than Marcus did.

As the guard's head lingered just in back of his shoulder, Marcus fought the sudden instinct to come up with his elbow, as he had been trained to do, and knock this prick out. This guy was sloppy about spacing and right now Marcus unexpectedly did not give a shit about the trouble he would face if he dropped this guy.

It was almost like the switch he had to keep off every day to stay out of trouble and stay on the team had been turned on and there was a suppressed, built-up energy wanting to be released to seek out confrontation. He wisely chose to be calm but he found a part of himself intrigued by this new state of mind that was slowly creeping into his thoughts. It was purring in the background of his terror.

Let's finally get an answer to this question, Marcus. Can you kick ass? Or are you a fucking pussy, kiddo?

The guard snapped, "Let's go! Today!" and Marcus was back in terror mode. It did not take much.

Since they were all soiled, Marcus picked up the nearest mattress and recoiled when he saw the bugs scatter as he lifted it off the pile. He trudged off with the guard trailing behind him, whistling softly to himself. Marcus knew from suffering through his Dad's music it was Elvis. Elvis sucked. He had just yelled that to his Dad this morning at home. And now I am in the jail? He missed his Dad more than ever and felt weepy again. Does he know about this? Is he fighting to get me out?

Pull your shit together, kiddo.

As they neared the door to the main floor, the guard ordered Marcus to keep his eyes straight down on his toes. This guy was a self-important asshole, Marcus could already tell. He should've thrown the elbow and knocked him on his ass. But he was now dealing with a guy who had Marcus on his turf. Marcus had no idea what was going on and he felt like not pissing this guy off would probably be the right thing to do here.

As the guard opened the door, he whispered to Marcus, "I got you right where I fucking want you. Welcome to my jail. You have no idea what I got planned for you, Mr. Superstar."

The door to the main floor began to open and the muffled background noise slowly began to roar to life. The jail was now ready to fully expose itself to Marcus Kelly.

He was going to need that new voice in his head.

Chapter 5

Dan Baker was opening his gym at 6am sharp as usual. He was pleased that the Boston Herald was waiting at his doorstep. As a former Marine, he valued punctuality and responsibility. Those traits had helped Dan get to his gym at such an early time every morning for the last twenty years. He loved training and teaching fitness.

As he opened the door to his gym the swarm of early morning fitness nuts emerged from their idling cars in the parking lot. Some were here for early morning classes, others just getting in a pre-work sweat. Many would be back after work to train again, too. Dan's gym had its share of zealots, Dan among them. He had already run on the treadmill at home this morning.

Dan held the door open as the members marched by in various states of waking up, many of them reading texts or emails as they walked in. Dan loved the ritual of exchanging a series of fist bumps, head nods and hellos from his regular clients as they all greeted him in their unique ways. He liked this gig, always had.

His gym had many different fitness areas and training rooms, but it also had a renowned boxing and martial arts section where Dan himself taught along with a group of black belts and other high level instructors. These classes were becoming more and more popular, much to Dan's delight. That was Dan's passion, teaching the finer art of kicking ass. Baker's Gym was a highly regarded boxing facility.

There were many very talented students and instructors at this gym and Dan liked and respected his fellow instructors. They fought hard and sparred often, but they shared their knowledge and worked to teach their students to the highest level they could. The message he conveyed to his students was that learning to fight and to defend yourself were no different than learning to swim. Both were great workouts that might one day save your life.

As he unlocked his office door he turned the paper to the back page and saw in the corner a picture of Marcus Kelly.

What had Marcus done now?

Dan grabbed a seat and began to read the article. It was entitled "Mr. Superstar" and was a tribute to Marcus, his high school hockey career and his bright future. Marcus was within a few goals and points of breaking several records held by some serious legends of the Valley area. He could break them in today's game.

The article speculated whether Marcus would be going to college or signing an NHL contract. As Dan read and saw the picture of Marcus when he was much younger he began to think about the first time he had met Marcus.

Marcus was ten years old when he first came into Dan's gym. He and his Dad had set up an appointment to meet Dan. As he ushered them into his office, Dan listened as he learned through a surprisingly mature Marcus that he and his Dad, Aaron, were Bruins' fans and Marcus was very serious about playing in the NHL in the future.

Kid, you're a runt, Dan remembered thinking. But Marcus was not abrasive or cocky when he spoke so Dan listened on.

Aaron interrupted his exuberant son and explained, "Mr. Baker, my son Marcus is certain he will be in the NHL some day." Aaron winked at Dan to let him know that although his son was certain of his NHL future

Aaron was not a fool, indicating he knew the odds were not good.

Marcus impatiently but politely interrupted, "Dad, may I do it? Mr. Baker, I want to be in the NHL. To be in the NHL you have to be able score goals and fight. I mean, even Bobby Orr had to drop his gloves, right? Will you be able to teach me how to fight?" Marcus held up his hands in classic boxing position.

Dan already liked the kid and he saw a good Dad in Aaron. Aaron had a hopeful expression on his face as he made eye contact with Dan.

"I will tell you what I can do," Dan said. "But I will need your full commitment, son."

Marcus nodded and saluted enthusiastically. The former Marine smiled on the inside, careful to keep his military persona while he told his new pupil the rules of engagement.

"I am a hockey fan myself, Marcus. I love the Bruins games, too. I watched them fight then and I see how they fight now. I can tell the ones who got the training and the ones who get their butts kicked because they never took the step that you took by coming in here today. Good for you, and you, Dad." Aaron liked this guy.

"But I take you at your word, if playing in the NHL is the goal then I will do my part to make sure that even if you fall short of that goal you will still be able to kick butt at an NHL level. Deal?" They high-fived and Aaron looked relieved as they shook hands.

Marcus looked at Dan and said, "I will be in the NHL someday, Mr. Baker."

Baker laughed heartily; what a kid this was.

They worked out a training schedule right then and there and Marcus was Baker's most loyal customer. They worked and fought hard over the last ten years.

Baker also advised Marcus on the principles of lifting weights and nutrition and guided Marcus in those areas.

Marcus became a fitness and nutrition junkie.

Many of Baker's students would burn out and not come any more or lose the motivation and come less frequently and work at a lower level. Marcus had done the opposite, every workout built on the last. Push me, Mr. Baker. Come on!

Baker had Marcus spar often and they worked on basic skills to exhaustion. Marcus took to boxing like a fish to water and showed he could take a punch when Baker put him in against much older and bigger sparring partners as he improved. Eventually Marcus turned the tables as he grew and now there were very few in the whole gym that could spar at the level Marcus had attained.

Marcus had recently expressed to Baker his frustration and concern that he had never really fought yet. Sure, there were some scuffles on the ice but he was protected with layers of equipment and there were refs who broke up the fights quickly.

Marcus was frustrated because his hockey practices led to hockey games, where he could use his skills at game speed. With fighting he had never been in a street fight and Baker had not allowed Marcus to enter any boxing or martial arts tournaments for fear of getting hurt and keeping him off the ice. Baker knew Marcus would compete for the title at every tournament anyhow, the kid was that good. Even when he was a runt.

He was working on alleviating the self-doubt that had appeared. During recent workouts Baker had been trying to impress upon Marcus that he need not be concerned about never having fought if the need to fight arises. Flush any self-doubt down the crapper, son. Trust me, Marcus. You will be fine. It was the other guy in the fight who should be worried.

Baker preached patience and pleaded with Marcus to use restraint when confronted both on and off the ice. With his strength and training he was a weapon and needed to be sure there was no way out of a fight before he got into one. Baker trusted Marcus to observe these rules and stay out of trouble and maybe a courtroom or, God forbid, the jail. He had too much to lose.

Dan was going to miss Marcus when he left the Valley to chase his dream. He had come to him as a boy and would leave as a very different man. He had grown physically and mentally in leaps and bounds. And boy did he grow. Baker had never seen hard work pay off in such a big way. The kid had earned every pound of muscle, too. His punches now penetrated the thick padding Baker wore around his torso during their training.

Dan chuckled and thought back to that scrawny kid predicting pro hockey for himself. And his supportive father willing to make such a commitment to his son at a young age like that? And it looked like the kid was right.

Chapter 6

Friday Night • the jail

The heavily armored door opened and the muffled growl of the jail turned into a violent, engulfing roar. It was a visual and audible shock to Marcus so he had to blink quickly to adjust to what he was seeing and hearing. He could barely hear himself think as his senses were assaulted. It was not a singular loud noise that made him wince upon hearing it; the cacophony consisted of a thousand different sounds blended into one that had his still fuzzy brain scrambling to understand where he was.

He was overwhelmed and felt extremely vulnerable, more so than he had ever felt before. He shifted the mattress on his shoulder as if it weighed a thousand pounds due to his suddenly weak knees.

The jail had made its formal introduction to its newest guest and it had the usual effect as Marcus fought as hard as he could against bawling and collapsing. He tentatively stepped forward as if he were on the edge of an imagined cliff. There was so much for him to look at. He was reminded of going to the Planetarium at the Museum of Science in Boston for the first time as a kid and being bombarded by the hundreds of stars on the black ceiling, not knowing where to look first.

The main room of the jail, about the size of a basketball court, was dark and cavernous. Due to the storm the only light tonight was from the sparse emergency lights. The regular lights were suspended in the semi-dark like bats in a cave hanging from the centuries old, fifty-foot ceiling.

The fear continued to come at Marcus like waves on a beach, crashing into his brain as if in a hurricane.

Then he would have moments of boldness that did not last, either. It was tiring.

The room amplified the acoustics by not allowing sound to escape through the thick stone, causing echoes to careen back and forth like a tennis match. The rare occurrence of a power outage had agitated the masses and they were now alert – like a napping dog snapping to attention when the doorbell rings.

Some of the inmates in their cells could see the new guy being led into the jail, which caused many taunts and threats to be yelled toward Marcus. Combined they all blended into the singular noise the jail produced and went unnoticed by him. Marcus had stopped to take it all in and was again on the verge of tears.

Jail? Me? How?

He was about to finally burst into tears when the guard shoved him and told him to keep fucking moving. The surge of newly found anger reared its head again from being touched by this fat prick and overwhelmed the fear. Marcus was learning to like this feeling. Touch me again, asshole. He had the sudden urge to kick backwards and hyperextend this jerk's knee. Then he'd knee the guy in the face and make a run for it. He quickly dismissed the idea but was picturing the guard writhing in pain.

The evil of Valley Jail was going to work quickly on Marcus. Virgin territory. And what an arsenal of weapons it had at its disposal.

Marcus could not help but still think that this was a prank and somebody was going to come rescue him and tell him not to drink and drive ever again. This would be a great time to end this cruel joke. He thought he had reached full terror alert until, during a rare break in the overall noise, Marcus heard a raspy, unseen voice cry out.

"New meat!"

It echoed in the suddenly almost silent chamber. The jail temporarily hushed as if it was digesting what it had just heard. The jeers and taunts recommenced and Marcus heard various "in the ass" and "sucking my dick" proposals being shouted at him now.

The guard behind him was obviously enjoying putting him through this as he chuckled and pointed Marcus toward his hell on earth.

Chapter 7

Dorothy "Dottie" Cataldo was always in a good mood when either of two things occurred – a Valley High hockey game was scheduled for later that day or if there was a storm coming. Today she was getting both, but at this time they were not sure if the storm would hit their area severely or just miss.

As a precaution they had moved tonight's high school hockey game from 7pm to 5pm to be safe. Heaven forbid they cancel a Friday night hockey game between these two rivals. It was versus St. Mary's tonight, the big one. Even Dottie knew how important this game was.

I will have to bake early today to make sure I have enough goodies for the fans, she thought to herself. Everybody in town seemed to be affiliated with sports at Valley High School. Dottie ran the bake sale table and also helped Sally with the 50/50 raffle booth at the home games for the Valley High hockey team. She had been doing this for years and loved being what she considered an important part of the team. She was able to combine her love of baking with her love of hockey and she got a team jacket for doing it, which she currently was proudly wearing. With the matching cap, mittens and scarf she had knitted in the Valley High colors, of course.

There were some years when the team was horrible but the past few years they had Marcus Kelly playing for them and the team had been fantastic, this year especially.

That Marcus was something else!

It was not so chilly for February in the Valley that morning and Dottie was taking her Jack Russell terrier

28

out for a morning walk. Dottie and "DH" were on their normal route, making a loop around the surrounding neighborhoods that she had figured to be about three miles. DH was small and that seemed like enough of a distance for him, and Dottie was almost sixty now (she heard often that she looked twenty years younger, thank you very much) and the walk was just right for her.

Most people assumed DH was short for "designated hitter," as her late husband was a huge Red Sox fan and defended the DH like few others, "Why should a pitcher hit when you can have a guy like Big Papi bat for him instead?"

But DH was actually short for what she had called her husband – Dear Harry. She missed him so much since he had died from cancer that she decided to get this dog as a companion. DH was a great little guy but she still missed her Dear Harry.

As she walked up the street she saw Marcus Kelly coming out of his house with his hockey sticks in his hand on his way to school. Dottie blushed like a schoolgirl at this ruggedly handsome and muscular teenager and she was ashamed of herself but excited about seeing Mr. Superstar on the day of the big game.

Although he does need a haircut and shave badly, she thought. Those hockey boys looked sloppy with their hippie hair and scraggly beards. She heard them call it their "playoff look." She did not like it.

She gave Marcus a huge wave. This kid was going to be a hockey star in the future and she could always brag that she knew him since childhood. Stop waving, you silly old gal, she thought as her arm kept waving, seemingly on its own.

Chapter 8

Marcus emerged from the shower that Friday morning invigorated and ready for the game later that day. He heard his Dad down in the cellar running on the treadmill listening to Elvis with the volume turned up high so he could hear it while he ran. Marcus thought it was great that his Dad still ran every morning. Unlike most of his buddies, Marcus had a pretty cool Dad except for his music. His Dad loved Elvis.

He screamed, "Elvis sucks!" at the floor, mocking his Dad's favorite singer. Marcus then stomped on the floor knowing it was right above where his Dad was running.

Marcus could be described as having been a mischievously funny guy most of his life. He loved to laugh and bust balls and that made him a natural character and leader in a hockey locker room. Even upon becoming captain of the team the past two years Marcus was still a peer and continued to prank with the boys. He was adored by his teammates and they knew they were playing with a special player and just an overall good guy.

As he was toweling off, a thousand thoughts were running through his head. Marcus attributed these to game-day jitters.

He was struggling with drinking. He liked it because he was with the boys and laughing and listening to music up at the Quarry behind the school while they drank Busch beer in a can. He also liked it when the girls who were also drinking would show up later at night. It was fun and everybody was there and he was having fun with Kaleigh when they were both drinking,

30

but he knew that drinking was the only thing he was doing that was not good for his future.

Hockey had a sudden urgency to it because even though his grades were OK he never really did the work. Each class was getting harder for him as he focused on hockey and training while his classmates all focused on their SAT scores and college applications. He needed to have a good tournament in the next few weeks. He wanted to get drafted in the first round of this summer's NHL Draft, his lifelong dream.

He was not ready to give up drinking beer, though. He was having inner-turmoil about it but a good buzz wasn't the end of his world either. He loved his time with his teammates after games, drinking beers and re-living the game they had just played. Good times, indeed. Those were his best memories of high school, actually.

He stopped to flex in the mirror now that the steam from his shower had faded.

He played no organized sports other than hockey while growing up. The football coach pleaded for him to play. The baseball coach drooled when Marcus hit the ball in the coach's gym class. Nope.

Skate. Fight. Lift. Repeat.

He was going to the NHL or die trying. He lived, breathed and ate for hockey.

His parents were great about his passion and saw the drive their son had very early on in his hockey career. He was determined and strong-willed and stayed that way. The financial sacrifices they made for their son's hockey life were deemed investments in a good kid. They considered their trips for hockey tournaments their vacations and made the best of it. They had no regrets.

He flexed again as he brushed his teeth.

Marcus had an enormous growth spurt in high school when he grew from 5' 9", 165 lbs as a freshman to his current 6' 2", 205 lbs as a senior. He was impressively chiseled due to his dedication to training and eating right. Couple that physique with the training he got in the ring at Baker's Gym and Marcus Kelly had become one badass motherfucker. At least Baker assumed that – Marcus wished he shared his confidence. Being untested in a real fight gnawed at Marcus a bit. Some doubt had crept in about that. Whether that was his way of trying to goad himself into a fight or not was the real issue. Was hiding behind the restraint he was begged to use really his way of being scared to fight?

Too much to lose – he heard that often. Too often.

He had sparred enough to know what he could do but he also realized he was, in simple terms, a good guy. He was not inherently a bully or a trouble seeker. He liked to have a good time and would rather laugh than argue or fight. But he was untested. Could he turn it on and fuck somebody up for real?

He gave the mirror another flex. Veins popped in his arms. His mother thought that was gross. The girls at school sure didn't.

He treated his body like a temple, other than drinking beers and his relationship with Mom's brownies. When he drank Marcus was usually careful to only get buzzed, not hammered, and just beer, no booze. Most of his buddies drank way more often than he did and they got hammered when they drank. He had noticed a lot of his buddies were smoking pot now, too. He had zero interest in that. He was pretty sure his good buddy Fowler was smoking now, too.

Stupid habit.

As he brushed his teeth he suddenly remembered a test he had later that day for which had not studied. Oh well. Not the first time he had forgotten to study and his science teacher graded Marcus pretty easily. While it went mostly unsaid between his parents and Marcus, they knew that academics were not going to be the road to success for him. Marcus was certainly not dumb, and his folks did have a college savings account for him. But if he could reach his goal of playing pro hockey then he could afford to pay financial guys and personal assistants to handle things for him. He wanted to reach the pinnacle of his sport badly. He was specializing. He was being allowed to coast in school and he took advantage of it.

It was not like he was lazy. He busted his ass. The alarm went off daily at 5:30am and Marcus would put his music on and lift hard and hit the heavy bag every morning before school. He'd make puddles of sweat on the cement floor of the cellar, especially if he was hung over. That was happening more and more and causing Marcus this internal strife as he considered again if he should stop drinking. It would kill whatever social life he had, which was already very limited because of hockey and training. He had a few friends who did not drink but most of his buddies and just about all of the hockey team drank. The guys who would tag along but not drink just made everybody else feel bad about their drinking.

Nobody really ever got in trouble because of drinking, either. They stayed at the Quarry mostly, caused no problems and chose the least drunk guy to drive. The few times the cops did pull one of the guys over they would either follow them home or drive them home. No big deal, nobody ever ended up in an accident or in the jail. The cops seemed to look the other way every time a Valley hockey player was caught drinking or driving drunk.

In the cellar of their house, Aaron Kelly heard the thump of his son's stomp just above his head and laughed as he sweated out his five miles. Each day that passed he began to despise running just a bit more than the previous day. Chronically achy knees, sudden left hip pain out of nowhere, things jiggling just a bit more and the whine of the treadmill engine were all getting more and more annoying.

Aaron was a runner and had been since high school. He knew that his body needed it now more than ever as he aged, but that did not make him like it any more. Aaron had never been a big lifter. But he saw that Marcus really wanted to take hockey to a very high level early in his life so Aaron did everything a Dad could to help. Dan Baker from the gym also helped him with equipment choices and workouts.

Years ago Aaron had read about a football prodigy named Todd Marinovich and how his father had ridden him hard and trained him non-stop when he was still a kid and never let go and blew it. The kid revolted and the story ended badly with drugs and suicide attempts and a busted father–son relationship. Aaron vowed he would never be that parent, but then he never had to be.

Marcus was the kid that got up on his own for the 5am departure for the long rides to the hockey games and he made his own breakfast. It was usually a muddy protein drink that still disgusted Aaron to this day. The results of the protein-rich breakfasts usually forced them to drive to the rink with the windows open in the winter to let the stink from Marcus get sucked out. Marcus would laugh and laugh. Aaron would clean the travel mug Marcus drank his sludge from and he would need a chisel if it had dried on. His protein bars looked like cement with chocolate chips to Aaron. But it had paid off for Marcus. Big time.

Marcus would be twenty this summer, his folks had held him back a year in kindergarten in the hope that Marcus would grow a bit because he was so much smaller than the other kids back then.

The plan, um, worked? His son was a block of granite now.

Directly above Aaron, Marcus sang a Ludacris song, which was playing on his iPhone, into his hairbrush. He then examined his ten-day-old playoff beard, which he had to do daily to pluck any scraggly outcasts – for the chicks, of course. He put on yesterday's jeans and a gray Boston Bruins shirt, his lucky game day shirt.

He flexed one more time as he shook the water from his long hair and went to the kitchen and ate a protein bar while swilling down his vitamins standing at the kitchen counter. He saw the brochure for the cruise his parents were leaving for right after his game tonight on the counter, his crumbs gently falling on the bikini-clad gal that caught his eye. They never showed the really fat fuckers who went on cruises for the unlimited food.

His folks were usually kind of tight with money and he knew his hockey was quite expensive. But lately they had been spending a bit on items like Dad's Lexus and this cruise. Good for them, they deserve it. Marcus hoped he would be able to do nice things for his folks with the money from the NHL someday.

He checked the fridge to see if his Mom had cooked for him for while they were going to be away. Sure enough, there were half a dozen foil-wrapped plates with notes describing each dish and how to prepare it, all signed with Mom's familiar smiley face. He loved his Mom and they shared a great relationship. Especially when she made brownies, which he saw on the counter as he closed the fridge. Marcus followed a strict diet ninety-five percent of the time.

The other five percent of the time was affected by either of two things. First, if he had a buzz and was out with the boys he'd go to get a late night roast beef sandwich, pizza or Chinese food.

The only food that got Marcus off his eating plan without beers involved was Mom's brownies. They were kryptonite to Marcus. He had no willpower over them and did not need to be buzzed to indulge when his Mom made them.

He made a mental note to chow some of these tonight as he fought the urge to eat half a dozen right now.

Can't. Game. Big game, to boot.

He checked his cell and saw that the coach had sent out a team text confirming the game was now on for 5pm. Marcus was getting pumped up for the game. That it was his last conference varsity high school game had not yet sunk in. There was another text from his friend Fowler, the goalie on the hockey team.

<st marys all fairies NO tourney for them!>

Marcus texted back:

<no tourney for them if you can maybe make a few saves tonight?>

He grabbed his three identically taped hockey sticks on his way out the door. He had re-taped them the night before, his ritual, and grabbed the keys to his rusty old Honda and headed out. He yelled goodbye to his folks, he'd see them later.

As he got to his car he saw the bake sale lady from the hockey games out walking her dog and waving like a lunatic at him. She was dressed in all blue and gold, even her earrings.

Valley High School Bulldog colors.

He smiled and waved back when she wished him a good game. It would amaze an outsider just how much this town loved its Valley High teams, especially when it had a superstar, can't-miss, future pro like Marcus Kelly on the team. Marcus liked the adulation and had gotten used to it. He had adults treating him with awe and youth hockey kids asking him for autographs at his games and practices. They would call him Mr. Kelly and tell him he was their favorite hockey player. Not a Boston Bruin. Marcus Kelly was their favorite. His buddies busted his balls about that as often as they could and Marcus would usually reply with a fat mama joke.

He thought the bake sale lady might dislocate her shoulder by waving so much at him. "Crazy bake sale bee-yatch," he chuckled under his breath to himself as he fumbled for his trunk key. As he opened the trunk of the car he had to move aside a few empty cans of Busch beer from the other night that he and Fowler had guzzled after practice.

They had almost gotten into a fight that night. Two idiots were sitting on Fowler's car when they were leaving the pizza place and laughed when Fowler asked them to get off his car. They did not move, daring the boys to do something. They were older than Marcus, but Marcus would have been able to strike and probably immobilize both of them before they knew what hit them.

Or maybe he'd get his ass kicked.

He had a feeling he was going to have to find this out soon. It was bugging him more than he'd admit.

These two guys taunted Marcus and Fowler and they just took it, they had to. Hockey was too important. Marcus heard Baker's voice in his head as he showed restraint. Fowler had been hoping this would be the chance he could finally see his buddy in action as he beat the shit out of these assholes.

Ah, the sacrifices.

Marcus then noticed a full Busch can among the empties in the trunk and hid it under a towel. Marcus liked Busch.

Chapter 9

Jamie Hickey was hung over badly and still coughing up a bong hit as he anxiously dialed the phone. Wake-and-bake was his hangover cure as it had been a rough night. He dialed the police station from his parents' cellar – which he still called home. He reminded himself – sound sick, sound sick.

"Hello, Valley Police Department, this is Chief Russell, this line is recorded, what is your emergency?"

Shit, Russell never answered the phone at the PD. Jamie was expecting one of the switchboard ladies. And Russell is the Chief now?

Since when?

"Hey Chief uh Captain, it's Jamie Hickey. Um, look, I got hit with this flu going around. I don't think I can make it in today."

"Hickey, why are you calling on the 911 line?"

Jamie had forgotten to dial the other number, actually. He forgot a lot of things. Limited bandwidth, he'd joke. To say Jamie was forgetful would be a kind way of labeling Jamie's short-term memory affliction.

Early morning bong hits did not help.

Jamie was twenty two and could be best described as somebody with whom you went to school your whole life but at future reunions nobody had any recollection of him at all. Dull was a word that summed up Jamie pretty well.

"Also, Hickey, if we were not so shorthanded right now I'd suspend your ass in a heartbeat. You got some nerve. What flu going around, you dumb jackass? I got a dozen cops out legitimately already and we got a storm coming tonight. Even though you are just a secretary, sorry, an auxiliary officer, I need you in here tonight to help on the dispatch. Is that understood, idiot?"

"Uh, OK Captain Russell Chief, sir…see you then I guess? Sorry." Jamie hung up quickly. That went well. Fucking prick! Jamie hated Russell and vice versa.

Jamie's uncle had gotten him hired at the PD, but his uncle's connection was with Chief O'Reilly and he had just retired. O'Reilly was a good guy, he was easy going and Jamie liked him. Russell was a douche.

For the first year he liked the police gig, it was cool and he felt powerful even though he was more of a secretary than a cop. But he liked the uniform and the supposed power it conveyed.

He had no gun and worked mostly crappy office shifts as dispatch assistant, but he liked the money it paid. He sucked at it, as Russell liked to remind him all the time. He just had no eye for detail and often made administrative mistakes that sent people to the wrong places or caused the PD embarrassment. Jamie had no desire to ever become a real cop, either.

He wished his uncle had different connections. But at least now he had a similar job to his fairly new buddy, Rat, the jail guard. They hung out often and partied hard, and Rat looked at him differently since Jamie had gotten on the force.

Jamie loved to smoke pot and he had a great connection now with these scary gang guys, The Boyz, that Rat was getting it from. The Boyz were a Latino gang that was getting incredibly good marijuana and selling much of it in Juniper Valley, MA.

The Boyz also controlled Valley Jail from the inside.

Jamie was planning on quitting the Valley PD soon enough to go to California to become a director and make video documentaries as soon as he could. He was a video buff and was quietly collecting a vast array of equipment. He and Rat had been working a second job together that lately had begun to really pay off for them.

He began to daydream about his future when the sound of his mother's yelling telling him to stop burning incense in the cellar snapped him back to his dull reality. He did another bong hit and laughed as he thought of how stoned he'd still be while in his police uniform later that day.

Chapter 10

Friday Morning • Harrison Residence

Tony Harrison smiled as his daughter Nicole came out of her bedroom for school dressed with her Valley High School hockey cheerleader uniform on. As a father he was so proud of her being a cheerleader, she was a part of something positive and he hoped that would help her to set some goals and go to college and not give up on life. She was the only sophomore who had made the squad and she was proud of that.

Tony wanted to throw a tarp over his recently developed daughter, too. The uniform was cut way too tight and short and he was not thrilled with the way some of the fans at the game seemed more interested in the cheerleaders than in the hockey game – especially the fathers.

Fucking perverts.

Tony was a laid-off, divorced father raising a teenaged daughter on his own and he was struggling. Nicole was the spitting image of his ex-wife so he was constantly reminded of that witch. She had run off with one of her spin class instructors two years ago and they had not heard from her since. That had been tough on Nicole.

Tony knew Nicole was partying a bit lately (like her Mom) and did not know the best way to approach her about it. He had found shot glasses and beer bottle caps in her backpack when he cleaned it out for her. He left them in there. What do I say?

They bickered often of late and he was in no mood to fight, he was saving his energy for the storm arriving later that night. He used to go to the hockey games but now that his daughter was parading around in a stripper's outfit he felt uncomfortable there.

"You look cute as usual, sweetie," he lied. She looked like she was in college. Cute was not the word.

"Thanks Dad, I am sleeping over Trish's after the party tonight, OK?" She had a big bag slung over her shoulder. The one with the shot glasses, actually.

"As long as her parents are home, sure. And keep your cell on."

She gave him a smooch on the cheek and held up her phone, grabbed a granola bar and headed out the door to an SUV full of cheerleaders waiting to drive her to school. He grabbed the Herald and sat back down for another day of shitty daytime TV while looking for a non-existent job somewhere.

He absentmindedly thumbed through the morning paper, pausing to read about Marcus Kelly. Nice kid who grew up around the corner. Tony was proud of the kid, good for him. The few times Tony had seen Marcus play hockey there were at least two or three plays he'd make that would amaze Tony. This kid could play and he was big now. He seemed nice enough, too. Why can't Nicole find a guy like that?

Tony's thoughts went back to Nicole. She was the only thing he lived for now that his wife had fled, that fucking bitch. He never loved her and she never wanted marriage, but the pregnancy had forced a shotgun wedding. She was gorgeous; that did not hurt. Nicole had gotten her Mom's looks for sure. Beautiful brunettes with bodies that did not quit.

Wonderful.

He never could have done to Nicole what his ex-wife had done to her by just taking off and never saying goodbye to their kid or him. He was bitter, he could not imagine what Nicole felt; she actually at one point in her life had loved her Mom.

Used to, anyhow. They had not talked about his ex-wife much lately. They had not talked much at all,

43

actually. If he could just get her through high school in one piece and not pregnant he would consider it a job well done. He just had to guide her through this part of her life. He was thrilled she now had such a great bunch of gals to serve as role models for her on the cheering squad.

He opened a Diet Coke and absentmindedly watched cartoons with the Help Wanted section open on his lap.

Chapter 11

Pierre Gauthier, nicknamed Goat to everybody big and small, was in his office at the usual 7am arrival time, cup of coffee in hand. As the head coach of the Valley High Bulldogs hockey team the last nineteen years his butterflies were usually under control on game day, but he knew this one was different.

This was the last regular season game for the best player Goat had ever coached, Marcus Kelly. It was also against St. Mary's, their intra-city rival. And they had a pep rally later that day.

Coach Gauthier loved hockey and he loved coaching hockey in da Valley, as he would say. He was French-Canadian and had been quite a good hockey player himself, carving out a decent minor league career.

He made it as far as a few steps below the NHL when a knee injury, coupled with the realization that he was just a bit smaller and slower as he progressed through each league, derailed his dreams. But he had been a player/coach on every team on which he played. He loved the game and thus a transition to coaching was an easy decision. His last stop in his playing career was nearby to Juniper Valley where, coincidentally, there was a need for a high school hockey coach. Goat had not looked back since.

Although the team had struggled for many years, the administration knew that Goat was a great coach and his job was never really threatened by the team's mediocrity. Goat sensed this and took advantage of the power he had earned when he needed it. He played the political game like the veteran coach that he was. This was Massachusetts Division One hockey, the big time.

He did what was needed to do to get the best team on the ice, and what a team he had this year.

He knew he had a busy day ahead so game preparations had taken place last night with his assistant coach, Bobby "Boots" Balboni. Boots, twenty-eight, was a player for Goat a decade ago and went on to a decent college career. Goat hired him after Boots drank himself out of lower level pro hockey in Europe and then fizzled out in the mortgage world when he came back to the Valley.

Boots worked well with the kids and was especially good with the goalies, from what Goat had seen. Goat had talked to the Athletic Director and gotten Boots a meager salary but a steady job and the opportunity to learn from Goat.

Because of the coming storm, Goat had needed to plead with the headmaster at St. Mary's to not postpone tonight's game. Valley High's Principal, Thompson, was a friend to both the coach and the hockey program, so his support to play the game was a given.

The storm that was coming their way tonight was not typical for February in New England. It was going to be warmer than usual so this potential Nor'easter was going to be complicated and it was due to come in around 8pm. By moving the game to 5pm they could be out of the rink before any storm hit. There was even a chance it could just be all rain. That was the argument that Goat had used over and over yesterday morning.

"If dis storm is just da rain den we all have da egg on our face," was how he put it and when he heard the laughs on the conference call he knew he had won. His cute French accent was a weapon and he knew it.

But the real reason Goat was so insistent to play tonight was that there would be dozens of scouts in the stands, pro and college, to see Marcus play. Goat had been fielding call after call about Marcus from pro scouts recently, so he did not want the game canceled and have the scouts in town for nothing. Although most of the scouts had already marked Marcus as a sure thing, Goat respected them as fellow hockey guys and did not want them to all waste the trip to the Valley if there ended up being no game due to weather. He may need them for other students in the future.

Because Goat had come so close to the NHL and gotten help along the way, he wanted to do all he could to see that Marcus got his shot at the big time, too. Marcus was a huge story in the Valley and Goat loved the kid. Plus, Marcus was light years better than Goat had been.

After their strategy meeting last night, Goat and Boots had been out with some of the scouts in town. Like the hockey knuckleheads they were, they tied one on and had a bit too much fun. Goat knew his limits and was only a bit groggy this morning. Boots was lit up last night but he told good stories and made everybody laugh, as usual. He was not in the office yet this morning.

Last night the scouts were asking Goat if Marcus had decided between pro and college. Goat told them he had no idea, but he knew. He and Marcus often talked about it. Goat felt it was his obligation to steer Marcus to college. Many college grads played in the NHL, and if the NHL did not work out he'd still have the college degree. But Goat's heart was not into it, he knew what Marcus wanted and Marcus had tuned him out on the college talk. School was not for Marcus. Marcus Kelly would get drafted and he would go pro.

Goat was worried about Boots and his partying. Goat sensed that Boots was doing more than making phone calls on his frequent trips outside last night, but he had too many things to do today ahead of the game to worry about that right now.

Chapter 12

Captain John Russell was not quite yet the Police Chief of Juniper Valley PD. But he liked the sound of it and had begun referring to himself as Chief Russell. He was hoping to be named officially in March, but today was not a day he had that on his mind. He had just hung up with that village idiot Jamie and he was trying to get back on the plan he was making for that day. He was severely shorthanded and had this potentially brutal storm on the way. It was the Friday before February vacation; therefore many of his officers had booked vacations and taken off earlier with their families.

When he coupled that with the fact that the Feds had urgently, and at the last minute, flown five of his guys for homeland terrorist training in DC he was so shorthanded that he was probably going to have to call for assistance from local towns if any problems arose. He hated having to call in for help from others. This was his town now. O'Reilly was weak and needed their help.

Not this Chief.

And then Jamie calls in sick, or tries to. That kid was trouble, but his uncle was a town politician and had called in a favor, or the return of a favor, however that goes. Russell was stuck with Jamie for now. His predecessor had been a much different cop than Russell was. O'Reilly had adopted a kind of "look the other way when you can, saves us paperwork" attitude and the force went along. Russell sensed that most of the cops in the Valley liked his predecessor's procedures just fine.

It seemed to Russell and many others if you were a Valley athlete you got away with minor infractions and

DUIs. They made up for the kindness by being extra strict with all the non-athletes and those who had no connections. Russell did not play sports as a kid so he never liked O'Reilly's procedures and was eager to change Valley PD into an enforcement department. No more favors.

As it stood now, Russell's hands were tied and Jamie could not be fired. But he sure as hell was never going to give him any breaks, not while he ran this shop. He was sure Jamie took sleeping pills before work – he was that lazy and sloppy. But, and it killed Russell to admit this, he needed that fucking idiot tonight.

Chapter 13

Nicole jumped into Kaleigh's car. Kaleigh was the hockey cheering captain and a senior. She was wildly popular at school, especially among the partying crew at Valley High. Pretty and fun, she had a reputation among the boys of being an easy score for the best players. Marcus knew Kaleigh well.

There were now five cheerleaders, counting Nicole, in Kaleigh's SUV. They all had Dunkin Donuts coffees and Kaleigh handed Nicole's back to her. Nicole hated coffee but wanted to fit in so she always took the cup. Kaleigh had spiked her own coffee with coffee brandy before picking up the rest of the girls. Just like yesterday. And the day before.

Kaleigh was the current alpha female at Valley High as she was the head cheerleader of the best hockey team the school ever produced. She was blonde, curvy and fun. She was a party girl and felt as if she was among little kids when she was with her classmates. She had dated the football captain during the fall and was now hooking up Marcus when he was drunk.

Among others.

Nicole sat alone in the third row of seats in the SUV, but she did not care. She was in the car! As a freshman last year she could not try out for the squad but she went to all the games and just watched these same girls cheer and learned their routines inside out. She had been a gymnast as a kid so she had that to rely on. She loved her new identity and really looked up to and emulated this new group of girls into which she had been immediately accepted when she made the squad. They drank, she drank.

50

Since her Mom had left them for that skinny cyclist asshole Nicole had been very lonely and sad. Her Dad was sad all the time. Or drunk.

This group of girls made her happy. She could not believe she had made the squad. Kaleigh began to scream over the music how she was hoping she was finally going to go out steady with Marcus. Marcus was the big catch for this gaggle. He was, according to these gals, hot, adorable, hot and hot.

Nicole had loved Marcus since they were kids playing pond hockey. Marcus used to make fun of her figure skates. She kept her crush on Marcus to herself but she really adored him. She saw Kaleigh looking at her in the rearview mirror as if reading her mind so she pretended to drink her coffee.

Nicole only listened to the girls' conversation, careful not to embarrass herself by actually adding to the chitchat. She just timed her laughs to make the other girls feel good. They were talking about the big party at Mr. Fish's house tonight after the game, a party she was headed to as well. Nicole had been drinking with these girls quite a few times after games, but she had always gone home at curfew on those nights.

Tonight was going to be different.

Chapter 14

Marcus flip-flopped across the main floor of the jail carrying the nasty mattress, the stiff orange jumpsuit rubbing roughly against his skin. Through three more locked doors and up two flights of stairs he was finally being led to his cell. He wanted to turn and ask the guard what the fuck was going on and how did he get here, but he was still afraid he'd start choking up if he tried to speak so he chose silence and unanswered questions.

What did I do?

As he trudged slowly ahead of the sound of his captor's jingling keys he mostly ignored the comments he had to endure as he walked by the many locked cell doors to his immediate left. There were inmates saying things to others as Marcus passed by within a foot of his tormentors' cell doors and Marcus now wished he had paid more attention in Spanish class. He looked calm on the outside but he was more scared with each step he took. His knees were jelly.

The guard led him to the end of the catwalk on the top tier of this block and Marcus stopped at the cell door, correctly assuming this was his new home. He shifted the lumpy mattress so he could step forward through the narrow doorway and stopped once he cleared the threshold. As his eyes adjusted to the dark cell, he noticed a triple bunk along the back wall so close he could almost touch it standing just inside the door. Three guys living in a tiny cell in which they would be locked at least eighteen hours every day, sharing a toilet that was two feet from their beds.

What could go wrong there?

The cell was small and cold and the brick walls were painted a light pink. It also had a stainless steel sink and toilet attached to the walls. This cell was mostly barren except for a laundry bag hung on the bunk bed, a checkerboard on a shelf and a few items on the sink. The bottom two bunks were occupied, so it was either time to climb or ask his new roomies if they wanted to flip a coin to see who got the top bunk.

Rock, paper, scissors?

The guard pointed to confirm that the top bunk was for Marcus and then backed out and locked the cell behind him loudly. At this noise there was movement in both lower bunks. The bottom bunk inmate suddenly shifted and Marcus saw a large, muscular Hispanic man staring at him coldly from below.

He had no shirt on, his blanket was tossed aside and he was lying on his back. He was the same size as Marcus and heavily tattooed, even on his completely bald head.

Any light coming into the cell seemed to surround his shiny, tattooed head. Marcus was able to see what was written across his forehead. In fancy script, "Bald Boy" was clearly visible.

BALD BOY

What the fuck? Marcus thought Mike Tyson would feel a lot better about the tattoo on his face if he could see what this clown had done. He almost laughed out loud at the guy, forgetting where he was for a very brief moment.

This tattoo was no half-assed jailhouse tattoo, either. It was professional and well done and scary because it was so prominent and in fancy font. He had no eyebrows, and if there were any hair on his head Marcus did not see it in the five seconds their eyes locked. Bald Boy's scowl was growing into a growl as his upper lip moved to reveal his stained, crooked teeth. He looked like a monster.

Marcus finally caught himself staring and looked away before his stare became a threat. Just before he turned his head he noticed Bald Boy eye the guard for a moment and then nod, as if something non-verbal had just passed between the two.

That Marcus was brought to this cell was no coincidence.

Marcus heard soft snoring that sounded like whimpering coming from the middle bunk and the thin, blonde figure beneath the gray wool blanket remained facing the wall and did not turn to look at him. He was moaning in his sleep.

Marcus climbed to his bunk, spread the mattress on the ancient bed frame and stretched out on the crusty bug haven. It smelled like he had lied down in an ashtray full of half-smoked cigarettes floating in piss.

Steward, there was no mint on my pillow.

The wise ass commentary in his head would not stop but he welcomed the return to near normalcy after the unknown buzz seemed to be wearing off. He was also continuing to sense an inner-change coming on stronger as the buzz faded.

As he lay there the whimpering from below faded away and Marcus's mind raced a mile a minute. He was trying to figure out if he knew the guard, how he got here and if Nicole was OK all at once. Then something in his brain overrode all other thoughts and blasted the alarm. Baker's training was about boxing and fighting but also about mental toughness. Marcus was drawing upon that as he fought back the tears that needed to express themselves by rolling down his cheeks.

Bald Boy, awake on the bottom bunk, was quietly waiting for the newbie to cry. They all did when they lay down for their first night in jail.

Time to think. Despair.

The way his mind was racing Marcus doubted he would ever sleep again but after a few minutes the exhaustion from all he had done hit him and he mercifully passed out. He never heard Bald Boy getting out of the bunk to talk to the guard who had led Marcus to his cell. They spoke quietly but it was evident there was tension on both sides of the door.

"We got another show in the gym tomorrow night. I want this kid busted up bad," whispered the guard.

Bald Boy looked up at the prone and snoring Marcus. He nodded. He spoke slowly, "Where is my stuff?"

"Not yet. Soon," replied the guard as he slowly walked away.

Chapter 15

Russell was trying to figure out how he could cover twelve patrol duties tonight with only five cops to cover them. He would have had seven guys but the old Goat at the hockey rink would not let them postpone tonight's game and two cops had to work The Fish Tank when there was a game. Russell knew the hockey game, even at 5pm, was going to cause problems and now he had to have a significant part of his workforce working the game. There would probably be close to five thousand people at The Fish Tank.

Why do the Feds have terrorist training? Why this weekend? Fucking Al Qaeda. He could not argue for postponement as vehemently as he wanted because he knew there would be a time soon when he would need many of these same people to help appoint him Chief of the force. Always fucking politics, he cursed.

He was praying that the storm would stay all rain – it would be a nuisance but snow would be a nightmare. Russell was going to pay a visit to Goat today as he was already scheduled to go to the high school to visit Principal Thompson today.

Russell saw in the "informal logbook" this morning that a cop had driven the assistant hockey coach, Boots, home last night. He recalled seeing the same entry a few times during the past few months. This meant no charges and nobody but the Valley cops would know about it. This logbook O'Reilly had started was filling up more quickly than the actual arrest book, thought Russell.

First thing I do when I become Chief – no more favors and this logbook is history, too.

Russell was officially pissed off. DUI was a serious offense and he felt like the Valley treated it like a minor nuisance. Athletes were coddled and connections were used to make phone calls the next day if the PD had the nerve to actually enforce something.

Russell was happy the hockey team was doing so well and that Valley finally had a legitimate star, but he did not want to be in charge of cops who gave out favors to DUI suspects. Russell had also recently heard of some kids on the hockey team drinking a bit too much and too publicly. He just hoped Goat and Thompson would listen to the warning of upcoming changes Russell intended to implement as of now.

Chapter 16

Jack Fisher was in a great mood. Why wouldn't he be? It was game day and Valley could keep that cocky St. Mary's team out of the tournament in a rink named after him. The rink was more commonly called "The Fish Tank." Fish was proud of his rink.

Fish was filthy rich. He was one of the few investors to have had the foresight in the dotcom-internet insanity to have cashed out at nearly the top and never looked back. Bulls and bears survived markets, pigs got slaughtered. He did not want to become a pig so he got out.

Fish had been a computer nerd his whole life and had a great software idea at a very opportune time and took advantage of it. When he sold to a big PC firm he made hundreds of millions and never left the Valley to do it. Now retired from software, he had some real estate interests, retail ventures and The Fish Tank.

He was also heavily involved in the Valley High School Athletic Department. He was by far their most generous donor. He was the money that fed the machine that Valley High Sports had become during the past decade. Winning was of the utmost importance to Fish and he conveyed that rather forcefully to the administration and coaches at Valley High.

Rules were bent and wins were celebrated.

Four underperforming coaches had been fired in the past year. Goat had not been worried about being fired but he was happy to have Marcus helping his cause and taking any heat from Fish off him.

Fish loved the Valley and had played on a Valley High hockey team that, until Marcus Kelly came along, was considered the best team Valley High had ever

58

produced. Goat was just starting out as coach back then and Fish was a very dependable defenseman on two teams that qualified for the tourney but lost both times in the first round.

Now they had Marcus Kelly and the expectations were huge.

After making all that money Fish wanted to do something nice for the town in which he and his wife had grown up. Due to his love of hockey and the pride he had for his alma mater the gift ended up being a thirty million dollar rink that was a short walk from the school. It was way over the top for a high school rink. It could hold almost five thousand fans. Tonight it would have more than that. Fish was thrilled to build the rink and now the Bulldogs had the best ice around, hosting many regional tournaments and other events like concerts and ice shows. The State Tournament Finals would be held at The Fish Tank this year. How nice would it be if Valley made it to the Finals? They were certainly favored to be there and it would be the storybook ending for the career of Marcus Kelly.

He and his wife had built a beautiful house in the Valley in a fairly remote area on the undeveloped side of the Juniper River. He had amazing views from his back deck, with Boston's skyline visible on a clear night. He could see the jail's lights at night, too.

They entertained often for the non-profits and charities in which they were active. Entertaining was part of who they were and they were both natural at schmoozing.

Fish was currently busy working on the final list for the big party he always hosted after the last regular season hockey game. Moving the game up to 5pm was a bit of a problem, but he had money and money seemed to solve most problems. Also, that meant that they could drink two hours earlier than usual. He erased the "1" next to beer kegs on his list and wrote a "2" instead.

This was a special night for Valley High and Fish knew how to do it up right. Screw the storm.

Chapter 17

Saturday Dawn • the jail

Marcus awoke with a start and blinked the crust out of his eyes while he stared at the unfamiliar paint chip pattern on the ceiling overhead. There were some initials and dates carved into the ceiling. One was dated 1965. He was groggy but much more sober than he had been just a few hours ago. He was instantly petrified as soon as his eyes opened and he remembered where he was.

Game on, kiddo. Not a moment of peace in the jail.

The jail at this hour was much more quiet than it had been when he arrived, but not silent. Never silent. The jail's echoed sounds were its heartbeat. To be completely silent would mean the evil also slept. Nope. This jail was always alive and ready to promote some violence.

On edge. The other shoe, or flip-flop, always dropped. You never had to wait long for that. An innocent argument over a checkers game would instantly become a melee. An inevitable shank would appear from nowhere and the corner of the checkerboard would be used to blind a guy who did nothing but win against the wrong guy.

The sound that had awoken Marcus was that of the bald Hispanic man returning to the cell after being let in by the guard who had taunted Marcus earlier. That guard was now blatantly staring at Marcus through the locked cell door. It was still not light enough for Marcus to get a good look at him, but now he was convinced that he knew this guy.

The guard caught Marcus looking at him and stepped back into the shadows. "Keep staring, Kelly. Nobody but me knows you are here, that ice storm

61

knocked down every wire and tower for a hundred miles and there are so many trees down that nobody can get anywhere near this jail. This is going to be fun, tough guy. Let's see how tough you are in here. You messed with the wrong family last night."

As he walked away the pudgy guard whistled an Elvis song Marcus instantly recognized. Marcus whispered "Elvis sucks" to himself and it felt pretty good. He continued to have unfamiliar flashes of snapping and unleashing the power he knew he had within him, his brain almost willing him to start something. He was becoming aware that he was in a spot where there were no ramifications or suspensions as the result of him getting in a fight.

He decided right there he was going to defend himself aggressively if needed. He had seen enough jail movies to know he could become somebody's bitch in here.

Are you finally ready to answer the bell, kiddo?

When did I start calling myself kiddo? He was really starting to notice how edgy he was. Bring it on. Fat fucking jail guard. Then, just as quickly, the toughness would fade away and an overpowering fear would dominate his thoughts.

What did I do to that guy's family last night?

Chapter 18

Friday Morning • Valley High School

As Captain Russell drove out to Valley High he was listening to the local news in the Valley PD Chief's SUV. He liked the idea of this SUV being his soon. He anticipated the power he was going to have and it felt good. He was ready to lead.

He noted that the radio microphone was still broken so he could not talk into the police radio in this SUV to communicate with the other patrol cars. That would need to be fixed. He needed this SUV as a symbol he was ready for the job.

He turned up the volume on the AM radio, and the serious sounding weatherman began: "We are looking for the storm to hit this area around 8pm in the form of substantial rain initially. There are three possible outcomes from this storm – first, we get really lucky and it stays all rain, we'll end up with three or four inches and the usual flooding by the time it ends. Second, if it turns to snow, we will have close to two feet of snow by tomorrow night. Third, and worst in my opinion, is the temperature hovers around freezing and is more freezing rain than snow. This will result in serious ice damage to trees and the roads will be an absolute flooding nightmare. So listeners, pray for rain or snow and stay off the road."

Russell's head sank to his chest. He felt as if his leadership abilities were about to be put to the test.

Chapter 19

Goat was in his office going through his emails when one in particular caught his attention. It was from the new French teacher, Irene Poulin, about his goalie, Eric Fowler. Apparently Eric was pulling an "F" in her French class and she was posting it today, which would mean he would be ineligible for the game tonight, his last home game as a senior. This witch would do that? Goat had to go see her quickly.

That was the nice thing about Fish putting his rink near school property. Goat could get over to the school to go fix things quickly, and it was time for him to use that power of his and mix in a bit of charm, too. This was not the first kid to need some academic assistance from da Goat.

Goat was deep in thought. After tonight's game they'd have seven days off until the tournament. He could deal with the school issues over that time if need be. But he needed his top goalie in the nets tonight. Fowler was not as important as Marcus Kelly, not by a mile. But the drop in talent from Fowler to his backup was too big a risk for tonight, especially with the ability to keep St. Mary's out of the tournament. He needed Fowler and he was going to convince Irene Goddamned Poulin to help him get that boy back on the team for his last game as a senior.

This is Division One Massachusetts High School hockey, dammit.

Chapter 20

Marcus parked the Honda and was walking from the student lot to his first class of the day when he saw Kaleigh's SUV unloading hot chicks, one after another. He wanted to avoid Kaleigh, she was looking for more from a relationship with Marcus and he just did not like her that much – unless he was drunk and it was late.

Then he really liked her.

It was like a clown car, only full of cheerleaders pouring out of every door. Marcus smiled and admired their uniforms, and his jaw dropped when he saw Nicole Harrison get out of the car.

Hello?

Her cheering uniform hugged her curves and Marcus was blatantly staring as he stopped walking to admire her.

Where the hell did she come from all of a sudden?

They had grown up near each other but to Marcus she was always Nic, the little kid with the figure skates following us everywhere. But today Marcus saw her in a whole new light. Wow, he thought. I was blind.

The other gals all said hello to him and giggled after they walked by him. Kaleigh playfully bumped Marcus and went to hug him to wish him luck but Marcus had already taken a step toward Nicole and Kaleigh's semi-drunken, awkward hug totally missed its mark. The other girls all saw this and quietly laughed among themselves, careful not to offend Kaleigh. She was mean in the morning.

Kaleigh turned to see Marcus heading straight for Nicole. Kaleigh was pissed now and she was a vindictive bitch. She was going to be the one who scooped Marcus tonight. Little bitch sophomore chicks don't take guys from me, thought Kaleigh. She was going to show this foolish little girl who she was messing with. Kaleigh and Marcus had hooked up more than a few times when Marcus had been drunk this season already. She quickly rejoined her group and they walked silently into school.

She liked being the top dog and thought of as cool. It was important to her. Her drinking had influenced some of her recent decisions in the back seats of the athletes' cars at Valley High and she found herself more than a few times driving to CVS to get a pregnancy test. So far she had dodged that bullet.

She tried a few times to get Marcus to go all the way but he was too focused on his future. He was the first guy to say no to Kaleigh. They did plenty of other stuff when he was drunk, though. She could not believe his body. He was like an Abercrombie model but way more muscular.

She would try harder tonight to get him to go all the way as she would not mind hitching her cart to his wagon and becoming Mrs. NHL with Marcus.

Kaleigh Kelly sounded right to her.

Marcus waited for Nicole, enjoying the view as she approached. Wow. He caught himself staring when Nicole looked at her sweater to see if she had spilled coffee on her chest, following Marcus's eyes.

He looked away and then quickly asked, "Are you going to Fish's party after the game?"

"Yes, are you?"

"I am. I wonder if there will be like a million people there again this year."

Nicole replied that she had never been to Fish's party but heard the house is incredible.

She was amazed that he was talking to her and checking her out. She was all too aware of what was going on with her body and she did not mind the attention it was bringing her way, especially right now. To break the silence she said, "I hope you break those records tonight."

Marcus blushed and blurted out, "Do you need a ride to the party?" He was shocked she would know about the records. She became even hotter, if that was possible. Marcus could not stop smiling and staring at her.

Nicole blushed right back at him, smiled and shrugged her shoulders as she playfully twirled her hair and ran off for school.

Marcus was left standing in his tracks and admiring Nicole's … uniform.

Chapter 21

Marcus had been in and out of sleep since initially awakening at dawn. He heard the doors opening all around him and heard inmates stir. Instant terror again awoke with him.

His cell was on the top tier of the block. The jail's layout was fairly simple, it looked like a bicycle wheel with four blocks of cells that jutted out like spokes from the hub of the jail, the main floor. Each block had three tiers and each tier had a three-foot wide catwalk that was covered by chain link on the side opposite the cell doors. There were stairs within each block so inmates could go from tier to tier but only within their own block.

There were, however, many secluded areas and alleyways within each block where the unspeakable shit happened.

Each tier had twelve cells that ran one after the other in a row and due to the width of the catwalk one had to turn sideways if trying to get by anybody standing or walking toward them. The open side of the walkway that was covered in chain link up to the ceiling gave the walkway a very claustrophobic feel. There were years of dried up mucus from guys spitting from their cells and hitting the fence. Nobody touched the fence for that reason. If the fence got shaken flakes of phlegm would fall to the floor like snow.

Nasty snow.

As Marcus lay in bed the cigarette smoke from the large percentage of inmates who started their day with a butt wafted to the unvented ceiling and then slowly expanded to give each block the look of a city covered by smog.

Because cigarettes were the most common form of currency used in bartering within the confines of Valley Jail, most inmates kept them in their cells. This led to many non-smokers becoming smokers out of convenience – yet another nice trait the jail bestowed upon its inhabitants.

Possible lung cancer? Here you go.

The routine for most inmates was to wake up coughing, spit up a big loogie, grab the butts and light one up. Cigarettes were coveted in the jail. They seemed to be symbolic to the inmates in a way. Each cigarette signaled a small passage of rare, peaceful time – a segment of their sentence that had gone by.

The first one of the day seemed to have higher significance than those that would follow. As each inmate smoked that first butt each day they seemed to be quietly pondering or reflecting. It was as close to peaceful as the jail would ever get. They were independent, isolated moments for each inmate imprisoned there – smoking the first of many butts as they savored their better memories, the ones that kept them going.

Family. Wives, girlfriends or both. Hidden money or loot. The next crime or victim. Revenge.

Most would then either roll back over to sleep the day away or head to breakfast and then sleep after eating. Sleeping during the day was the routine as daylight was not a factor affecting sleep in Valley Jail. The only natural light entering the blocks was from the thirty-foot high arched windows in the granite walls opposite the cells. There were two of them in each block and they were made of steel bars and wire-meshed, extra-thick glass. The glass was stained brown and yellow by years of smoke, grime and bird crap, giving the block a muted light that left the blocks still dark during the day.

This morning the emergency lights remained the only effective lighting in the jail as the generators were still being used due to the power outage created by the storm. It produced the light of dusk at best. It was eerie.

Before being allowed to head to the chow hall, a guard called out cell numbers and the inmates in that cell walked out to the catwalk and announced their names. The guard's voice reminded Marcus of his junior high gym class with Mr. Bruce taking attendance, but Mr. Bruce did it while they were naked and showering.

Marcus heard the guys in the cell next to him shuffle out so he shifted his feet over the edge of his bunk to ready himself for the jump down to the granite floor. As he did this he noticed that the bald guy was getting down from the middle bunk and then he heard the whimpering guy move to get down.

Marcus almost kicked the bald guy in the head when he swung his feet down. He thankfully missed and Bald Boy left the cell, ignoring Marcus but aware of him somehow.

He heard the guard say "twenty" loudly and Bald Boy and the thin guy in the middle bunk shuffled out. Marcus jumped down and headed out.

"Hernandez," shouted Baldy as he was walking over to the steps taking him back to his assigned cell in the same block. He disappeared down the steps.

Cell 20 was just his love nest. His real cell was in the same block but on the bottom floor. Unlike the outside world, the penthouses in this jail were on the bottom floor. The powerful and their crews resided on the lower levels.

"Pinkham," whispered the skinny blonde guy in a very feminine voice. He went back into his cell and lay down facing the wall again.

"Kelly," stated Marcus as bravely as he could but his voice squeaked like a pubescent teen's.

Nice, Marcus. Don't drop the soap.

Thankfully nobody lifted an eyebrow and he focused on his toenails, which badly needed trimming, he noticed. Fowler always joked that Marcus had "bad toes," whatever that meant. Marcus skated with no socks so his skates did do a number on his feet. He caught himself not focusing and got back on task.

Jail, not toes, kiddo. The new voice in his head was cracking the whip. He had to get serious, no choice.

Breakfast was being served in the cafeteria but their block was not going for about twenty more minutes. The other blocks ate first.

That gave Marcus time to observe the inmates as he stayed where he was on the catwalk outside his cell, afraid to move. He caught a few sideways glances and some murmuring as he was noticed as being the new guy for the first time. He decided to look straight ahead through the fence but did not dare touch the fence – it was full of nasty, dried-up loogies.

He sensed that there was danger lurking in this place for him but also remained hopeful that somebody would notice his presence, or absence, and get him out soon. He put his hands in the pockets of his jumpsuit. They were trembling and he did not want the guys assembled on the catwalk around him to notice.

As he looked around him he noticed some guys pointing at him and whispering. Fuck! Marcus immediately looked down through the fence, suddenly sweating and flexing his hands in his pockets.

He could see down to the bottom floor where the inmates housed down there were starting their day. Those on ground level could move about a bit more than those housed in the top two tiers, but they ran the risk of being hit with things thrown, or spit, from the top tiers.

That had been the start of many fights in the jail. An innocent spit at the fence would land on one of The Boyz and within an hour the spitter would be facing five guys with shanks.

To Marcus it looked like a men's social club – like the members of the golf club where he had once caddied. They were all smoking, some reading sections or single pages of newspapers – Marcus saw a picture of himself in yesterday's Herald. Others were drinking jailhouse coffee (old grounds filtered through old socks) and chatting, mostly in loud Spanish. Spanish music blared from somewhere in the block.

This jail had a routine to its day and when things were smooth you could not discern one day from another. Every uneventful day in the jail was like the other ordinary days, more or less. But many days in jail were far from routine or peaceful and it did not take much to light the fuse and make it memorable.

Today would be one of those days.

Marcus noticed guys now moving toward their staircase slowly; there was very little talk among the inmates. Many had gone back to bed. Soon their block was shuffling down the catwalk, down the two flights of stairs and into line with another block of inmates in the cafeteria. There were about a hundred inmates in total with two guards overseeing the process of feeding them.

Two guards total?

Marcus was shocked and even more scared now. Guys were noticing him and gesturing toward him as they whispered with others nearby in line.

As they entered the cafeteria a tall, skinny white guy bumped hard into Marcus and stood in front of Marcus, forcing him to stop. The skinny guy was four inches taller than Marcus and had incredibly long nose hairs bursting from his nostrils.

"Your ass is mine, new meat." He raised his eyebrows and laughed hard at what he had just said. Two associates of his laughed and mocked Marcus as they all cut right in front of him in line.

Marcus almost did two things. Cry was the first one. Throw a vicious sucker punch was the other. He chose neither as he just stood there staring at the number on his jumpsuit.

What the fuck am I going to do to survive this?

Marcus heard the wiseass that had threatened him blurt out loudly and to nobody in particular, "I love Saturdays. Always steak and eggs here in the Valley, boys!"

The English-speaking inmates that heard it all laughed, catching the guard's attention. Marcus heard the guard shuffle over their way but he was timid and powerless.

"Guard, Guard! My dick is hard!" yelled the same guy, able to remain anonymous in the long line.

Even the Hispanics laughed at that one.

The guard was feeble and old. He knew he had no backup, especially today. He had to take the insult and look away.

Pitiful.

Marcus kept his head down but stayed alert. He wanted badly to look around and take this all in. He still felt like this was a bad joke and he would be released before he could sit down to eat. But his parents were on a cruise and out of touch and from what the fat asshole guard said the storm that hit last night crushed this area and the jail was basically cut off from society for the time being.

He risked a look around. He initially noticed that many of the guys looked like normal guys, and he was right. Many inmates at this jail were drug abusers and drunks. In jail, where booze was almost non-existent and drugs were hard to get and too expensive for the average inmate, these addicts returned somewhat to what they looked like before the booze or pills got its claws in them. They regained weight and worked out in the gym. Their faces looked healthier, especially around their eyes.

Most would return to their former ways the day they got released and be back in jail shortly after, looking skinny and sickly once again. It was a vicious cycle repeated too many times.

However, not all of the guys looked normal. There were many guys who looked like the killers they were, Bald Boy among them. The tattoos all over their bodies and the malevolent look in their eyes gave them an aura of viciousness that surrounded them like an over-perfumed hooker. You recoiled upon seeing them and did your best to avoid any conversation or interaction with them.

Marcus was beginning to worry again that nobody on the outside knew where he was, at least not for a while. He suddenly wanted to cry again. He would've cried had he known that only two people knew where he was being held. The asshole guard was one. His buddy, the cop, who was sedated at the hospital and would not wake up for the rest of the day, was the other one.

No Dial-A-Friend, no Lifeline.

He had to stay strong and he had to be ready. He risked a look up once more to see where he was in line and caught Bald Boy, who was surrounded by similarly scary, heavily tattooed Hispanic men, staring at him.

Bald Boy did not look away but Marcus quickly did.

Do not cry, kiddo.

Chapter 22

Jim Ratkowski, like most guys with that last name, was called Rat. However, unlike most of his Rat peers, he actually loved the nickname. Some would say he spent his life doing things to live down to the nickname.

He had always been the biggest kid in his class until high school. His size allowed him to be a bully and he played the part to perfection. It also made him the perfect jail guard.

Just ask him.

Rat grew up in the Valley but went to St. Mary's at his asshole father's insistence. He was not the ideal student and was often in trouble with the school administration for both academic and behavioral issues throughout his four years there. The school had tolerated his antics because his father was an alumnus and often donated to the school.

Rat had been a clumsy but hard-hitting hockey player, nothing special and just mediocre all around. But he was dirty and vicious as hell.

Sports were very important at St Mary's. Rat took advantage of his athletic status, on the ice and off. Rat was the leader in penalty minutes every year he played hockey and led the school in principal's office visits every year, too.

Rat was twenty two now and still lived at home. He had become very out of shape and pudgy. Most of his weight had been gained since high school because that is when he really started drinking beer. He loved drinking and he loved the effect it had on him. He smoked pot here and there with Jamie but he preferred beer. He truly believed that when he was drunk he was cool and better able to talk to women. The women he spoke to at bars would not agree.

At all.

Rat was arrogant and pushy, two great qualities for a jail guard but not great to bring out socially. He also had a pudgy, babyish face that blushed in the cheeks when he drank.

As he awoke he was shaking off a bad hangover he had from drinking the previous night with some co-workers and Jamie Hickey, the guy he had nicknamed "half a cop". He lifted the curtain on the window so he could see the driveway and saw his pickup parked in the driveway, albeit a bit askew. Phew.

"Don't remember parking there," he said to himself.

Sgt. Rat worked at the jail and had been there since he quit community college after half a semester. The promotion to Sergeant had been recent. He was one of the few guards who stayed working at Valley Jail long enough to be considered for a promotion, actually. Many guards worked only a few shifts and never went back.

It was his dream job. He had applied after deciding that college was not for him and the Warden had loved Rat from the moment he met him and hired him on the spot. The Warden was still puzzled as to why anybody actually wanted to work at the jail at all, let alone somebody so talented like his boy Rat.

Rat loved the power he had in the jail over the inmates. He used it to his full advantage, too. He could play God and get away with it. He was all-powerful for eight hours a day because he had the fucking keys. He loved hearing the inmates plead with him to allow them to go here or there within the jail as he pretended to not hear them and jingled the keys to taunt the inmates. They were all guilty pieces of shit to Rat.

During his shift he controlled who went where and always made sure he was aware of who needed what so he could leverage that into something for himself. It was all a game to him, a game he loved to play.

When he began working at the jail he kissed the asses of those above him to move up. He volunteered for duties other guys shunned. One time a guy had broken into a jewelry store and hurriedly swallowed a diamond ring when the cops showed up. He got arrested in the act and taken to the jail to "process the ring".

The Captain needed a guy to go sit with this creep in the holding cell and wait for him to shit the ring out. Nobody wanted that duty so Rat jumped at the opportunity to get paid while making sure the Warden knew he was doing it. Sure enough, after ten hours there was a "ding" in the metal bucket into which the thief had shat.

Rat always wondered which unfortunate bride ended up with that ring.

Rat had been a schemer in the jail, almost from day one, and now he had accumulated enough power that if any fucking inmate ever pissed him off he had the means to take care of it without getting his hands dirty.

He had Bald Boy now. Bald Boy was the leader of The Boyz, the powerful gang inside the jail and out. And he was bought and paid for by Rat.

Cross Rat at your own risk. To Rat, being feared in the jail by the inmates had become very important to him – he had never been allowed so much power before. He was "the Boss" and the inmates better remember that.

Or Bald Boy reminds them.

Rat was on the rise in the jail. But he impatiently wanted more.

Money. Rank. Respect.

For a guy with the flawed and cruel personality traits Rat had, to be able to find a job where he excelled was indeed a match made in heaven. He had failed in society and just bullied his way through school and life, but in jail he was in his element and was able to gracefully connive and deceive his way up the ladder. It was in stunning contrast to how he stumbled and bumbled outside the walls.

As Rat got out of bed he suddenly remembered there was a big hockey game tonight. Rat's younger brother Joey was on the St. Mary's team. Rat loved hockey but rarely went to Joey's games. Joey was smaller than Rat but had the aggressive Rat gene and played dirty.

Rat was not going to the game tonight, he had taken a shift from a guard whose cousin played for the Valley High team and gotten the guy to pay him an extra $100 to take his shift. Sucker! He also had a few illegal things to lug into the jail and tonight was a perfect night for that.

Rat paid for Bald Boy's services with lugged items. It was too easy, or so it seemed to Rat. Who gives a fuck if the other guards know or don't know? Fuck you, bitch. The other guards were most definitely aware of the connection between Bald Boy and Rat but they already fucking hated Rat and there was a weird honor code about ratting out a fellow CO.

Even if you despised him and wanted him fired.

Rat wanted that punk Marcus Kelly to get his bell rung and he might even bribe Joey to take a run at him. Rat smiled as he remembered his big moment, crushing a then-freshman Marcus Kelly with a very dirty hit back in his high school days. Marcus was considered a young phenomenon even back then – more promise than production if you asked Rat.

Rat smoked him good and still smiled when he recalled that hit, which was often in bars.

To impress the ladies.

He had wanted to teach the little all-star a lesson that day. His hatred of Marcus had stayed with him ever since.

Rat was also thinking about Bald Boy. He had detected some things from The Boyz that smelled like trouble and he wanted to address that soon with Bald Boy.

Last night he had picked up a big package of ganja from The Boyz with Jamie that he had to lug in to Bald Boy tonight. He needed to have a conversation with Bald Boy and regain his control. The scale of power was tipped in a direction he did not like and needed to be fixed. Bald Boy and The Boyz had been getting bolder and bolder. He knew just what to do, but it would take some planning.

He needed to get some jailbait.

For the show.

He smiled and looked for the Advil.

Chapter 23

Marcus was in first period Algebra 2 class and daydreaming, as he often did in class. He had never been an honor roll student but since the beginning of his Junior year there seemed to be a drop both in the expectations of his teachers and in his effort in their classrooms. Which came first is neither here nor there, but it was not coincidence that he stopped trying when the teachers stopped asking him to.

This had led to Marcus's getting the best grades of his life the past few years despite barely any homework being done or tests being passed. His parents were thrilled. Marcus and Fowler had a big laugh when Marcus made Second Honors last year. Fowler knew what was going on, he did not blame Marcus for coasting.

Marcus hardly called what he did coasting. He had hockey, lifting and fight training so that left little time for homework. It had evolved into a free pass at school and nobody complained, certainly not Marcus.

His teachers all knew that Marcus was capable of more effort in class but they seemed to have become more of a fan of Marcus the hockey star than Marcus the student. He considered it the perks of where he was headed. Maybe it was a sign of things to come for him, perhaps?

Freebies and endorsements.

It was almost as if an unspoken bond had emerged between Marcus and the school's teachers – "Marcus, you show us you are at least trying and we will do our part to keep you on the ice. Oh, and a few tickets my way when you play for the Bruins, OK?" Wink.

Go Bulldogs! This was just one cog in the machine called Valley High Sports. Superstars get a pass? Check.

During this morning's class the only points the math teacher taught that Marcus tuned into were the end-of-class life lessons that math could teach us all. He called them fireside chats and let the kids put their pencils down and relax as he spoke.

He was talking about Venn Diagrams – the math theory showing intersecting circles and sets. Mr. Burns made his point, "In life, it is not so much where the circle that represents a lifetime starts and ends – that part is perfectly expressed as three hundred sixty degrees, that is constant. That circle is pre-determined and certain. What is uncertain is where and when your life circle intersects with other circles as it completes its arc. That part is where randomness comes into the equation. Which circles meet and where the circles intersect, this gray shaded area, forever affects each circle as it completes its trek. Although the trajectory of that life circle is not altered, the mark it makes as it moves onward is different. What would best show the effect of each intersection would be a color change of the circle as it exited the shaded areas it had shared with other circles. Unquestionably, life circles cannot intersect without affecting the other. This holds true for both animate and inanimate objects. A purple circle intersecting with a pink circle will inevitably bring some pink with it the rest of the way around."

The bell rang but Marcus wanted this sermon to continue, he found it fascinating. Marcus pondered this deep life parallel his teacher had preached and he really understood what his teacher meant here. He would have to be careful what circles he intersected with going forward. He did not want any excess baggage as he worked his way to the NHL.

81

As his teacher was giving homework equations Marcus had stopped listening. He was thinking about the game tonight. It was his last regular season home game after having been on varsity for four years. He remembered when Coach Gauthier had visited him in eighth grade and implored him to come to Valley High to let Goat coach him up. It was never a hard decision for Marcus, he had been going to Valley games since first grade and he considered it an honor to play for Goat. His folks loved Coach Goat's background and that he had almost made it to the NHL.

Valley and St. Mary's were bitter rivals in every sport and in every way. These kids had grown up with each other and played on the same youth and middle school teams. They lived next door to each other.

That all changed if somebody chose St. Mary's instead of Valley High. Instant hatred occurred. Longtime middle school relationships that seemed as if they would last forever would end in a break-up within a week of starting at the two different high schools.

Valley High and St. Mary's played each other in every sport two times per year – the first and last regular season games in every sport, it was tradition. Marcus had already scored four goals in that first game of the season in an 8-4 rout of their rivals.

Now Valley High's record was 19-2 on the year and headed for the tourney while St. Mary's was having a bad year and their record was 10-10. They needed at least a point tonight to qualify. Valley High could keep St. Mary's out of the tournament by winning – that was the talk of the town leading up to the game.

Marcus loved the Goat. Goat had taught Marcus all about hockey, details that only a guy who had played up to a high level would know.

Instinctive stuff, subtle stuff.

Da devil is in da details, Goat would often say to him. Goat and Mr. Baker were great role models and mentors for Marcus given his goal in life.

Marcus knew how lucky he was when Goat would invite him over to watch game film or a Bruins game. Goat would see minute details that Marcus found fascinating and eventually Marcus had learned so much from Goat that he would see things before Goat would.

Passing da torch, as Goat had called it.

Goat always had a Busch beer in his hand those nights. His beer.

"I can't afford da Molson on da coach's pay."

Chapter 24

Marcus arrived at the service window and slid his tray to the large opening. He guided it to the spot where the oatmeal was put upon his tray. The fat white guy with bright orange hair slapped the paste on his tray like a large bird shitting on it – splat! Marcus poked at it with his flimsy spork.

Only plastic sporks were used at Valley Jail now, no more metal forks. There had been an incident last year and a guy ended up with fifteen forks painfully and forcefully stuck all over his body in a coordinated assault by The Boyz. "He must have tripped," wrote Rat in his incident report later that day.

Fifteen forks.

Marcus then slid his tray to the toast server and got one piece of toast from a huge black guy with the biggest bucked-teeth Marcus had ever seen. He noticed all the other guys had gotten two pieces of toast but Marcus did not say anything as Black Bucky ate a piece of toast with one hand and gave Marcus the finger with the other. He was also supposed to put scrambled eggs on his tray but pointed to the quite full pan and said, "We be outta bambled eggs." He kept his middle finger up the whole time and kept smiling and showing the big beaver teeth he was apparently proud of.

Meeting some great guys in jail, Mom.

Marcus again had that new feeling of violent behavior and imagined grabbing the guy by his hair and smashing his fucked-up teeth into the eggs. He nodded and smirked at the guy.

Fuck you very much.

Marcus grabbed a milk carton and a banana and looked for a seat. He noticed the black guys were all with the black guys, whites with whites and Latinos with Latinos. There appeared to be cliques just like high school only the groups were not based upon popularity – just skin color. Marcus wondered if there was a handbook to which he could refer to find the section on where to sit so you stay alive in this hellhole.

As Marcus re-entered panic zone about where to sit, the new owner of his ass bumped him to remind Marcus of his existence. His two pals chuckled and pointed at Marcus as they walked by.

Where the fuck do I sit? Please God, help me here. His knees almost gave out on him.

As Marcus was freaking out and looking for a safe seat, Rich Contorelli was eyeing him. Conti, his jail nickname, had been an inmate at this facility for eighteen months, his first time in this jail. He had been held in Concord State Prison for the previous four years. He was transferred to this jail after his sixth fight causing bodily harm at Concord Prison. He was not to be treated lightly.

He had four months left on this sentence but had been in prison for half of his adult life. The last time he was out he had tried being a law-abiding, job-holding citizen until one fateful day. He had been rightfully convicted of beating a man, with his bare hands, to within a centimeter of death. The guy had busted up Conti's younger sister. He paid a dear price.

Conti was now paying his. Again. No problem, he did time like a bear shits in the woods – it came naturally to him now. He was the leader of the white men's gang in Valley Jail, The Gringos. He was a ruthless man whose power came from brute force and attitude. He was a mean motherfucker.

As he eyed Marcus being bumped by the skinny jackass, Conti thought he knew this big, scared kid who was walking around like a lamb in a wolf den. He had that look of most new guys – terrified toughness with a smoldering, piss-your-pants fear bubbling about a centimeter below the surface.

Big kid, though. Even through the jumpsuit Conti could tell Marcus was jacked. Hmmm. The CO who was working today, Officer Wilson, Conti's lugger, had given Conti his Herald yesterday and Conti saw the picture of Marcus and read the article.

He grabbed the Herald from the guy next to him and flipped to the page with the picture of Marcus. Same guy? And now he was standing in front of him in the cafeteria in Valley Jail? This was definitely the kid he had read about. How is he here on a weekend? This jail rarely took guys in on the weekend.

Marcus Kelly. Mr. Superstar. Mr. Inmate.

Conti knew that something stunk here and it would not be the first time something illegal or immoral was done by a guard to somebody within the walls of this dump. This one smelled like a freshly run over skunk to Conti. He also knew that piece of shit guard Rat was involved.

Conti also smelled opportunity. How though?

As a seasoned convict, Conti was a selfish prick because he needed to be, it was the law of this land. The only end game in jail was survival. Especially in this dump. Power was how you survived in Conti's jail handbook and that had been his motto throughout his many stays in jail. It had done well by him so far.

He had learned early in his career in State Prison that if you showed any weakness you were prey. You befriended somebody and they stole from you. Inevitably you would have to fight at least once to save your virginity. Once was enough for Conti to show the other inmates not to fuck with him. The big, fat guy who made a move on him one night ended up with a broken face and weeks in the infirmary. Word spread quickly in jail. Information was a commodity that could be valuable and bartered, like everything else inside.

Conti was deep in thought. How could this Marcus kid being in here work for him? He immediately began sizing up this situation to see how he could make it work to his benefit. If it helped the kid, too, fine. He's white. But I ain't babysitting this newbie. No fucking way.

As he was pondering the situation Conti observed that his main rival, the Cuban Bald Boy, was staring at Marcus and talking to The Boyz, gesturing wildly. He knew he had to act quickly.

Something was cooking here.

Anxiety had been high in Valley Jail recently. That fucking Cuban was really getting on his nerves lately and he seemed to be daring Conti to make a move. There was a simmering tension in the jail that Conti felt needed to be addressed soon. Like a typical communist, Bald Boy had gotten a taste of the life that power brought to him in the jail and wanted more, more and more. He was exerting his power a little at a time. Bald Boy was a skilled organizer and leader. The Boyz had transformed from being a sloppy mix of Puerto Ricans, Dominicans and Mexicans into being one Latino gang under Bald Boy's leadership.

But that meant less for Conti and his guys, The Gringos. Like any good leader, Conti knew that his guys were watching his every move and he needed to be cautious but forceful with his next strategy. These two respective leaders were not on good terms. Their Cold War was warming up, but The Boyz far outnumbered The Gringos and Conti did not think he could take out Bald Boy one on one.

It was not coincidence that the two respective leaders of the most powerful jail gangs were also the primary recipients of the lugging guards.

It was Conti and his lugger, Officer Wilson, versus Bald Boy and his lugger, Rat, in this race for power. Wilson had no desire for power, he did the lugging for money alone. To Rat the money was important but secondary.

Conti had evolved into an unfeeling animal in the jail out of necessity. He had done things to people in jail that shamed him when he reflected upon them, so he reflected very infrequently. He was a brutal savage but he justified it more and more easily and his crises of conscience seemed to be coming less frequently.

Valley Jail was desensitizing him.

He thought back to the day his sister came to him after she had absorbed a heck of a beating and needed his help. Marcus was a young white kid who needed help quickly, too.

Conti motioned for Marcus to join them and he looked around for the Rat as he did so. He did not want to attract attention from Rat, that guy could make Conti's remaining time very unpleasant and powerless.

That motherfucker needed to be dealt with, too.

He had to act fast. Get over here, kid.

Chapter 25

After her walk, Dottie was busy in the kitchen baking for the big game tonight. She was in her glory. DH was dutifully sleeping nearby, ready to defend the castle from mailmen and other intruders.

She loved to bake and she loved being in her kitchen. Dottie was humming along to her Anita Baker CD and measuring ingredients for brownies, cakes, cupcakes and muffins to be sold later at the game. She rarely left a game with leftovers. Her baking abilities were well known at the games. As she sang and mixed she snuck peeks at the picture of Dear Harry. He used to love her horrible singing. She smiled at him.

Today there was one ingredient she had to be extra careful with.

When her Dear Harry had gotten the cancer he was suffering with the chemo and radiation. His brother had driven from Vermont with the promise of some amazing medicine, which ended up being a big bag of green, sticky, stinky marijuana. Dottie was horrified at first but it seemed to really help Harold and he learned to roll joints and smoked them daily until he died. It was the only thing that worked to give him some peace from the nausea and pain from both the cancer and the treatments.

After treatments he would quietly roll a joint and then go to the garage and sit in his car, which he always backed into its bay. He would open the garage door, put on Sinatra, gaze outside and puff away to ease his pain. Dottie would sit in the kitchen where she could see him through the open door to keep an eye on him, always wiping tears away as she did so.

They were extremely private about the marijuana. Dottie was initially ashamed and not on board with the plan, but as she saw how well it worked to ease his pain she relented and was thankful his brother Paul had brought it with him. She was never proud of it being smoked in her house, so they kept it their secret.

Dottie had jokingly bought him reggae wigs and other "ganja" joke gifts to make him laugh at the irony of him taking up smoking pot so late in his life. Those little laughs seemed to help ease his pain, too. Despite Harry's pestering, Dottie never indulged in smoking the pot with him. She needed a clear head to deal with his prescriptions and instructions from the doctors. Dottie had recently stumbled upon the huge bag of pot that was still in the cupboard.

She had been on the brink of depression and contemplating suicide.

She kept her house impeccably clean but one particular day she was finding peace in an all-out cleaning. As she pulled things out of cabinets she was bawling hysterically. It was the lowest she had been since Dear Harry had passed. She was aware of how close she was to giving up on everything so on a whim she smoked one of his already rolled joints.

Right there on the kitchen floor.

Although she did not like the smoking part of it, Dottie loved the buzz she got from it. She went from borderline suicidal to joyful as she spoke aloud to her Dear Harry for the first time since he had died. She talked on and on as she puffed away. She hated herself for it but it was undeniably helpful, especially given her current state of mind.

Dottie had been puritanically innocent most of her life, but this felt good. She deserved this. It really helped her cope with her loss.

She justified it.

As the baker that she was she began to bake pot brownies. She had gotten the recipe for "Buzzed Brownies" from the Internet. Since she wanted the buzz and not the calories she naively tripled the amount of pot in the recipe. They were extremely potent so she would nibble on them as she read a book or watched TV with DH on her lap.

Leno was even funnier on those nights.

She saw it as harmless and a way to reconnect with her deceased husband. The marijuana stimulated her brain and she remembered things about him that she otherwise never really remembered at all. She liked that the most about her brownies.

But she was eating them more frequently, even if she was hesitant to admit that. She was not hurting anybody and being extra careful to stay home on the nights she indulged. She was at peace with her special brownies.

She deserved them!

As she took out the plate she always put them on, she remembered the day she found the marijuana. As she emptied the cabinets feverishly, she spotted a really tacky plate that said "Dottie~n~Harold" that she had rarely used. However, that day it was the nicest thing she had ever seen. Just seeing his name made her smile, so she reached out to hug it to her chest and continue to have a good cry.

As she picked it up she found Harry's marijuana hidden in the salad bowl beneath it. She almost felt as if Dear Harry guided her to it and said, "This will make you feel better." He was, as usual, correct. She tried marijuana for the first time right there on the kitchen floor, smoking one of his doobies, as he called them.

She had recently run out of her last batch of the special brownies, her pet name for them, but still had that big bag of ganja. That is what the brownie website had called it. She liked that name.

She was baking her special brownies alongside the bake sale goodies today for the first time. She was being extra careful. She had to make sure she remembered to use the tacky plate for the special brownies to keep them separate. God forbid they get mixed in with the bake sale items. She giggled as she thought of that.

Can you imagine?

Chapter 26

Friday Morning • Kelly Residence

Aaron Kelly had finished his run and was happy he got five miles in before his right knee began to bark a bit too much. They had moved the old flat screen into the gym in the cellar a few years ago and had also thrown an old love seat among various weightlifting paraphernalia that Marcus and he had accumulated over the years.

They also had a ping-pong table upon which they engaged in epic battles. Aaron could play well and Marcus had gotten better as the years progressed. He had the amazingly quick hands that Baker loved but he was also a teenager and always went for the slam. Aaron was able to goad him into blasting errant shots when he set him up for them.

The rule was whoever won the last tournament (always best of seven, just like hockey) controlled the music while they played. So it was either mostly rap if Marcus had won or all Elvis if Aaron won. Elvis still was played the majority of the time, but as time went by Aaron was able to sing along to Ludacris and Snoop, too.

Aaron had seen his son go from a scrawny kid with God given talent to a very powerful force on the ice who had made the most of his gift. He had seen almost all of Marcus's hockey games and he hoped to see his son play in NHL games. He had been hoping for that a lot more lately as he had spent some college money they had saved over the years on the new Lexus instead.

But for good reason.

A few weeks ago Aaron had seen a scout he recognized from Montreal who had been nearby to see a college prospect but then stayed over in the Valley to see Marcus play again. The scout had no idea who Aaron was but Aaron had caught the guy chatting up the grocery store manager about Marcus and why he was in town. Although Aaron had not heard all of the conversation, he lingered by in the frozen food section long enough to hear him say, "Marcus Kelly is just the real deal, NHL potential, size and speed, but he most likely won't be there when we pick."

Aaron just smiled. He had dipped into the college fund for the Lexus and he suspected that Claire knew this and thus had insisted on their first vacation in years. She had booked them for a cruise with upgraded cabins and all sorts of massages and cream treatments. They were leaving for the cruise tonight.

If you can do it then so can I, she seemed to be daring him. If losing this tug of war to her meant that a pro team would draft his son and he had a Lexus and went on a cruise that was fine by him.

After hearing the scout making such positive comments about Marcus and his potential, Aaron felt as if a college scholarship, a full boat, would be the worst they could expect if Marcus could keep his grades up. Could he? Aaron had never pushed Marcus academically. Their focus had been hockey, lifting and fighting. He hoped that would not bite them in the ass if college became the choice.

NHL draft? That was a better fit.

After a quick shower and cup of coffee to go, Aaron was whistling as he got into the Lexus and began to back out of the driveway to head to work. He loved this car more every day. Sure he was rolling the dice on Marcus's not needing the money for college, but why not bet on such a great kid and great car? He still could not picture Marcus in college.

Marcus had been a gifted skater since he began playing, anybody could see it. Marcus could score goals since day one, just one of those things. He had vision on the ice and he could skate faster than everybody else. He had a few years where he was smaller and got punished by bigger guys, but he still scored the most goals every year. He had hockey smarts.

But his kid could shoot a puck, too. Boy could he shoot a puck. He used to work tirelessly in the backyard shooting street hockey balls into the net. Slap. Slap. Slap. It was background noise in the Kelly house. Their garage door was a mess, having absorbed thousands of errant shots and having the dents and scuff marks to prove it. That thought made Aaron laugh and remember when he learned the hard way that his son's practice had paid off.

When Marcus was twelve years old Aaron took out his baseball glove, an old hockey glove and his old hockey stick and strutted over and stood in the net where Marcus had been practicing his shot in the backyard. He taunted Marcus with his glove – bring it on. Marcus laughed and shook his head.

Claire, who had been out back gardening while Marcus shot the dozen or so bright orange street hockey balls about a thousand times that day, warned Aaron to be careful. Even with her back turned she could sense how fast those balls were whizzing into the net.

Aaron dismissed her warning with a macho smirk and waved Marcus in closer to the net. He told him if he could score one goal in five shots he would get five dollars. Marcus did not move the balls closer and when he chose not to Aaron gulped a bit and looked to Claire for help.

Marcus asked if they could make it five dollars per goal. Aaron was now wondering what he had gotten himself into. He regained his composure and agreed to the five dollars per goal.

He had not seen Marcus shoot in a while, thought Claire, who was now standing up and silently betting on her son winning this one even as she said, "Get ready, Aaron."

"Can I get in on this bet?" she asked with a smile. Aaron looked at her and rolled his eyes.

Marcus nodded to his Dad and Aaron meekly smiled and readied himself in his best goalie imitation. He thought of the stitched-up mask that the Bruins' goalie Gerry Cheevers had worn and suddenly wished he had at least worn his sunglasses.

Can I call a time out?

Marcus took position and wound up for a slap shot from about forty feet away. Aaron was distracted by how good his windup was.

The kid had been practicing.

Aaron never had a chance.

The rock hard missile hit Aaron in the balls with a dull thud. Claire gasped as Aaron groaned and dropped his gloves and stick. He was bent at the waist, trapping the ball in the exact spot where it had made full contact with his genitalia. He dropped to his knees, his mouth stuck open but making no noise. The ball dropped and rolled slowly away as if to say, "Marcus made me do it."

Before Claire could move to help her husband Marcus had skillfully shot four quick snapshots into the net, whizzing past Aaron, who was still kneeling and silently in an inordinate amount of pain.

He walked by his frozen-in-pain Dad to pick up the balls and said to him, "You owe me twenty bucks. Sorry about your balls, Dad." Aaron replied through gritted teeth and with quick breaths, "Make sure you are wearing your cup all the time when you play, please."

To this day Marcus insists he was not aiming for his Dad's balls with the first shot. His parents are not so sure.

Hockey dominated their lives. He and Claire made sure that they got him to every game they could get him to as a kid. He played year round and for many teams. It was expensive and initially they had to travel great distances by car just for one game. The Fish Tank was a godsend as many of the regional tournaments were then held locally and greatly reduced their travel time and costs.

They had sacrificed and worked hard to earn the money for this expensive sport. The Lexus was his reward, how Aaron had justified it. He was Marcus Kelly's father and he had an image to project now, also.

No?

Aaron had played some hockey as a kid, most boys in Massachusetts at that time did. But he never reached anything near the level at which Marcus had been playing these last two years.

Who had, really?

Valley residents stopped Aaron and Claire constantly to talk about Marcus. Everybody knew about Marcus. He was overwhelmed by the adulation and the fanatical way in which they rooted for Marcus. It was overwhelming to Claire and him so he could only imagine what Marcus went through.

But he and Claire ate it up and enjoyed their status.

The autograph requests at restaurants from kids were a sign of things to come, hopefully. Marcus ate it up, too – it was part of the plan. Expected but not taken for granted.

The NHL never really was truly considered an attainable goal until Marcus had his growth spurt.

Initially Marcus was undersized in high school. Sure, he was talented and fast with a goal scorer's touch and a reputation that preceded him. He scored seventy-nine goals one season early on in youth hockey and had told Aaron that was "more than Espo ever scored for the Bruins!"

During his freshman and sophomore years Marcus had shown signs of being a superstar but overall his production did not match the hype and Aaron sensed disappointment from the other parents. Marcus paid no attention to any criticism and just kept working hard and working out.

Skate. Spar. Lift. Repeat.

He was vastly undersized despite his skills and speed but he was slowly adjusting to the more physical play. Because of his reputation he was targeted by the bigger guys on the other teams and even by his own guys in practices whenever they could land a hit on him. It was like a secret club they were trying to get into and putting Marcus through the boards was the initiation fee.

Marcus was amazingly durable, though. He had taken a severe cheap shot from a St. Mary's player during his freshman year but only had to miss a few games with a bum shoulder.

A guy named Ratkowski hit him dirty.

Those were the only games he had ever missed for Valley High. His ability to take a hit was up there with his skill level.

He worked hard at the rink but he may have worked his hardest at Baker's Gym. He often came home from sparring sessions with black eyes, bloody noses, split lips and other bruises. He was sparring against seriously good trainers and other students. Even at the gym the other students seemed to be trying to get into the "I Hit Marcus Club". He usually had sore knuckles from landing good shots, too. They wore padding everywhere but they went at it. He never let a sparring injury keep him from playing a hockey game but he played through a lot of pain. He would hide most of it from his parents.

Tough kid playing a tough sport, as Goat would say. Goat's support was unwavering and his faith in Marcus remained strong as he saw something in the kid that others were too impatient to notice.

Things began to really change for Marcus physically as he trained the summer before his junior year. He had scored twenty-five goals in his sophomore year but the Bulldogs missed the tournament for the sixth straight year.

Marcus was determined that Valley would qualify for the tournament his last two years. He had helped the team achieve that goal. He doubled his production from sophomore year to junior year and was on a similar pace this year.

He worked harder than ever and his body finally responded. Claire was initially astonished at how much food a kid who was growing this much this quickly consumed. She would look in the fridge and wonder if she really had just gone shopping two days ago. She joked they should buy a henhouse and a cattle farm.

He was becoming a finely tuned hockey machine. Youth was not wasted on this kid. This was his homework and he did the extra credit assignments. He was a bitch to play against now. He was not dirty but hockey was a contact sport and Marcus was a two-way player. He took the body and he shielded the puck by initiating contact with unsuspecting, oncoming opponents. He had uncanny timing with open ice hits. Guys that used to push him around two years ago were now unable to budge Marcus off the puck. And in the corners it was Marcus delivering the huge hits, not taking them.

As his legend grew, the stands were more and more crowded with each game he played. His slap shot was well known now as he had two "broken-Plexiglas" moments at The Fish Tank. He shattered the glass with the puck. Fish did not mind that expense at all.

Marcus knew which teams' coaches would want to goon Marcus up and have their boys take runs at him all night. The poor goons were in for long nights now. Marcus always gave as well as he got and he was much stronger than most of the guys who tried to goad him into retaliating. That was their motive. They wanted Marcus in the penalty box instead of on the ice. Marcus had to use restraint and absorb abuse. The refs did not feel the need to defend the biggest guy on the ice.

The scouts loved his on-ice demeanor. "Bring it on," he seemed to say every night. And Marcus prided himself on showing up every night to play. There were more scouts as the seasons progressed – college and pro. The Boston papers had guys covering his games now.

There were also a few times when, if a kid had been going after Marcus on the ice, Aaron would be pissed off and nod from the stands. That meant that Marcus had permission to retaliate or defend himself. These happened very infrequently and Claire would elbow Aaron knowing what he had just unleashed, but she never really protested. She, like Aaron, knew that this was part of the process of their son moving up the hockey ladder. He had to show others that he was not incapable of dishing it out, too. And boy could he dish it out.

Hockey was a vicious, beautiful sport to Aaron. Claire saw the danger but knew denying her son the game he loved so much would be a huge disservice to him.

Marcus was no saint on the ice. He played hard.

A while ago, a kid was really swinging his stick at Marcus and hitting him with dirty hits all game. He got the nod from the stands. With a hockey glove on he knocked out the kid with one perfect punch. The poor kid was wearing a wire cage over his face and a top of the line helmet. Marcus was eleven at the time.

Out cold. Kid had it coming in spades that day. Baker still loved hearing that story.

Chapter 27

Aaron beeped when he saw Dan Baker inside his gym as he drove by on his way to work. Baker turned and had no idea who was driving the fancy car. Aaron had not shown him his new car yet.

Aaron and Baker had become good friends since the day they met almost ten years ago. Until Marcus got his license Aaron drove him to the gym for his workouts and often stayed to observe.

Marcus and Baker had a special relationship, too. Baker the Marine had loved Marcus from day one. He taught Marcus everything he knew about fighting and was impressed with how easily Marcus took to the training. Baker was a specialist in many disciplines and the perfect pupil had shown up at his door – clay ready to be molded, fervently.

Marcus showed up for every lesson ready to go. He absorbed instruction, and beatings, like a sponge and Aaron loved the way Baker was so hands on with Marcus as he instructed him. They sparred frequently. They always hugged at the end of their sessions, something Baker did with few other students.

After watching Marcus's training on one particular day, Aaron had learned that he never wanted to fight an Israeli soldier. This guy was diminutive but was by far the most badass fighter Baker had ever hosted at his gym. He taught Marcus many things but he showed Marcus some elbow techniques that Marcus had never been taught. Marcus loved the guy and hugged him after the lesson in which Marcus was thrown and smacked around like a car-crash dummy.

They had a great relationship and Aaron was relieved that Marcus communicated with him. Aaron knew Marcus drank a bit but felt assured that Marcus was too focused on his future to waste it with booze and drugs.

Suddenly Aaron was jolted out of his thoughts as he drove over an empty can in his parking lot.

He got out and picked up the can. "Busch? Who drinks that piss?"

Chapter 28

Friday Morning • The Fish Tank

Captain Russell walked into The Fish Tank and found his way to Goat's office. Russell had been there before but it had been a while.

"Hey, Goat. Word is the Valley Alumni Association wants you hung by your French Fries if you lose this game tonight."

"That is no joke, Captain. Or is it Chief yet?"

"To you, Goat, it's Russ, please." Russ wanted to warm up to Goat before he told him why he was there. Goat did not let him. Goat had home ice advantage here.

"What is on your mind, Russ? I got a busy day." Goat tapped his foot anxiously, wanting to get over to the school to sweet talk his goalie back onto his team. He was distracted and impatient.

Russell picked up on Goat's insubordinate reply and got right to his point, too.

"Boots is on my mind, Goat, among too many other things, thanks to you hockey guys. He is using cop cars like they are his personal designated driver. Only problem is we are catching him drunk driving and then giving him the ride home. Plus some of your players are being a little too brazenly public with their drinking. I know this city loves a winner and you are certainly providing us with one this year – thanks to Marcus."

Goat signed the cross and whispered a prayer in French, winking at Russell as he did this, trying to lighten the mood.

Boots was becoming an issue.

Russell ignored the wink, "And I know that Chief O'Reilly was a bit relaxed in regard to enforcement of the law when it came to drunk driving and other offenses, especially to Valley athletes and coaches. Thankfully, we have not had any serious incidents that have stemmed from this relaxed approach to the enforcement of a very serious crime. Yet."

He continued, "Therefore, I am putting you coaches on notice, Goat. Things change. Today. Tonight. Going forward. I am telling my boys that DUIs are enforced regardless of what team you are on or who you are or whom you know. No exceptions. No favors."

Goat was steaming mad. "Seems to me, Russ, that you should be talking to da damn football coach, da lacrosse coach and all da other coaches in here before you come into my office on a day like this!" Goat barked at Russell, surprising him.

Time to shift gears.

"Goat, take it down a notch. I am here to ask that you address your team and alert them to this chat we are having, that's it. Your team is in-season and easily assembled. I am trusting that you will do this for me and for the kids."

"I will. Anything else?" asked Goat, composing himself and slightly embarrassed.

"Ya, can you cancel your game tonight, please?" pleaded Russell.

"Ha, can't do that, Chief, rivalry and all. I gotta go write my speech for da big pep rally, eh?" Goat stood up and dismissed Russell from his office.

Goat knew the boys on his team drank, probably a bit more than other years. But hockey players drank and this team was heavy with seniors. Senior hockey players were a thirsty lot but he just had to coach these guys for a few more weeks. They would be fine.

He reminisced about his playing days and his fondest memories were sitting around the room after a game and drinking beers with the boys. That is how he

105

viewed his players' drinking – an innocent and vital part of the bonding among hockey players.

Fucking cops.

Chapter 29

Claire Kelly was so excited. She had finally talked Aaron into taking this fancy cruise and their dear friends Matt and Kelsey were coming with them. It was only for five days because they had to be back in time for the first tournament game that Marcus would play next week.

She loved going to the hockey games. Because Marcus was the star of the team the other Valley Hockey Moms treated her a bit differently. She was considered the leader of the pack and she liked it that way. Her suggestions were followed and when the teams traveled throughout the years she got to decide where to stay and where to eat on the road. She had grown accustomed to it and liked it that way.

Marcus was her son, after all.

She was so excited about this cruise. It was their first non-hockey vacation in years. They should be leaving this afternoon to be safe but since the game was moved to the earlier time they could watch the game and then head out quickly. They hated to miss such a big game and chance at the scoring record. Logistically it was a bit of a mess, but they should get to Logan in time if the weather cooperated.

She was a little surprised that Aaron would be so willing to spend money on a cruise after buying the Lexus recently, too. However, she had played her hand perfectly, using the Lexus as leverage for her to finally get the vacation.

Aaron handled the finances for the Kelly family. They were frugal but only had one child and had saved some money for Marcus for college early so it had grown as Aaron invested it through the years. But Claire had sacrificed enough.

I earned this.

Chapter 30

Friday Morning • Hickey Residence

Jamie called Rat on his cell. Rat saw the name "HalfCop" on his screen and did not want to pick up but figured it might have to do with something from last night. Rat's brain was still a bit fuzzy about the night before. He and Jamie and a few other jail guards had really tied one on. He vaguely remembered seeing his newest female target, Darlene, last night. That made him smile.

"What's up, Half-a-Cop?" Rat answered using Jamie's newish nickname that only Rat used. He considered himself a nickname inventor. Like most of Rat's actions it was considered annoying by all he anointed.

Jamie hated his new nickname, he was sensitive about his auxiliary status which Rat and Russell liked to bust his balls about. "Hey Rat, how's the hangover? I am hurting, man. That was some night."

"No shit, Jamie, I can smell the bong smoke from here by the way. I thought you had to work today?" Rat could always tell when Jamie was stoned.

Jamie coughed and said, "I do, ha – stoned cop should be my nickname. I should film a documentary about my day today, never been this fucked up before work. I tried calling in sick but they need me I guess. I hate Russell. He sucks!"

Jamie continued, "Hey, you were funny last night. After about our sixth tequila shot you were telling that chick Darlene you know from Dunkin Donuts at the bar that you wiped your ass lefty but jerked off righty. You kept asking her if that was weird. It was fucking comical and sad at the same time! She was not laughing but we all were."

109

Rat was horrified. But he was happy to hear that he was at least talking with Darlene. He had been trying to ask her out the last few weeks but so far had chickened out. He tried to fluff off his emotions at the mention of Darlene so he joked, "Ha, that is true. What hand do you use?"

"I am righty-righty, fella. You were hammered."

Rat felt his pocket and said, "I have all those drugs and the ounce of ganja for Bald Boy, minus a few joints for you, of course. You better have not taken out too much, that Cuban notices that shit. Oh, when I went in to get the pot, Bald Boy's cousin paid me two grand, I'll give you your cut soon."

"This is working out quite well for both of us, buddy," said Jamie. He was using his money to buy video gadgets such as hidden cameras and microphones. "Is this bald Cuban dude going to keep needing us? I hope so." Jamie was going to leave for California soon and wanted to maximize his money before he left.

"I told you, Bald Boy runs the inmates, especially the Latinos, because there are about a million of them in there. He is the king of the fucking Spanish inmates. But that is like you being king of the half-a-cops. Who fucking cares, right? Sorry, but it's true. But know this – Bald Boy is my bitch. He needs me, without me he is nothing! I lug him these drugs and all the other shit every week and I let him have his way with that drag queen when he gets that sick urge and he takes care of my problems in the jail. It works out for everybody." Rat eyed the three stripes on his uniform shirt. Sergeant Rat. He was so proud of those stripes. He was moving up.

He was a fucking Sergeant, motherfucker!

He needed to start acting like one now. He was anxious to get to work to see if he'd be in charge of the

110

whole jail tonight. If so he needed to pick his jailbait wisely. There were no obvious choices among the current population so he'd have to give this some thought. He needed to use the power he had over Bald Boy. Going in and telling him he had to fight, put on a show, was the ultimate weapon Rat had in his arsenal. It was a way to tip the scales of power back to him. You do what I say, Cuban.

But whom does he fight? This one needs to be special.

Rat hesitated before saying, "I am a Sergeant, Jamie. I have rank now."

Rat was trying to believe what he was saying to Jamie but he knew that Bald Boy was trying to change the dynamic of their relationship to better fit his needs, not Rat's. Rat was desperate to change that.

Jamie chimed in, "That Boyz gang we are getting the dope from is fucking scary, man. I don't want to go with you for those meetings any more. That guy and his crew are serious people. There were about twenty of them just looking at me in the car last night while I waited for you. They have some serious tattoos, too. Who the fuck gets a tattoo on their face? They look stupid." Jamie shuddered at the memory of being looked at like that by so many gang-bangers.

Rat was holding his fully loaded nine-millimeter pistol and pointing it at various spots in his room, fake target shooting with his finger on the trigger and then pointing it elsewhere like the idiot that he was.

"Jamie, relax. I deal with the real bad guys inside the walls. These so-called gangsters from last night are nothing but talk. Besides, I got my nine-mill with me at all times. I will fucking use it if we need to. You need to drive me, remember? Why else would I be paying you? So you are most definitely still coming every

111

fucking time, ka-peesh? Don't wet your pants, though, I'll protect you with my gun, Half-a-Cop."

Jamie remembered Rat pulling out his gun last night and said, "You took out your gun at the bar last night, man. Everybody scattered. You gotta watch that shit when you are all fucked up like that, Rat. I had to talk that hot bartender out of calling the cops. She was looking at me like, "You are a cop, do something!" Darlene was screaming at you, too. I don't think she likes you much."

Rat knew Darlene liked him and he got hot in the face and pointed his gun at the phone. "You are only a half a cop and you don't know how to read ladies like I do. Plus you got no gun."

That was true but Jamie did not like seeing a drunk with a gun even if it was Rat. He changed the subject. "You ever fear getting caught lugging all this stuff into jail, man? I mean, it is illegal."

"I am in total control, relax." Rat saw that he was aiming the gun at himself in the mirror as he said that and pulled it down to his leg.

Rat was working himself into a rage on his end, "Jamie, don't you fucking doubt me! I am God in the jail. I say jump and they jump until I say stop. Don't doubt my power in the fucking jail, you fucking half-a-cop dope head!" He slammed the phone down.

Jamie knew that Rat's forehead vein was throbbing like a swollen river when he hung up on Jamie after his rant. Rat was becoming more and more volatile and Jamie was attached at the hip to him with this lugging into jail scheme of theirs. Jamie was in this thing up to his eyeballs and those face-tattooed Boyz had seen him more than once.

That scared him.

Jamie wanted to leave for California soon. He was itching to film something.

112

Chapter 31

Goat found Irene Poulin in the teachers' lounge and asked if she had a minute.

Over the glasses perched on her nose she replied, "Certainement, monsieur."

Goat laughed a fake laugh and replied, "En anglais, s'il vous plait." His French was rusty and he preferred English at this point in his life.

As he sat he pointed to the open sports page next to her with a picture of Marcus and the Mr. Superstar headline. Goat had just read the article this morning and found it thoughtful and well done. Goat did not know some of the things about Marcus that were mentioned in the article. It was a tribute to his career and a look back at his achievements.

"Nice article on Marcus, eh?" asked Goat, turning on the French Canuck charm like he had a switch.

"Yes, he sure is a good hockey player. I never had him in any of my classes, however, so I've no idea what kind of a student he is other than from what I hear in places like this," she said as she motioned to the other teachers seated in a separate area of the lounge.

Goat looked around at the motley crew of burned out faculty and said, "Marcus has had a great career and it has been a real joy to coach him. He is a true leader and da most talented kid I've ever seen at this level. Which brings me to my visit, eh? I was hoping you could postpone posting Fowler's grade by just a few days so that he can work on his grade to get it up to da level where he can play hockey and also get to play his last home game as a senior here at Valley High."

Goat sensed apprehension so he made eye contact and shifted forward in his seat, "We have this nice celebration tonight for Senior Night. His folks walk him out to center ice. They get a nice rose and some applause for being da chauffeurs all these years, paying those bills, tightening those skates. This is their small tribute."

Goat paused for effect, nodding, letting the importance of his poignant speech sink in.

He had done this many times before.

Irene cleared her throat and said, "Coach Gauthier, I know how much you care about hockey. It is as much as I care about teaching. If your player had broken a rule for your team that affected his participation in my class, I would honor that and trust your judgment and back you up. I hope that you will do the same for me, to offer me the same professional courtesy. Mr. Fowler was a decent student until a few months ago. All of a sudden he just turned off the switch. No homework, no participation, bad test scores. Mr. Fowler has not done a thing in my class and he deserves an F as much as any kid ever has. So for you to ask me to postpone this grade so he can play a stupid hockey game really gets my goat, Goat!" She smiled at her play on words, proud of her stand on this issue.

Goat knew what he was up against here. He had heard this professionalism speech many times. This young idealist was making a stand, something the Goat had seen too many times. He knew it was futile to continue this conversation.

He smiled, left the lounge and walked toward the principal's office. This was a chess match. His cute French accent had no effect on that new gal, now it was time for his next move.

Goat needed his fucking goalie.

He walked in and shook hands with his friend, Principal Thompson, who was an old buddy and sometime drinking partner. Thompson was reading the

114

Marcus article and smiling. Thompson knew that the school board liked him a lot more when Valley's sports teams were winning so he really liked Goat now.

Goat explained the dilemma he now faced with Fowler to Thompson and added, with some forced fake emotion, how sad it would be if Marcus went out on a losing note after all the good his success had done for the school's, and the town's, pride.

But he really got Thompson when he suggested how upset Fish, Thompson's biggest backer and an invaluable donor to the Principal's every need, would be. Fish would not be pleased to hear that the starting goalie was now benched because of a bad grade that could have been posted later. Thompson shook Goat's hand and nodded, indicating he knew what to do.

A teacher who was new to town and needed a reminder about how things worked in Juniper Valley was fucking with the machine.

Thompson immediately headed down to the teachers' lounge and found Irene. The other teachers quickly remembered they had other places to be when they saw the angry, familiar look on Thompson's ruddy face.

"Irene, Coach Gauthier just explained to me that you have the option of posting Fowler's grade next week but you are choosing to post it today instead? Is this true?"

Irene did not like being put on the spot for doing her job. She replied through gritted teeth, "That is one way of saying it, yes." She was nervous but steadfast.

"Irene, this seems silly. I applaud your professionalism, I really do. However, this seems vindictive. Is this a personal vendetta against this young man?"

He did not wait for an answer, "Because I am appalled that you would do something so cruel to our

115

young athletes. This city loves a winner and this hockey team has provided so much civic pride and, if I may, joie de vivre, that I think it is fair of me to ask that you hold off on posting Fowler's grade. No major rules would be broken by doing so, I assure you." He broke into his politician's smile and awaited her acquiescence via a small nod or simple yes.

Irene removed her glasses and spoke in a quiet but terse, almost disrespectful tone. "Principal Thompson, I have only been teaching here for five months but I have observed things I believe are horribly detrimental to these kids. Stupid levels of bending over backwards to accommodate athletes, fanaticism of these kids by the teachers and adults that is borderline extremism by any standard. Cops that look the other way if you have a sports jacket on. You are teaching these kids that as long as you can score a goal or hit a ball you are special and deserve special treatment. This city pampers these kids like no other I have ever seen. You are bringing up a generation of drunks and drug addicts by being so lenient. And now you are saying it is OK to not teach them to a high standard?"

Principal Thompson was fuming. He quickly glanced over each shoulder to make sure the room was empty. He then leaned forward, "Now you listen here, Missy. This machine that is Valley High Sports is bigger than me and certainly bigger than some first year teacher who, may I remind you, has no tenure here. If you and your noble aspirations want to try to stand in the way of this machine you just might find yourself out of a job. Think hard about that!"

Irene wanted to continue to argue about doing a disservice to these kids by ignoring warning signs. She wanted to reiterate that Fowler had been a decent student until recently and she suspected drugs were involved. And how these kids were better off being educated than futilely hoping to make millions playing sports.

Thompson smiled but said nothing as he watched the expression change on her face. From determined to unsure to surrender. He knew he had pulled the trump card – unemployment.

Irene thought about the Mini Cooper convertible she had just leased and remembered the new car payment she had just taken on to get that car. She loved her new loft apartment, too.

She needed this job.

Through gritted teeth Irene said she would be glad to be of help.

"Sorry for the misunderstanding, Irene. Will I see you at the game tonight? I would hope so. Stop by the box."

He stood with his crotch just a bit too close to her face for a moment as he squeezed her shoulder and looked down her blouse. Irene was now the one fuming. She looked down to hide her tears and nodded her head.

Fowler became a C- French student just like that.

Tres bien.

Chapter 32

As the student body gathered in the field house for the big pep rally to celebrate the hockey team and rally support for today's game, Marcus quietly slipped in and took his spot among his teammates. He knew that he was at his best among this crew of guys. There were seven other seniors and they had played together since they were six-year-olds. There were a few other hockey players who would be going to college and playing at that level, but they all knew Marcus was the reason they would be heavy favorites to win the tournament.

He loved this bunch of guys and he felt good about their chances in the tournament. As the number one seed they'd get a home game or two at least and probably open up against a team playing just decent hockey all year. Valley would be favored to win it all. Their two losses this year were to non-conference teams but Marcus was still pissed they had lost.

As he was waiting for the rally to start and looking at his texts Fowler landed with a thud beside him, laughing.

"I got the best video, check this out. Santorelli tried to drink a gallon of milk in less than an hour – this is a video of him puking it up and he only got halfway!"

Marcus watched the video with about ten hockey players watching over his shoulder. It was so gross that it was funny and they all hooted and hollered as it was played over and over. Santorelli watched them from the end of the bleachers with a silly grin on his face as he still looked like he may puke again. Marcus recalled Santo trying to eat a dozen Dunkin Donuts in a short time and puking that up, too. And there was a time when he tried to eat Saltines and failed. Then he had

118

tried something with cinnamon. He kept trying, had to give him credit.

Marcus bragged that he had not puked since he was ten years old. He was proud of that streak, too. Fowler said that was because Marcus drank like a chick and all the guys cracked up. Marcus punched Fowler on the shoulder and Fowler fell off the end of the bleachers but landed on his feet, rubbing his shoulder.

Marcus and Fowler had been best friends since grade school, always being the star player and goalie on whatever team they played. Fowler loved being on any team with Marcus. He could let in seven goals and still win because Marcus would score eight. Marcus made him look good in the win/loss column and that was all that mattered to Goat. Unlike his best friend, Fowler knew this would be as far as he would go in hockey.

But he was sure he and Marcus would be friends forever.

Marcus noticed the whole gym was silent and the boys were very focused as the hockey cheerleaders stood ready then began to perform during the rally. They had skimpy uniforms and danced and moved in ways that made all the boys in the stands take notice. Kaleigh was the choreographer so the routine they had chosen for the rally was their most provocative.

Fowler elbowed Marcus and pointed to Nicole, "Where the hell did she come from all of a sudden?" Marcus did not reply, he just watched her shimmy and shake. He never noticed Kaleigh leading her squad.

Coach Boots was leaning on the stands, watching the gals perform and wondered who the hell designed those uniforms? Give that guy a gold medal. Should I be getting some dollar bills for lap dances? He had been with Kaleigh a few times already. She was so hot and young. He chuckled to himself as she gyrated and made eye contact with him. He was hung over and hurting from last night but he had business to conduct ahead of February vacation. His pockets bulged a bit. Because of Kaleigh and because of the contents of his pockets.

Baggies and money.

Boots had begun smoking pot when he went overseas and failed in the pro hockey league over there. He came back to the Valley and worked the mortgage gig for a few years but hated it and quit that. He then ran into Goat and before he knew it he was coaching the hockey team with him. He loved hockey and The Fish Tank was a great rink.

He made shit for money so he had to supplement that.

He initially began dealing prescription pills to the kids at the school. Then he got a connection with The Boyz and started buying big bags of marijuana and selling small baggies to these kids, and some teachers, for a large profit. It was a captive audience. He was making good money from it now but the high school kids were constantly calling him. Last night he noticed Goat was watching him take the calls outside the bar.

Fucking kids.

The Boyz got great marijuana from Mexico but they scared the absolute shit out of Boots and he found their tattooed faces disturbing. He was making more and more trips to see them as he made more sales but they got no friendlier with him. They spoke Spanish and laughed in his face when he went inside to buy the drugs.

Why did he take French?

Marcus could not take his eyes off of Nicole as she performed. Had she been this gorgeous all along and he had simply missed it? Was he too busy hooking up with Kaleigh, whom he did not really like but who was hot and easy?

After the cheerleaders did their thing Principal Thompson took the microphone. He was very popular among the athletes as he was, like the Valley PD, never ashamed to look the other way when an athlete got into minor trouble. He evened that out by being extremely hard on the non-athletes.

"Welcome to the home of the Bulldogs! Who is going to win tonight?"

The gym went bonkers with the kids barking like bulldogs in unison, the Valley tradition. Thompson settled them by holding his right hand up.

"A few things to take care of first. This is the last day before February vacation so let's be sure to be safe and smart wherever your travels take you."

OK, Captain Russell? I did my part. Fucking cops.

The Principal continued, "As many of you know, this game against St. Mary's is the last game of Mr. Superstar Marcus Kelly's Bulldog career!" Marcus suddenly wished the Herald had chosen a different title for the article. Fowler and many teammates nearby began to jokingly raise their arms up and down in praise of their Mr. Superstar. Marcus gave them the middle finger so no others could see it.

Thompson calmly waited for the Boston-flavored chants of "Mah-kiss" to die down before he continued. Marcus ducked behind Fowler as his buddies all pointed to him and prodded him to stand up, to no avail.

"The other important aspect of this game is that if we can beat St. Mary's we can keep those rascals out of the tournament!"

The place erupted again; they all hated St. Mary's.

Fowler turned to Marcus and asked, "What the fuck is a rascal?"

"Some little dudes on this old TV show I think?"

They both laughed and bumped knuckles.

Principal Thompson continued, "We are going to need all of you to show up tonight at The Fish Tank and cheer the Bulldogs on to victory! Let's show St. Mary's what a home ice advantage really is! And, let's behave and make the Valley proud of its high school and its students, please. Be smart, be safe, and be sober!"

Captain Russell had visited Thompson after his visit to the Goat and asked him to read that last sentence verbatim. Thompson thought it was silly and over the top, but he played along.

He was aware, through his snitches, that the football players had already dragged three kegs of beer up to the quarries behind the school for the big party before the hockey game. Word of the pre-game kegger was spreading quickly and they might need a fourth keg. Everybody was going. Thompson chose to look the other way.

The football guys looked for Boots to give him some more money to buy the kegs.

Chapter 33

As Marcus placed his tray on the cafeteria table two guys shifted down so he could sit across from Conti, who had mercifully waved him over. He risked a look around at the scruffy crew of guys with whom he now sat. He looked like he fit in, more or less. Because Marcus had been growing his hair out (hockey hair) and not shaving (playoff beard) he almost looked like a peer of these convicts. He was just missing about a thousand tattoos, bad teeth and pasty white skin.

"The only thing I'd eat on that tray is the banana," said the really scary guy who had motioned Marcus over to the table. Conti.

Marcus sporked at the pile of crap that was called oatmeal and saw small rust colored legs sticking up at him. A cockroach. And two bright orange, curly hairs. Then he saw the curly black hairs on his toast. He almost puked. Again.

Conti laughed and said, "They screw with the new guys. What the fuck is Mr. Superstar doing in here, by the way?" asked Conti.

All white men, all almost as scary looking as the next guy, awaited his answer. Marcus thought to himself, Group picture, fellas? A memento from my time in here?

He refocused quickly. "I got DUI'd last night," guessed Marcus without looking up. The memories of being pulled over were coming back to him as his head cleared. Bits and pieces of being brought here were slowly returning to him, too.

"DUI does not get you in here without going to court first. Play straight with me, what are you hiding?"

Marcus hesitated. "I am telling the truth. I think the storm affected the police station so there was no place to bring me. I was hammered, I forget most of it." Marcus again remembered being way more fucked up than he should have been given what he drank. Why? He usually handled that amount of beer so easily. He had eaten nothing at Fish's party but then eaten those brownies in the car with Nicole.

"Well, you just got dealt the worst fucking hand in the history of DUIs," said the convict across from him, snapping Marcus out of his thoughts.

"Tell me about it," said Marcus. This strange state of mind he was in compelled him to look up and stare at Conti menacingly.

Time to deal with this, kiddo.

Conti did not notice the act across from him as he said, "I know who you are, saw you in the Herald yesterday. Big hockey stud, Marcus Kelly. I am your new best friend in here, Mr. NHL, not that you have much to choose from."

He pointed to himself and said, "Conti," as he slurped some milk from the carton and shoveled a big sporkful of eggs into his mouth.

Marcus wondered how the Herald got delivered to inmates in jail.

He continued to look at this man before him. On the street he would have either run from him or dialed 911. His hair was shoulder length and graying a bit, his beard was bushy and salt and pepper, too. His eyes were sky blue and had bags under them. In truth he looked exhausted. But he was mean-looking and had the arms of a football lineman. He had hands the size of a bear's paws. He was thick and hairy all over, scars and tattoos having a fight for supremacy of his skin.

This was a guardian angel? He had his jumpsuit rolled down to his waist exposing a stained tee shirt that had a picture of a hand grenade with the words "Japanese Motorcycle Repair Kit" below it.

Harley guys to the rescue. Harley's Angel?

"I only got a few minutes before they run us back up to the cells, so listen to me. You'll figure out why I am doing this someday. Pay it forward and all that happy horseshit," Conti lied. He had his reasons to help Marcus and they were all selfish. Wilson, his lugger, had told Conti all about Rat bringing in this kid under dubious circumstances when he had dropped off some cigarettes to him this morning.

"You gotta remember what I am about to say here, so shut the fuck up and open your ears. You do not belong here but here you are. You are in the worst fucking hellhole on the planet." Conti slurped more milk as his crew all nodded at what he had just said.

"This place is being run by a dirty CO called Rat – he is as dirty as any convict in here. The storm is keeping any change of guards away from here so this is his domain until they clear things out. That probably won't be any time soon from what we hear. He has an agenda today. This guy has a hard on for you. I don't know what you did to him but that ain't important now. He is a sick fucker. He probably killed neighbors' cats and shit when he was a kid." At this the other guys at the table all laughed.

"You are his fly today and he wants to pull your wings off, kid." Conti hated Rat and hoped their paths would cross when Conti got out of jail but he dared not fuck with him inside. Rat had a stacked deck inside the walls.

"He has the bald Cuban fucker working for him and if I know the Rat like I think I do I am going to guess he is either going to have Bald Boy go at you one on one or have a dozen of his little Hispanic Boyz come at you like a hive of killer bees. Today."

Marcus fought the urge to run back to his bunk and hide. What the fuck?

Conti went silent as if an idea had just hit him.

"Although Rat will probably make this go down as a sanctioned fight in the gym, make it all legit looking, he likes those public displays of power. Yup, he will probably put on one of his shows." Conti got very serious and was pointing at Marcus with his spork as he said, "Rat knows he has a limited time with you, he knows somebody fucked up and they will be coming for you as soon as they figure out what happened. This fight is going to happen today, it has to. He cannot risk you getting noticed by somebody and released before he can put on the show."

Conti again paused and took a bite of his toast, leaving the crumbs hanging from his beard. He looked at Marcus and asked, "You been in many fights, kid?"

Marcus shook his head, not wanting to explain his training.

Conti rolled his eyes and blew out a big breath.

Conti was getting antsy as he said, "I hear you are cellmates with that drag queen that Baldy fucks around with, is that right?" He sprayed the remaining toast crumbs from his beard as he said Baldy. Marcus was amazed at how much information this guy had already gathered. He nodded as he peeled his banana. He wanted to ask questions but was afraid to speak right now. He was fucking starving, too.

"Ok, when we get back to our cells I am guessing you are going to be reassigned quickly to a new cell by Rat. He needs you away from the Cuban fucker until the fight because he loses his show if nobody witnesses the fight. When you get back to the cell you tell queenie to give you the shank he bought from me, OK? Tell him I will make him another one."

Conti wanted Marcus to survive a surprise attack and fight Bald Boy where it would help Conti the most instead. Do it in the gym. Sanction it, Rat Fucker. Give this kid a chance. I gotta make sure that is how it goes down. This kid might fuck Bald Boy up for me.

He looked at Marcus for a long spell. Jesus, thought Conti, this was just a kid. "When you have it in your hands you hide it here," he said as he pointed to the waistband in his orange jumpsuit. Marcus was too terrified to even speak.

Conti saw this as an opportunity. He was going to use Marcus because he wanted Bald Boy taken out badly but he lacked the numbers to take The Boyz on and he feared fighting Bald Boy one on one.

This kid in front of him was a physical specimen. Conti wondered if he could fight and kick Baldy's ass in a sanctioned fight? He could really leverage that to his benefit. Conti knew that any power that existed in the jail was a finite amount. Whatever he gained or lost was gained or lost elsewhere.

What a lift it would be to his status among his crew if he could orchestrate it just right. Bald Boy would be the shame of The Boyz if he lost and there would be an internal fight among them as to who takes over after the Cuban goes down. Weakness exposed. Conti was really hoping that this fight would be sanctioned and not an ambush where a dozen Boyz will jump this kid with knives. That would just get them more power and more in business with that fucking Rat. Conti got nothing out of that deal.

If this worked out, Conti could then make his move and get Rat lugging to him instead. That was the key to this whole thing. He had that old fucker Officer Wilson bringing him cigarettes and porn magazines but he was retiring soon and he would not lug drugs or phones. When Wilson retired Conti would have to cultivate a new relationship with a lugging CO and that took time, which he did not have. Butts and drugs were power in the cellblocks. Conti wanted what Bald Boy now had. Conti had selfish reasons for helping this kid but he did start feeling sorry for him as he watched Marcus stare blankly at his tray.

This kid had no idea what was coming his way; how could he?

Chapter 34

Nicole was thrilled! Her squad had played a big role in the rally and the field house had gone nuts. She was a part of it, finally. As she left the basketball floor of the field house Kaleigh caught up with her. They sat together to take in the rest of the rally.

"That was fun, you did awesome," said Kaleigh.

"Thanks Kaleigh, I learned from the best," Nicole said as she sucked up to the captain of the squad shamelessly. She really liked Kaleigh and admired her.

Kaleigh laughed then got serious. "Nicole, I saw you and Marcus talking this morning. What was that about?"

Nicole paused, unsure where this was going. "Nothing, just wished him good luck in the game, that's it," lied Nicole. She was not a good liar to anybody but her father.

"Well, Marcus and I are kind of going out, so why don't you remember your place here. I can make or break you, remember that, OK? Back off Marcus." Kaleigh's early morning buzz had worn off and she was lashing out at the bitch that was trying to steal her man. Nicole was crushed.

Chapter 35

The name Rat was familiar to Marcus but he still could not figure out from where he knew him. He was groggy but way better with that banana and milk in his belly.

As he was trying to comprehend all that he had just been told Marcus heard the guard who was running the cafeteria yell, "OK convicts, back to your holes!" The guard then guffawed at his own lack of humor. Marcus saw a dozen convicts' middle fingers shoot up at him when he turned his back.

As Conti stood up he went right over to the three guys who were giving Marcus a hard time on the way into the cafeteria. Conti grabbed the skinny leader of the group, the guy who claimed to own Marcus's ass. He pushed him against a wall and pushed his forearm into his throat. He pointed at him and said, "I do not like you. I will knock you out and then piss in your open mouth if I see you even look at that fucking kid again."

Leave the new kid alone, motherfuckers, was the message Conti was sending to the whole jail. Bald Boy barely noticed and stood to walk out of the cafeteria.

As he stood Marcus saw Bald Boy staring at him and sizing him up, stirring the new violent streak Marcus had been given by the jail. Marcus gave him the best "fuck you" look he had. The evil of the jail was still working its way around inside Marcus but he was obviously affected. There was no flight left in Marcus, he was all fight now.

He had trained for this but he just thought it would be on an ice sheet against a big Canuck farm boy. Not against a Cuban in the local jail. As he continued to glare at Bald Boy his brave façade faded and was

130

replaced by the total fear he had been carrying with him since he arrived.

He also hoped that he had not just pissed his pants, it would show up on his orange suit.

Chapter 36

Fish was driving to the rink from his house. It was only a short drive there and Fish was talking on the phone to the caterer about the menu and the time changes. Even though there was a potential storm, Fish knew to expect upwards of three hundred people (more if Valley won!) and they would drink the place dry because that is what hockey people did. Fish had invited all alums and anybody ever associated with the program. Why not? He figured since Marcus was graduating why not really celebrate this? Should he order car service for the guests tonight, just in case? Nah, the storm just had to cooperate, he thought. We'll be fine.

Chapter 37

Rat still slept in the room in which he grew up. It was remarkably neat and tidy. Mama was the reason for that. Rat was a slob. There were no hints that this was the room that once belonged to a young boy. There were no pictures of family or teams. No trophies. He had not removed them over the years. He just never got any trophies. They did not give out trophies for being a bully and a prick.

He went into the kitchen and saw his brother getting up from the table. Joey cleared his plates and kissed Mama and thanked her for making him his game-day breakfast. Mama Rat did not cook much any more after almost burning the house down the last few times she had cooked bacon. Mama's screws were getting looser and looser and the boys saw it more every day.

Joey was going in late today. He was a senior hockey player at St. Mary's. He was considered a nice kid, unlike his brother, but once he hit the ice he played like the Rat that he was. Joey was smaller than Rat, but where they both lacked talent on the ice they more than made up for it in tenacity.

Joey hated being called Rat and he vowed to change his name as soon as he could. He preferred Joey and nobody really called him Rat. St. Mary's teams had their names on the backs of their game shirts and Joey had insisted on "Joey" on his back above his number thirteen.

Joey asked his older brother if he was coming to the game tonight.

"No, I got a shift at the jail, sorry little bro. But I hope you take a run at Marcus the pussy for me."

Joey was disappointed. His father never went to the games but he was used to that. His father was never really home, he traveled for work. Joey was hoping Jimmy would be there tonight.

Mama smiled and said, "I'll be there honey. That Marcus Kelly had better have his head up all night." She smacked her fist into her palm as she said this. She was wearing only one slipper and her bathrobe was on inside-out.

Although they loved her and Mama Rat knew her hockey, she was becoming "a bit off" as the polite among us would say. The boys made fun of her behind her back for it but they did love her and worried about her, especially Joey. He was around Mama a lot more than anybody else. She was slipping and getting more forgetful. She was only fifty-six.

She was getting crazier, too. Last week she frantically called Joey into the living room. Joey ran in and Mama told him she was calling her sister on the phone but was only getting cartoons. Puzzled, Joey asked her to show him what she meant, so she dialed her sister's phone number and handed the phone to Joey who held it up to his ear as his heart broke.

It was the TV remote control, not the phone. She was "dialing" the remote and the last three digits she had pushed put the TV on the Cartoon Network. Joey was concerned but what could he do? He told Jimmy and Jimmy just laughed his ass off and called that idiot Jamie to tell him the story.

Mr. Ratkowski, Jim and Joey's Dad, was never home. He was always away on weekends and was out of town again tonight "making sales," as Mama called his absences. He was taking advantage of Mama's somewhat recent decline and becoming bolder with his trysts.

Instead of making sales, he was actually shacked up with his newest girlfriend in the next town over and they had booked a hotel for the weekend. He missed almost all of the kids' games and events. Rat hated his old man and knew exactly what he was doing. It kept him away from the house, so that was fine with Rat. He did not step up to fill his Dad's void, though. He looked at it as one less asshole to deal with.

Joey did not really know his father so he only had Rat to emulate. He could not have picked a bigger asshole to look up to.

Rat sensed his brother's disappointment and laughed. He did not give a shit if his brother wanted him at the game. Rat was not a good guy in any way to anybody. Rat broke the silence, holding up the Herald and pointing at the picture of Marcus on the back cover.

"Yup, this is the last chance a member of this family has to take a run at Mr. Superstar. Remember what I did to him in his first game we played against him when I was a senior?"

Of course they did, it was Rat's shining moment on the ice in his sick mind. He told the story about a million times, each time the story growing a bit more. Mama Rat ducked her head in and said, "You dropped him like a sack of hammers!"

Joey rolled his eyes at Rat and said, "You were the dirtiest player I've ever seen and that was the cheapest hit you ever threw."

They bumped knuckles as Rat hissed, "Fuck Marcus Fucking Kelly." He had worked up a loathing for Marcus out of jealousy without ever having met him off the ice. It was an unhealthy and weird hatred. But the more the legend of Marcus Kelly grew the better the story it would make for Rat. I crushed an NHL player.

The chicks would like that story even more.

Rat said, "Well, now that torch has been passed, little bro. I know what I'd do if I was the last Rat to play against him." He stared at his brother and sliced his throat with his finger. Mama saw it and smacked her hand into her fist as she nodded.

Jimmy threw a twenty-dollar bill at his brother and said, "I better fucking hear about an ambulance ride needed at The Fish Tank over the radio tonight, little bro. Make me proud." The jail had a radio that Rat religiously listened to while he was at work. It picked up all EMT transmissions as well as the police radio broadcasts. Rat paid attention to that so he could keep an ear to the ground on all fronts. By listening to the police radio he'd know who was coming to visit him at the jail and he could stay a step ahead.

Again Mama Rat entered the conversation, "I will make sure he does just that, James. Now go clean up the piss in your closet from last night. When will you stop that drunken sleepwalking and start pissing in the toilet like a normal drunk?"

They all laughed as Joey headed out to school.

Chapter 38

Saturday Morning • the jail

Marcus remained in shock and scared stiff but successfully walked back up to his cell without making eye contact with anybody who wanted to cause him physical harm. Even up here in the blocks Marcus could see that the guards were few and far between, not that they would be of any help if he got jumped. He was praying he would be out of this nightmare soon. Conti's speech had scared the shit out of him but he was happy to see Conti stick up for him, too.

He wondered if the storm had passed, but the thick granite walls gave no hints from the outside world, nor did the windows. He suddenly pictured his folks on the cruise, eating like royalty, and got depressed. He prayed they knew he was here.

When he walked into his cell he saw the whimpering figure from the night before sitting up and smoking a cigarette. He had long blonde hair and a thin build. His face was very thin but pretty like a woman's. He had fingernails shaped into pointed claws that would make a tiger jealous. Marcus could not take his eyes off the talons as they were each sharpened to a fierce looking point, even the thumbs. They still had chipped red polish on them that gave the appearance of dried blood from a recent victim.

The whimpering man cleared his throat and offered a hand and said, "I am Jacob Pinkham at your service, young stud. You can call me Jake, if you prefer." He was skinny but lean and wiry. His skin was almost translucent making his bluish veins appear to be on the surface.

As he stated his name to Jake and went to shake hands, Marcus noticed the limp way in which Jake offered his hand. He was feminine in every way.

Marcus clumsily grabbed his hand, careful to avoid Jake's claws. Marcus was a mental mess as he further assessed his current situation. That Conti guy had said a gang of those tattooed guys might come for him and to be ready for it. How exactly does one prepare to fight twelve armed convicts?

Marcus could not stop looking at the unlocked cell door. There was a lot of commotion out on the catwalk as inmates bartered and traded cigarettes, food and magazines ahead of being locked up until lunch. He heard somebody saying Rat was headed this way and they all scattered back to their cells.

Rat? Where have I heard that? Marcus was nervous and wanted to see if Bald Boy would be coming back into this cell so he stood facing the door to be ready for either a gang of guys or one Bald Boy. He hoped the doors would close soon.

"Where is your boyfriend?" asked Marcus without taking his eyes from the still open cell door.

Close the fucking door! He was on full alert. He flexed his hands into and out of fists. Had he asked Jake he would have known this happened to be a cell that you could close manually by pulling hard on the door and getting it off its tracks. There were about a dozen throughout the jail that the inmates knew about. The guards did not.

Rat screamed "All in!" and the cells all closed via a remote panel still being run by the generators. They rumbled shut with a steady hum followed by the thud of a hundred doors slamming shut at once, echoing off slabs of granite. This place even had scary noises in daylight, Marcus noted. But it was music to his ears to have the cell door locked and nobody else in their cell.

His senses remained on high alert and it was a strain on his depleted system. He felt exhausted from the fear and lack of sleep and food. He was drifting toward a state of panic when Jake interrupted his nightmare.

"Did you call that animal my boyfriend? Jealous, Marcus? Ha! Boyfriend? Not by my definition anyhow. He has his own cell so he just comes up here to visit his favorite blonde at night when he has the urge. God, you are sooo young and hot and big and muscle-y, what are you doing in a place like this?"

"DUI last night," replied Marcus, anticipating the follow up question as he said it. He was trying to act cool but Jake sensed his fear and Marcus was too tired to hide it.

"DUI? Did you kill somebody?" He offered Marcus a Virginia Slim.

Marcus shook his head, "I wish I knew. I cannot remember a thing about it. I am trying to focus on this place and survive this. I have no idea how I got in here but I do know that I got some shit to deal with while I am in this fucking nightmare. Conti said you could help me. He said something about a guard named Rat making me fight against that Bald Boy. A show?" For the second time his voice cracked as he said this. Jake did not seem to notice as he lit another cigarette.

Jake signaled to Marcus to have a seat beside him on the middle bunk but Marcus smartly chose to lean on the sink and motioned for Jake to begin. He did not want any part of those claws being near him.

"OK, story time in Jake's cell, kids! First a brief history about me." Jake liked talking and he really liked Marcus. Marcus squirmed. He knew he had very little time but what could he do? At least the cell door was locked now.

"I am here because I like heroin but my various ways of making money do not make me enough money

139

to actually afford a heroin habit. That is a problem if you are not familiar with heroin, Marco Polo. If you need it you need it, cash or no cash. But I have something some men like better than cash, of course." He motioned to his body and stuck out his abnormally large tongue and touched his nose with it. Marcus chalked it up to yet another strange thing happening to him since he got here.

Marcus nervously chuckled and blurted out, "I know, I heard you guys last night. Can you tell me about Bald Boy?" Marcus was amazed at what he was talking about and with whom he was having the conversation. He wished he could text Fowler.

Marcus noticed that Jake took his voice down to a whisper at the mention of Bald Boy and looked nervously out the door.

"Bald Boy runs the inmate side of this jail, make no mistake about that. The wimpy Warden might have the title, and that absolute piece of shit guard Rat might think he has the power in the blocks, but Bald Boy and The Boyz in his crew are the undisputed power in these blocks. The guards are outnumbered, old, corrupt and scared. The other gangs and crews of inmates are nothing in comparison to The Boyz now that Bald Boy is leading them. I have been here six months and I have seen them do some things to people that would make you shudder."

Marcus just stared at Jake's claws and asked purely out of curiosity, "So why are you in here?"

Jake nodded and puffed away, careful to blow the smoke from his Virginia Slim away from Marcus. Like that mattered in this unventilated hellhole.

He lifted his other hand and wiggled his fingers at Marcus as he playfully growled. It was menacing even in jest.

Jake began speaking while exhaling, "I used my claws in a way a customer who did not pay for services which he had already received did not really like. He was the brother of a cop. Voila, here I am, six more months to serve on an indecent battery charge, not my first and probably not my last." He playfully pawed in Jake's direction and meowed, "I can be a fierce bitch, especially when I need a fix." Marcus withdrew and thought for a minute.

"And you are Bald Boy's, um, guy in here? I thought that was just made up on TV?" Marcus knew he did not have much time but when would he be talking to a drag queen in jail any time soon? He was trying to be cool but his façade was slowly fading. This was fascinating to hear.

"Look, I ain't like all the other fellas in here, if you had not noticed? So I have a choice. Either let that Cuban animal have his way with me and have him protect me from the other assholes in here or I can try to fight off every horny idiot in here. I ain't proud, Marky, but I gotta survive. When I first got put in here there was a big guy who was assigned to my cell and I could not claw him off me so he began viciously raping me at his leisure. I had to eat a light bulb to get the fuck out of that hell. Ever eat a light bulb?" He did not wait for an answer from Marcus as he sat quietly for a moment, thinking about that horrible time. His hand trembled as he brought the cigarette to his mouth.

Jake blew out another lungful of smoke, "Bald Boy, aka Angel Hernandez, is Cuban. He was in jail in Cuba and he has a bar code tattooed onto his right forearm to prove it. He had been held in the worst jail in Cuba for seven years before his family bribed the Castro government and then somehow got him to Canada, or some shit like that. His tattoo that says "Bald Boy" is actually a very feared symbol that is from his Cuban

141

prison days. I asked him why he got his Bald Boy tattoo in English and he laughed. He said he always knew he would be coming to the US one day, where the real money is, and he wanted to scare the fuck out of us in English. He always laughs when he tells that story. He is creepy in every way." Jake blew out more Virginia Slim smoke and absentmindedly hugged his knees to his chest.

"How does he have all this power in here?" Marcus asked as he kept his eyes on the claws.

"He has been locked in here for a while. They got him on some drug and immigration stuff, but the Feds seem to have forgotten about him, leaving him to rot here I guess. And he is happy in here compared to Cuban prison. He is a brutally savage man with The Boyz backing him up inside and out in the real world. Plus he has Rat bringing him whatever he needs. He is a brilliant leader of these guys and they fear him. He has an iPad and cell phones and a ton of marijuana to sell or smoke or bribe. I actually got to smoke a joint with him and watch a documentary about a male lion the other night on his iPad because I let him do certain things to me. Again, I am not proud but a gal has to survive, Marky Mark."

Marcus was gathering his thoughts as quickly as he could while trying not to laugh at the names this guy was calling him. His mysterious buzz from last night was gone and he was just about to have a revelation about the Rat name when Jake began again.

"So Bald Boy gets drugs and pre-paid phone cards, porn magazines, among many other things that he needs or guys in here ask for. He sells or rents them for a huge profit or whatever he needs at that time. This jail thrives on barter, so if you have the stuff people want then you have the power if you can back it up physically. Whatever he needs, well almost anything,

142

Rat brings him and he then works out a deal with inmates who need what Rat lugged in. And if you don't pay you get pummeled by The Boyz."

Jake continued, "In jail there are three kinds of currency: sex, cigarettes and drugs. If you got any of those three you can get almost anything you need. Most guys in here won't give sex as payment – funny, they all have no problem forcefully taking sex. Anyhow, where was I? Oh, yes – so that leaves drugs and cigarettes. The white boy Gringos seem to dominate the cigarette market so I guess they got their own lugger for that. I think it is Officer Wilson actually. See, the jail canteen only sells generic cigarettes but they taste like the tobacco was rolled in dog shit and they are very harsh to smoke and give you a headache. We all still smoke them, of course, being the addicts that we are. But if you can get a good pack of cigarettes to smoke it is very valuable and guys will trade for them, especially menthols. Those give you a nice buzz. And of course I need my Virginia Slims, baby. I asked Bald Boy to bring me some more and I must have been a good girl because he said he would today.

"So, where was I? Oh ya, Rat brings good marijuana and a lot of pharmaceuticals from Bald Boy's gang's connections and that seems to be trumping the cigarettes lately as the preferred currency in here. There is way more marijuana in here since Bald Boy took over. So that is why there is some friction in here because Bald Boy wants Rat to start bringing in cigarettes, too, as he wants to fuck with Conti and The Gringos. Then he'll have drugs and cigarettes and more power."

"And you like Conti?" asked Marcus.

Jake coughed as he laughed with a lungful of smoke, "I only like him because he does not force himself on me. He is just like Bald Boy, just a different

143

color and different ways to get the same thing – power. In here that is important to guys like them. In their ruthless pursuit of power there just happens to be a lot of convenient tragedies along the way and the guards look the other way. Be careful with both of those guys, they only want to help themselves, not anybody else. Remember that, Marco."

Both men stopped to think.

"Where is this jail fight going to be?" asked Marcus, quickly getting back onto the information he so badly needed.

Jake rolled his eyes at Marcus and shook his head. He stubbed out his cigarette on the metal bed frame and looked at Marcus, holding up the filter and about a quarter inch of tobacco left to smoke, "I can get a package of crackers for this from a newbie," he coughed as he stuffed the butt into a can by his bed.

He continued, "They call this a sanctioned fight or a show. So this is my take, the female point of view, if you will. In this jail things seem to simmer just below the surface and jail life goes on with just a few interruptions here and there. It is a very delicate balance. However, every now and then the tensions will be so high that even the idiot guards can figure out that something just isn't right with the natives. So, the brilliant idea was to sanction fights – but unofficially, no records or any disciplinary forms and nothing is ever said over the radio about any fights. Only a few guards will even allow them. Of course Rat loves putting on a show for many selfish reasons, but he also uses the fights as a way to remind the inmates not to fuck with him."

Jake continued, gesturing in a very feminine but fitting way as he spoke, "Whoever was having the problem – say a white guy and a Hispanic – rather than have the issue blow up to an all-out white on tan war

144

inside the jail, the guards will let it be known that they will allow the two guys with the problem to fight in the gym to let the pressure off the cooker, honey."

Marcus was shocked. This really went on? "Where is the gym?"

"The gym is on the top floor. Two guards and two blocks of inmates at a time go up there for workout time and they rotate different blocks who can be up there on any given night. So when a fight is sanctioned the guards lock the gym door and the inmates make a circle on the basketball floor. The rules are no weapons and nobody can jump in to help. The guards referee but usually one guy who is fighting has to be unconscious before they will allow the fight to be stopped."

"Does it work to help cool things off?"

Jake paused. "More or less. Things in here are never good so I don't know what the ultimate goal of the fight is, but usually each side agrees beforehand that whatever happens, happens and they live with the results. Then things seem to go back to the fucked-up normal we all strive for in here. Until the next time."

Jake quickly remembered one more thing, "Oh ya, in the case of you fighting today – sometimes Rat just wants to see an inmate get beaten up, too. Rat calls it "jailbait" and Rat and Bald Boy often do this. Rat likes the population to see his guy kick ass. Rat seems to think it makes him look better, don't ask me how. He basically pays Bald Boy to beat guys up for him in public. It's sickness on a whole new level if you ask me. These poor jailbait guys never stand a chance. Oh, sorry?"

"Has Bald Boy been in many of these fights?" Marcus gulped.

Help!

Jake shook his head at the innocence, "Marky Mark Wahlberg, so innocent you are. He is the king of this

145

jail for a reason. He fights all the time. And he wins. That is why I chose him to be my protector, silly, haha. But I fucking hate that man when it comes right down to it," Jake said as he hugged his knees even tighter and stared blankly at the cell's pink wall. All the cells in Valley Jail were painted pink in the 1980s. It was based on a study that said it was calming to violent animals. It looked like it belonged in a newborn girl's bedroom. Pink? Marcus guessed that if Jake had a choice to paint the walls a different color he'd say no, he likes it pink. And can I have comforter and throw pillows to match?

Marcus suddenly remembered he had to ask for the shank. "Conti said you had a shank thing for me."

Jake nodded and quickly reached into his mattress and pulled out a flesh colored toothbrush handle that was melted into a spike at one end with a razor blade from a disposable razor inserted on one side. It was sharper than a box cutter and easily hidden.

Jake handed the shank to Marcus, "They give us disposable razors but they won't give us forks – fucking idiots. I would say that every razor that is bought from the canteen is used for shaving and then made into a weapon. So this is just the standard jail issued toothbrush melted with a match and then the blade slides in where it was melted and let dry. I've seen guys get cut up bad with this kind of shank – it is lethal. You can have it, I have three more in here." He motioned to the sink and toilet. This thing was a vicious implement. Marcus was looking at it and holding out hope he would be let go before he might have to use it.

Would he use it if he needed to?

Jake got serious and looked at Marcus as if he knew what Marcus was thinking, "You do not hesitate to use this. They won't."

146

Chapter 39

Rat was in his room stuffing the ounce of pot into his jail bag and looking at his latest bank statement. He now had almost twenty five thousand dollars in his lugging account. He had collected it all from The Boyz for goods delivered to the jail. Lugging was paying off nicely. Most luggers felt remorseful for their actions. Rat could not care less what others thought of him.

As he got his uniform out of the closet, Rat had a flashback to his first day of working at the jail when he saw his red sweatshirt that had just been hung by his mother. He had worn that on his first day working at the jail because he did not yet have a uniform to wear.

As he stood with the officer in charge and soaked in the jail's interior for the first time, there had been a terrifying scream from Block 2 so he rushed over with Lieutenant Lattrell and opened the cell from which the noise was coming. As soon as the cell door opened Rat could see a big Latino guy emerge from the cell with bloody bumps all over his head and face.

When the guards entered the cell they saw a skinny guy, Jake Pinkham actually, with foamy blood coming out of his mouth lying on the bed. A black guy was holding a cut off broom handle and begging for the guards to listen to him as he stood screaming and breathing hard. There was blood and hair on the wooden club in his hand.

Lt. Lattrell told him to talk as he took the broom handle from him and looked out to the bleeding inmate in the common area and told him to go to the nurse.

Rat was actually smiling and nodding as he took this all in.

The black guy pointed to the bloody man going up the stairs and said, "That asshole was not giving this guy a chance to come up for air. He was fucking this guy every hour and making him blow him in between attacks, for Chrissakes. This guy here ate a fucking light bulb to get the fuck out of this cell. The guy was fucking him like a rabbit! I could not listen to it any more! Enough is enough!"

Rat knew right then and there this was the place for him to work. He had found his calling.

He was now making what he considered good money by his standards. He was going to buy a big gun safe and start accumulating guns. No rifles, you could not wear those out in public. Handguns. Pistols.

He was so cool when he had his gun on him. He saw how Jamie looked at him when he was wearing his gun and he always had it on when he went to see Darlene to get his pre-shift snack.

Rat wished he could bring a gun in when he went to see Bald Boy today but guns were not allowed inside the jail. He needed the power it gave him to forcefully deliver the message he had to convey to the convict who was trying to bully Rat. He'd make the piece of shit inmate fight again, in the gym and against whomever Rat told him to fight. If not? No drugs. No phones. No porn.

Lugger strike.

That fucking Cuban was not going to like what Rat had to say today so Rat had to make sure he followed through if necessary because it was getting out of balance. Bald Boy was becoming more demanding about his requests and he disrespectfully treated Rat in front of The Boyz. He initially thanked Rat when he dropped off the goods. Now Bald Boy accused him of stealing some of the drugs or phones.

Since his arrival on a drug charge and subsequent immigration issues Bald Boy had been an immediate leader in Valley Jail and Rat observed him whenever possible. His tattoo was a well-known symbol and instantly respected. His size and intimidating aura did the rest. Bald Boy made sure he got into a fight almost immediately to show this new jail exactly who the fuck he was. He picked out a weak, pretend tough guy and destroyed him in front of a large crowd in his block. Shortly thereafter the guys above him in rank within The Boyz finished their sentences and he assumed the top spot.

The other guards were visibly scared of Bald Boy. Rat took a different approach, a capitalist's method.

To lure Bald Boy in Rat looked the other way when one of The Boyz was caught doing something or being somewhere they should not be. He always made sure Bald Boy was made aware of Rat's kind gestures. Although they were subtle messages initially, Rat knew how this game was played.

He was a step ahead in jail. He acted and they reacted.

Eventually Bald Boy asked him to meet in the laundry room and Rat knew his plan had worked. Stupid fucking convicts, so easy.

Here kitty, kitty, kitty. Time to make some money.

Rat showed up for that meeting ready with his directives for how this relationship was going to work. Bald Boy had other ideas. He walked in and silently handed Rat a list of things such as drugs, food, money, cell phones, phone cards, ink for tattoos, condoms, sewing needles. Next to each item was an amount that Rat would be paid for lugging it into the jail. Bald Boy explained how his cousins would give Rat the money they agreed upon.

They always paid, usually hundred-dollar bills, crisp new paper. Rat got the money up front.

"Angel, you got yourself a partner. But I won't bring in anything that can be made into a weapon or that can be used against us in a fight," Rat declared, like he was dictating the terms.

Bald Boy stared through Rat, chilling Rat to the bone. He had immediate regret about not being ready for this move. "Call me Bald Boy, and we are not partners, Rat man. No, no, no. Not partners. But we do have a deal," and he cackled as he slapped Rat on the shoulder on his way out. Rat bristled at being touched by a piece of shit Cuban inmate.

Inmates don't touch God.

So it had started badly and was now getting worse. Bald Boy was asking for more and more and that meant more trips to see The Boyz. He did not admit it to Jamie but those guys scared the shit out of Rat, too.

But it also meant more money and more power.

As Rat looked at the list of stuff Bald Boy wanted lugged today he noticed Bald Boy had put two cartons of cigarettes on the lug list for the first time. Rat would make two hundred dollars for doing it, but why cigarettes and why now? Butts were harder to bring in – they were bulky. An ounce of pot could be hidden easily and Rat made more money for that.

Rat was already bringing him a pharmacy worth of drugs, now he wanted butts, too? This had to stop, but as a good-will gesture Rat would get the two cartons on the list. He would include this issue in a chat with the Cuban tonight, too. The more he thought about it the more he realized how deeply into this he had already waded. Too late to back out.

Rat was thinking about how he would handle the meeting with Bald Boy later that night as he absentmindedly walked a few blocks to the local convenience store. It was owned by that prick Mr. Gordon with the pussy son who was Rat's age. Rat had tormented the Gordon family his whole life but the store was close so he went there whenever he needed something.

He was distracted by his jail situation and he was also planning how he would ask Darlene out when he stopped by Dunkin Donuts on his way to work later today. Big day! His demeanor was upbeat despite his worries. Money and girls did that to him.

He was totally sidetracked by his contemplation about his shift tonight and Darlene as he opened the door and heard the familiar chime above and saw Mr. Gordon himself behind the counter.

His state of mind totally changed. He hated that old fucker and Gordon also disliked Rat very much. It was a mutual dislike and neither hid their feelings well. That was not unusual. Nobody liked Rat, but Gordon was beloved by Valley residents and his store, Gordon's Grocery, was frequented by most families who lived nearby.

Rat had bullied Gordon's son, Gates, mercilessly when they were kids. Gordon's son was a nerd in his youth – small and timid but smart and polite. He worked at the store throughout his youth and had to endure Rat's horrible abuse almost daily. Rat was a big asshole to everybody but he saw Gates Gordon whenever he came to the store and laid into him even if there were others in the store.

"Well, will you look at the piece of trash the cat dragged in?" shouted Mr. Gordon, greeting Rat in a hateful tone of voice. The store was empty other than the funny guy behind the counter.

Rat scowled at the weird, old asshole and barked, "I killed your cat, Gordon, remember? Your faggot kid cried for a month." That was true. Rat had shot the cat with his first BB gun.

"I need two cartons of cigarettes," Rat blurted out, pissed off already.

Rat suddenly realized he had fucked up by coming here for this order. Being sloppy gets you caught, Rat. Gordon was a sharp guy who had many customers who worked at the jail throughout the years. Gordon missed nothing.

"I did not know that you smoked, you don't seem cool enough to smoke, Rat." Gordon eyed Rat suspiciously, as if they both knew something was happening here.

Fuck! Rat was boiling mad at himself for his carelessness but was somehow able to maintain a rare restraint on the outside. He already regretted not having foreseen this happening and was pissed at himself for not having driven a few miles where he was an unknown to buy these cigarettes. He could have been in uniform and worn his gun; who knows, maybe there would have been a young hotty to impress with his gun belt move. He immediately thought of Darlene again. Should I take her to some place fancy like Golden Corral? He was shaken out of his thoughts by the door's chime as another customer walked in. He wished he could walk out right now.

It was too late, the toothpaste was out of the tube on this one, "One carton of Marlboro Menthol and one carton of Virginia Slims," Rat sighed and shook his head as he finished. Virginia Slims? How had he not put that together? He was buying cigarettes for Queenie?

What the fuck?

Gordon spoke mockingly, "Virginia Slims? Those must be for you. I have those out back. And the menthols I got out back, I think. Be right back." He looked over his shoulder at Rat as he walked toward the back door.

Gordon saw an opportunity to bust Rat's balls again, "Oh, I know that while you ladies smoke your Virginia Slims you might want to douche or change your tampon. I have those in aisle five."

Rat was daydreaming about Darlene again and blurted out, "Go fuck yourself, Gordon, you piece of shit." That was Rat's standard line in the jail to idiot inmates and it seemed to work on the outside, too, as Gordon's smile faded when Rat laid into him.

Gordon came back a few minutes later than Rat had expected it would take. Slow asshole, too. Both types of cigarettes were in opened cartons. That was fucking weird, too. Oh well, easier to lug in.

Gordon turned to Rat, "Now I hear the inmates love the menthols because of the flavor and the slight buzz it still gives you every time you smoke one. Would you know anything about that, Rat? Since you work inside a jail and all, that's why I am asking?"

Who did this old buzzard think he was playing with here?

Gordon rang up the sale and Rat threw the money on the counter, "Here is your money. You know, for being in a shitty economy you'd be better off being nice to your fucking customers instead of being the asshole that you really are! And say hi to your son for me, I miss him."

Gordon replied with a thin smile, "What is the word I am looking for here...hmmm...rhymes with hugger. Oh, that's it – lugger. Look you piece of shit, I have hated you and your fucked up family since I opened this place. You have stolen from me and been a prick to my kid. And now you come in here and buy cigarettes for the first fucking time in your life and you don't think I am smart enough to put two and two together?

Look, you stupid jackass, I got friends who worked at the jail and they spoke of luggers like they were lepers. All the luggers thought they were so smart, so secretive. But these other guys all knew who the luggers were. They'd have a fancy car or take a big trip, showing it off like nobody could ever figure it out.

"And you? You are not even smart enough to not go to your local store to buy cigarettes for the first time in the seventeen years you have lived down the street. Just let me warn you about what my friends spoke about back in their day. These luggers were on an island. The other guards did not have their backs, not by a long shot, on anything. And the inmates who were paying these fools? They were in control, not the guard. They could turn them over to the Warden any time they wanted because they're already in jail, Einstein! You are an ignorant rodent! I hope you get caught."

Gordon had just let out a decade's worth of pent-up venom on the Rat. He would have to sit down for a half an hour after this just to compose himself.

"Go fuck yourself you fucking piece of shit," was all a stunned Rat could muster as he walked out clutching the stuff he'd be lugging into the jail later.

He wished he had his gun.

Chapter 40

Aaron and Claire had gone over to the high school to see the last pep rally Marcus would be in at Valley High. They stayed in back so they were hidden from view but they could take it all in. Aaron had his camera.

He had snuck out of work early. He worked in Boston as a mid-level financial manager. He had been there for twenty years. The pay was only decent but he loved his co-workers, many of whom had come into his office that morning to congratulate him on the article in the Herald about Marcus. Aaron was incredibly proud and just shrugged when they asked if Marcus was going pro or to college. His bosses were very supportive and allowed Aaron to adjust his hours to see his son's hockey games.

Coach Goat was up at the podium using his accented English to inspire the student body to show up en masse tonight if they could. He then asked for silence as he introduced the eight seniors who were graduating this year and all of whom had played a big role in this year's success.

Time for me to French this speech up, "Dis next guy I am going to talk about…dis kid is a special one. We have seen him grow from a scrawny freshman to what he has become today. He is as great a guy and leader on dis team and he is a great, talented hockey player. Boys and girls, you will be watching dis kid play pro hockey in a few years, mark my words! Maybe even for da Boston Broonz!"

Goat calmly took a sip of water as the crowd erupted and "Mah-kiss!" chants took over again. Goat held up a hand.

155

He pointed a finger to the crowd and said, "And tonight, if you don't get over to da Fish Tank to see dis guy play his last conference varsity home game for da Bulldogs den you will be a damned fool!"

Aaron and Claire were both choked up as they watched Marcus stride across the floor to shake hands and get an unexpected hug from Goat. The field house was a mass of students screaming their son's name. They had never been so proud. What great kids at this school, they thought.

Little did they know that ninety percent of those "great kids" would be making the short walk up to the Valley Quarry behind the school to get all fucked up at a major pre-game keg party.

Chapter 41

Jamie was getting ready to go upstairs for lunch before heading into work. As he was putting on his uniform shirt and badge he noticed the mini-camera that he had recently bought with the money he was earning from selling ganja with Rat to the convicts.

The camera was in the form of two pens side by side, one for video and one for audio. It was pretty fucking expensive and it took great hi-def video along with incredibly sensitive audio. He had used it a few times when he went out with Rat and then played the video on his laptop the next day. He wanted to test if anybody would know it was a camera. Nobody had.

Although Jamie had never before worn the camera to work, he remembered joking with Rat that he was going to make a stoned-cop documentary. I am going to fucking do it, he thought as he slipped the camera into his uniform pocket next to two similar looking pens. Perfect.

Action!

He hated that prick Russell, hopefully he could catch him doing something unlawful and get it on film. He turned the camera on and did another bong hit.

He emerged from his cave in the cellar and had to squint as the sunlight hit his bloodshot eyes when he entered the kitchen.

"I hope you don't burn down the house with all that incense you burn. It does smell good I have to admit. It reminds me of high school," said Jamie's naïve Mom.

Jamie grabbed a bag of chips and a two-liter Coke and headed back downstairs. He wanted to burn some more incense before he headed into the police station with his camera rolling.

Chapter 42

The rally ended and Marcus was hanging among his teammates. They were reading texts and busting each other's balls about girls and hockey. There was a nervous energy among the players. St. Mary's was no pushover.

Marcus saw a text from Nicole. She has my phone number?

<hey, see you at fish's after the game? Going with squad drinking first>

Marcus replied, <sure>. He was trying to play cool but he was now very motivated to play well today. And hopefully celebrate a win and catch a nice buzz tonight. He would be driving the Lexus after the game, had to keep it to a buzz.

Life was good for Marcus Kelly.

Fowler made eye contact with Boots and they walked out to the student parking lot. Boots was the unofficial goalie coach and he and Fowler had a good relationship. Part of that relationship was Boots selling ganja to Fowler as well as most of the students who did drugs and that list was growing. Boots was becoming very popular among the student body.

The faculty, too.

Fowler was the typical kooky goalie. But Boots noticed when he first started working with him that he was too amped up, even for practice. Before games Fowler would always puke in the toilet stall of the locker room at The Fish Tank. It had been part of the pre-game routine: speech from Goat, Fowler pukes...game time!

But the last few months Fowler had not been puking before games. Everybody assumed maturity and confidence were the reasons. Nope.

Fowler had been buying pot from his assistant hockey coach since Boots had spoken to him about ways to control his nerves. Fowler was shocked initially that his coach would push drugs on him and resisted, but after trying it once before practice he knew he had the answer right there. He still kind of sucked but at least he was not afraid of the puck.

"Fowls, I got the goods," said Boots as he handed him a baggie when they got in Boots's car outside the field house as the students conspicuously made their way up the hill to the Quarry to tap the kegs.

Fowler paid him and smelled the pot, "Nice work, Boots, I was out. You got a rolling paper?"

Boots slapped him on the shoulder and handed him his ceramic pipe while he suggested one or two hits first. "This shit is legit, Fowls, be careful." And with that Boots was off, he had many more stops to make in the student parking lot.

And the faculty lounge.

Chapter 43

Steve Murphy had been the head hockey coach for St. Mary's for the last ten years. He loved this job and he taught physical education at the school during the day. He had been very successful most years, but this hockey season was a down year by his standards. He desperately wanted these guys to make the tournament but he knew what they were up against.

Valley High was good and Marcus Kelly was fantastic, the best player Murphy had ever seen at this level. Because Valley High loved being the top team in the Valley this year and last, after years of abuse at the hands of Murphy's much better teams, Murphy knew that Valley was not going to lie down and let St. Mary's walk into the tournament. St. Mary's would have to earn any points today. Goat would see to that. He hated that French Fry as much as he respected him. Murphy had to admit – that guy knew his hockey.

Valley kicked their ass in the first game of the year, so Murphy had been working on a better game plan all week. He knew he had the better goalie; he had tried to recruit Fowler but he knew that if Marcus went to Valley High that Fowler would follow like a puppy. It was a good miss, St. Mary's goalie was Chris Joseph and he was a conference all-star. Murphy heard Fowler was a druggie, for what that was worth. He had seen film of Fowler's last few games and told his guys, "Just shoot on this guy, he looks terrible."

Because of their advantage in net, Murphy knew that the rest of his team was maybe only just a little worse than all but one player on Valley. If he could neutralize Marcus his team would have a chance at the point they desperately needed to qualify for the tournament.

Murphy looked at the stats, Marcus needed three goals to reach fifty goals scored for the year.

Not today, Marcus … not today.

His plan was to put Joey on Marcus all night. Joey could skate fast but he lacked size. Murphy's plan was to piss off Marcus – he was going to have Joey cover Marcus all night and hack and whack at Marcus with his stick, nothing dangerous, just enough to get Marcus off his game and maybe into the penalty box.

Joey was coachable, unlike his older brother. Murphy hated Jimmy Rat and he spat into his wastebasket as he thought about that punk. Joey would want to please his coach, he was a good kid and he was a pest on the ice already. He was going to pull Joey aside as they boarded the bus and let him know what his assignment was going to be. He did not tell him earlier this week because he knew Joey would not get a wink of sleep knowing he had to cover Marcus.

Chapter 44

Rat was still pissed as he got into his uniform and was strapping his gun belt around his expanding gut. The shirt had ketchup stains from last week on it.

Fucking Gordon, piece of shit he is. He was pissed off as he eyed the cigarettes in his lug bag.

"Fucking belt shrunk again?" he bellowed as he sucked in the gut and finally snapped it closed. He looked at himself in the mirror. That gun looks good, my man! His mood changed as soon as he put the gun on.

He loved wearing the gun publicly. He had to leave it in his locker at the jail so the gun was all for show in public. Rat always saved his errands for when he was in uniform with the gun on his hip. He liked to have people notice him and his gun. Rat adopted a different persona when he had his gun on and visible. He went from quiet bully to more of what he was like within the jail. Chest out a bit, arms out from his sides like he was carrying imaginary watermelons in his armpits, slow strut to his gait and gut sucked in as much as he still could. People noticed him and respected him at the convenience stores, fast food places and gas stations where he stopped while in uniform and with gun on hip. That they mistook him for a cop was lost on Rat, never hearing those around him say, "Is that a cop? Oh, he's just a jail guard," as they looked him over when he walked by.

He jumped in his pickup, backed out of its awkward parking spot in the driveway and headed to the jail for his shift, lug bag on the passenger seat.

He had one stop on the way to work in particular that he was anxious about today. There was a Dunkin

Donuts on the way to the jail and Darlene from the bar last night worked there on Friday afternoons. Darlene was a divorced mother of two who had married a guy Rat knew from high school. He was a dickhead and Darlene had finally figured that out and kicked him out. He ran out and kept running, there would be no child support from that guy.

She was somewhat recently divorced and Rat had been in the donut shop quite a few times since, dipping his toe in the water to see what the temperature was. He was getting good signals, he knew how to read ladies, he was sure of this one.

She was actually way out of his league.

And she abso-fucking-lutely did not like Rat.

He just wished he remembered if he had left it off on good terms with her or not last night.

Time to find out. He patted his gun.

Chapter 45

Darlene was miserable because she hated having to work since the divorce, especially at Dunkin Fucking Donuts, her pet name for her new employer. At least she could bring leftover food home for herself and the kids. Money was tight since the divorce.

She also had a hangover from last night. Last night sucked. She was trying to go out more lately but every time she did she just got hit on by idiots and regretted going out at all. She was still far from ready to date anybody yet but that did not stop every guard from the jail up the street from hitting on her on their way to or from work. Life sucked.

Just then it got worse.

As she was thinking about the jail guards the king jackass of them all was strutting into the shop. Wonderful. This guy was the biggest prick in the world as far as Darlene was concerned. She had come close to throwing her drink at him last night.

Arrogant, ugly and chubby – you got a mirror at home, Rat? Yet he walked around like he thought he was a stud or something. What is wrong with his flabby arms? Is he carrying something invisible under his armpits? She was repulsed by his presence.

Plus she had to run into him at the bar last night? He was hammered and being the typical idiot he was. She had sworn at him and left when he took out his gun. Jackass.

"Hey Darl," said Rat with a big smile as he approached the counter. He had been saying Darl out loud on the ride, he liked the way it sounded, he was sure this nickname would be a keeper. He liked the sound of Rat and Darl as he said that over and over in his car, too.

The shop was empty and Darlene's co-worker was on break out back. Perfect, thought Rat.

Darlene thought to herself, Who is Darl? Nobody has ever called me that, you loser.

"Hey," replied Darlene without looking up and with no emotion as she wiped imaginary crumbs off the counter that was thankfully between them, awaiting his order.

Rat did not pick up on any of the obvious "I fucking hate you" clues she was throwing his way. He confidently said, "The usual, sweetheart," as he pulled his gun belt up, making sure the gun was visible to Darlene. It was his patented move.

Chicks dig the sidearm.

"I have no fucking idea what your usual is," Darlene replied in a monotone, loathsome voice that Rat finally picked up on as she stared holes through the back of his head.

Had she not just seen the power move? Nine-millimeter, bitch!

Rat stammered and blushed, any momentum from his patented gun belt move had vanished. "Ummm, medium regular, please? And two chocolate frosted."

What happened here?

"Yup," she robotically answered and gladly turned away from him and his still stained shirt, mumbling "fucking loser" under her breath as she turned.

I need to ask today before somebody else gets her, he thought as he worked up the courage to ask her out. He stared at her ass in the polyester brown slacks of her uniform and stifled a yelp. She was so hot.

He tried to tap into his jail bravado so while her back was turned to him he asked, "Darl, would you want to go out some night? Grab some chow or something?"

He habitually performed the gun belt move again out of nervousness even though her back was turned. Little did he know the move looked like a fat kid unsuccessfully trying to pull a hula-hoop over his gut.

Darlene poured hot coffee on her hand because she did not expect to be hit upon by this asshole. After what she had said to him last night?

"Fuck!" She swore loudly as the pain of the burn kicked in. Rat stepped back.

She stared at Rat while running her hand under cold water at the sink and she spoke slowly and with purpose. "Look, my name is Darlene! I think you are an absolutely repulsive jackass. I'd rather screw every inmate in your jail than go out with you to dinner and watch you stuff that fat, ugly face of yours, Rathole."

That felt good. Ok, maybe a little harsh, but Rat was nothing to her but a complete asshole. "Oh, and next time you want to talk to a girl about jerking off and wiping your ass? Like I told you last night, go stroke that stupid fucking gun you love so much and stick it up your ass!" Darlene wished she could have been so eloquent to her ex-husband when she left him. She was smiling slightly as she finished her rant.

She was now leaning over the counter and pointing at Rat, "Did you really think I would ever go out with you?"

She laughed the same cackle that Bald Boy had when they began their business together. It was as unsettling then as it was now.

Rat grabbed his coffee and donuts. He was humiliated and he noticed Darlene's co-worker giggling behind the swinging doors after having witnessed the whole scene.

Rat was pissed and now some poor inmate was going to pay a price for that slut's stupidity!

Chapter 46

After breakfast, Conti was in his cell on the bottom tier of Block 2. He had already forgotten about the incident that had just happened, in his world that was less than a blip on his radar. To Conti, threatening the idiots was like pissing on a hydrant.

Lift your leg, move the fuck on.

All of the cells on this level housed white guys who were in The Gringos. It was as close to a mutually respectful atmosphere that you could get in Valley Jail. They self-policed and delivered punishment when deserved. They looked out for each other in the common areas and they shared whatever ill-begotten goods they had. They were a melting pot of white supremacists, Neo-Nazis, Red Necks and Yankees. The one bond they had inside the jail was skin color, but that was all they needed.

It was the lowest common denominator.

They were very bad men who had done horrible things but they were mostly true to each other out of need.

Conti's cellmate was a jailhouse tattoo artist and he was inking a new tattoo on their other cellmate. The tattoo artist, Wally, used melted plastic from blue plastic disposable razors as his ink. The razors were used, tail to snout, after their primary use, shaving, was in its past. Blades for weapons, handles melted for tat ink.

He had a sewing needle that he inserted into an empty Bic pen and the needle was hooked up to the motor from a cassette Walkman that spun around at high speed. That caused the needle to move within the pen rapidly up and down, grabbing the melted razor ink as it did, forming the tattoo under the skin. It was amazing to watch and an ingenious set-up that Wally had devised. It was far from clean or safe, though, as the same needle was used on multiple recipients. These guys did not think long-term on anything.

Wally was either sleeping or tattooing somebody while he did his two years for selling meth. He was paid in cigarettes or joints. He was a very talented artist and these guys protected Wally, who was meek and timid. He was a drug abusing tattoo artist inside the jail and outside of it. His work was spectacular – when he was straight.

Conti had told his guys to give him a heads up when they saw Rat walking their way and heard the guys yell "Five-Oh" just after the cell doors opened for the afternoon. Five-Oh was short for Hawaii Five-0 and was shouted to alert all inmates within the block to the presence of a CO coming into the block. There was nothing the CO could do about it – so much for stealth and surprise.

Conti snaked his way through the inmates moving out and about to the front gate of the block and asked Rat for a minute of his time as he crossed the main floor. Rat looked toward Bald Boy's block but nobody was at the front gate to see him so he quickly opened the door to Conti's block and motioned for him to go to his cell and he would meet him there.

It was unusual for a guard to enter a block alone. Protocol was two guards at a time all the time. Rat always felt safe on his solo trips, although he rarely ventured into this block alone.

Enemy territory.

Conti kicked out his cellmates and Rat entered cautiously. It was unlike Conti to request a meeting with him. It felt like treason to Rat just being there.

Conti began, "I know you got something up your sleeve with this Marcus kid. I gotta ask you on behalf of The Gringos and this kid being white. Let him fight one-on-one, don't jump him with the attack Boyz. Put on one of your shows. He is a young kid who does not belong here and you know it as well as I. You have him jumped and I am going to cause trouble. You let him fight Bald Boy and I condone your actions. Let it be a fight in the gym. Sanction it."

Rat had already decided to sanction it and hold it up in the gym. He had told Wilson about his plan just after breakfast so the old buzzard would be the other guard up there in the gym when it went down. Rat could not risk having a newbie up there.

It was a risk telling Wilson but he was old and lazy and would not do anything with that information. Little did Rat know that the only reason Wilson had not run to Conti to tell him was because he was too busy doing something behind Rat's back at that very moment.

Rat knew Wilson lugged and vice versa, so there was already a shaky, unspoken alliance between the two of them – thick as thieves. Neither one trusted the other but they also dared not run to the Warden with accusations about the other. Their bond was an uneasy partnership based on dishonesty. Wilson, like most, hated Rat. The fact that the Warden had put Rat in charge this weekend gave Wilson the green light to lug all the stuff from his trunk in to Conti easily but he loathed having to take orders from that prick.

Rat being Rat, he simply nodded at Conti and said, "You got a deal, but you owe me one big favor. Remember this." With that he walked out quickly, hoping his time with Conti went unseen by The Boyz, another future favor secured.

While Rat spoke with Conti, Marcus was being moved from his current cell just as Jake had finished talking. It was entertaining but Marcus had learned nothing about how to win a fight versus Bald Boy, just that it was not likely he could. And he now had a serious weapon in his jumpsuit.

Well, Marcus wanted to know how he would do in a fight and he was about to find out. He would have preferred the two jackasses at the pizza place sitting on Fowler's car, though. This was like starting your fight career against the world champion.

Thinking about the upcoming fight did nothing to lessen his sense of total panic. He hoped this guard had some answers. He seemed nicer than Rat.

As he followed the older guard, Marcus was still in total disbelief as to his predicament. He was hoping this would be where his parents would greet him and make him sign a pledge to never drink again.

They came to a door and the guard had to play with the key a bit but the door squeaked open and Marcus wondered if the door was ever used. Where the hell were they going?

The guard seemed nervous and edgy.

The door was to an unused hallway that led to the old incinerator room. The guard shut the door but did not lock it. He wanted privacy but did not trust the old lock to open again. He turned to Marcus.

"Look son, what is going on here is making me fucking sick. I only got two months until I can make full retirement, so I am just biding time and making no waves until then. But this? You ain't supposed to be in this jail, this is wrong. But we cannot radio or call anybody so I cannot do anything about this shit. There is something I have to warn you about. This fucking Sgt. Rat is breaking laws just having you in here. But here you are, he is in charge and we gotta play the cards in our hand.

"You just remember this name – Wilson. OK? Officer Wilson was nice to you. When this all blows over and you end up having to tell my bosses what went on in here and what this prick Rat set you up for, you just remember Wilson was nice to you, OK?"

As Marcus nodded his consent, he noticed Wilson drifted off for a brief moment.

Wilson was often preoccupied with how to replace the money he made from lugging for Conti when he retired. That money paid for his wife's expensive hair stylist, nail treatments and massage therapists. He mostly loved her, she was gorgeous. She paid him back with amazing blowjobs but he knew she was going to be expensive to maintain during retirement. He wanted to survive this weekend and not lose his job because of it.

He needed his pension. He had a bad feeling about this whole fucking weekend. Rat had put him in a bad spot.

Marcus was processing this and starting to accept his reality and his head was totally clearing. So it was true, Rat was coming for him. Or Bald Boy was. He again felt as if he was being unleashed – finally. He was anxious and ready, the evil had awoken the nasty in Marcus and he felt invigorated by it.

"Do you know what I did to get in here?" Marcus asked pleadingly.

Wilson was shaking his head disgustedly as he replied, "Probably nothing. I know Rat and his cop buddy are in on this together. Whether the storm had anything to do with this is beyond me, we are shut off from the world right now because of that storm."

Marcus asked, "Why do you need to warn me? What is going to happen?"

172

Wilson hesitated, ran his fingers through his hair and said, "You got a jail fight. In the gym, first session due up in there tonight, one-on-one fight versus Bald Boy. I am going to go up there with your block so Rat will be the other guard up there. He gets off on this shit. Sick fuck he is. He calls you his jailbait and this fight is a show to him."

Wilson paused and stared hard into Marcus's eyes.

"It's up to you how we do this. I can sneak you out of the gym and lock the door after us to buy time. Then we can run you down to the office. Maybe by then the phone lines and cell towers will be operable again. For now nobody can get anywhere near this place and Rat is in charge.

"Or you can fight this maniac, your call."

Marcus thought about this for a minute. He had no idea when he would be able to connect to the outside or if anybody would be able to get here even if they found out where he was. This guy Bald Boy was a big motherfucker, no doubt about that. But Marcus did not want to run.

Fuck it, kiddo.

It was time for his first real fight. Plus, chances are there would be many Boyz between him and the office door if he tried to make a run out and they'd probably have shanks. He'd rather take his chances one on one.

"Wilson, are there ever weapons used in these arranged fights?" Marcus asked, suddenly aware of the blade against his hip.

"Dear Lord, you are going to fight this prick, aren't you?" Wilson asked. He shook his head and broke into a grin, like a proud uncle.

"You got some balls, kiddo. I'll give you that. No, no weapons allowed, goes against the code of conduct for sanctioned fights. This guy is legitimately a bad man who can absolutely kick some ass. He's had some

173

training and he seems to get off on maiming other guys in these fights." He lit a cigarette and blew the smoke toward the ceiling as he looked back to Marcus.

"Kid, can you fight?" asked Wilson sincerely.

Marcus made serious eye contact for the first time back to Wilson and replied, "We are about to find out together, Wilson."

They trudged off to the new cell Marcus would call home for a few hours.

Chapter 47

Rat was pissed. That slut Darlene had some nerve. He was eating his second chocolate frosted donut as he cut off an eighteen-wheeler and chirped his tires pulling into the jail access road. Elvis blared on his truck's stereo.

The only road to the jail passed over the Juniper River and the bridge that spanned it was an old wooden bridge. It was rickety and in need of some care, but it was not giving any hints of severe instability so it was ignored. Rat called it the "Jesus Christ Bridge" because every time he went over it he said a prayer, or what he remembered of one.

He was still pissed about Darlene's insults but he put his jail face on and noticed how empty the parking lot was, even more so than the usual Friday. Warden Davis was here, his car in its usual spot.

Rat was really in need of a convict he could use as his jailbait but was struggling to come up with anybody who would fit the bill. Maybe somebody new was brought in today. The jail was in a state of constant flux with guys being brought from courts and other jails or prisons within Massachusetts daily.

He grabbed his coffee and lug bag and trudged in as donut crumbs tumbled off over his gut. It was still warm for February but clouds were thickening and the jail looked gloomy against that backdrop. Not that it ever looked like Disneyland.

Rat thought of the hotel in the movie "The Shining" whenever he looked at his jail. As he knew all too well, physical appearance was not the only characteristic the jail shared with that evil hotel.

Redrum, baby.

Chapter 48

Marcus was in the locker room with most of his teammates. He liked to linger in there early and take his time getting ready before games. He was not a rah-rah kind of player because he did not need anything but his own thoughts to motivate himself to play well. He left the pre-game speech to Goat because he was really good at getting the team up for any game.

The image of Nicole in her skimpy uniform was interrupting a few of his game preparation thoughts. He was nineteen after all.

Marcus was a bit nostalgic as he sat quietly, so he was just observing the pre-game antics. He would miss this shit. Some guys were joking with Santorelli about the milk incident, from which he had thankfully recovered. Time passed and players were all dribbling in, it was an hour before the game and all but Fowler were accounted for. Marcus knew that Fowler liked to walk around the rink before the game now and it seemed to work, he was not puking any more. In a weird way Marcus missed the puking. Fowler's play the last few months had been on the decline so Marcus hoped tonight would get Fowler back on track for the tournament. Marcus knew he was a major question mark going forward but he was the best they had.

Fowler eventually came in laughing with the backup goalie and quickly dressed as game time was approaching. Boots was right behind them.

Their locker room at the Fish was beautiful and spacious. Painted in the Valley High colors of blue and gold with a huge Bulldog on each wall. Every varsity player had a locker with his name on it. There were speakers and a docking station for an iPod. Santo controlled the music – he was their locker room DJ.

Marcus only had one rule for the music – no Elvis!

Goat walked in as the players were taping pads and lacing skates to go out for the game. As the locker room door opened the familiar sound of the Zamboni was drowned out by the noise of the crowd awaiting the game. The Fish Tank was rocking.

Boots slammed the door shut and Goat began, "OK fellas, take da knee."

Goat said his usual prayer in French and nobody knew what the fuck it meant but it worked, right? He opened his eyes and began.

"Guys, I love coaching Valley hockey and I have loved every minute with you guys. This is a special group with some great players. This group will go down as da best team ever graduating from Valley High. Now I know that most of da attention goes to Marcus and he probably deserves some of it. But it is da team that won the conference. It is da team that set all the records. It is da team that is going to win da tournament next week!"

The players all let loose their Bulldog bark that was heard over in the St. Mary's locker and Goat waited patiently to continue.

"But guys, come on. All of that can happen but if we lose today NONE OF THAT IS GOING TO MATTER BECAUSE WE LET THOSE MUDDAFUCKERS FROM ST. FUCKING MARY'S INTO DA STATE TOURNAMENT, THAT IS ALL WE WILL REMEMBER! NOW GO FUCKING WIN!!!!"

At that, a nodding Boots timely opened the door and the players were professionally guided by Goat to be at peak emotion as they emerged onto the ice. Goat was good at all aspects of coaching. As Marcus passed by

177

Goat he grabbed Marcus and waited for the room to clear, asking Marcus to sit.

Goat had seen the scouts before the game and they had indicated that most of them were leaving after the first period to get out ahead of the storm. Goat seethed inside because of all the points he had used to keep this game from being postponed, but he understood that these guys were flying all over the country and they had places to go. They could not afford to get stuck overnight.

They assured Goat they loved Marcus and needed to see little more of him to know. The college guys were mostly going through the motions, they sensed he was going to be drafted by a pro team and head there.

Goat considered it a nice gesture they gave him the heads up, as if to say, "Play Marcus early and often, please." Goat would oblige. He usually did not like to tell Marcus or any previously scouted player he had that a scout was in the stands, it tended to backfire. Tonight Goat was going to risk it. And, there were officially thirty four scouts on hand tonight, college and pro.

"Son, I am going to ride you hard in da first period. Da scouts are here and they are leaving after that to get to da airport. You need to show them what you got early on. So, I am going to double shift your line in da first. You need da breather you tell da Goat or Boots, OK? Otherwise I am going to showcase you until you cannot skate."

Marcus smiled at his coach. He loved Goat. He understood. He said nothing as he jumped to his feet and rubbed Goat's balding head in his hands and kissed his forehead. He would reward his coach for his loyalty.

As Marcus strode out, Goat wiped a tear away. Was this kid really perfect?

178

Chapter 49

Jamie pulled into the police station and was late as usual. But he had driven around a bit to make sure he was late as he was looking to get material for his video. He knew his time at this job was limited.

He looked down to make sure the pen camera was on and the tiny red light indicated it was. Jamie was very stoned; good film guys needed to be; he remembered reading that in some magazine as he pulled into the deserted parking lot.

He said "Action" and looked around as he opened the door to the meeting room. That prick Captain Russell was standing up addressing a group of six cops who were seated at desks. This meeting usually had twelve cops working this shift. Wow.

Russell stopped talking, saw Jamie and looked at his watch. "Well, Jamie. I do hope you are feeling better. Thank you for not being as late as usual, you useless idiot." The other cops laughed. None of them respected Jamie.

Pure video gold, thought Jamie as he carefully backed his way into his seat, making sure his camera was catching Russell berate him.

Russell composed himself. "OK, where was I...oh, yeah – the fire department is short guys, too. They sent five guys to DC. That terrorist training is worth it but we are the ones paying a price tonight. The weather is the key tonight. If anybody knows a rain dance please perform one at once."

He waited for a laugh that never came. Jamie loved this. Smile, asshole!

"Slattery, you and Anderson take The Fish Tank tonight. I need you to get those folks out of that rink as

179

soon as the game is over. Let me know when you are good to leave there after the game and I will assign you to where we need you. Evans, you got the state highway region. Brown, you got downtown. Condon, you and Halloran get the North Side. I'll take the Riverfront and I will be in my squad car and mobile so I can get anywhere I am needed quickly. Communication has never been more important than tonight, guys. Be safe, be smart." At that everybody stood up but Russell instructed Jamie to sit back down and allow the others to leave. Jamie was smiling inside.

"Jamie, if you are capable of being something other than dumb as a rock, I need that tonight. You got that in you?"

Jamie squirmed in his seat to make sure he was getting Russell in his shot. "Define 'other than dumb as a rock'?" he asked, smirking.

Russell turned crimson. Jamie was happy he paid the extra money for the ability to record in color.

Russell came back down. "Let's try this another way. You are going to be doing dispatch alone tonight and handling the 911 calls. I know you have never done this on your own but I think you can. Can you?"

"Yes I can and I will, sir." He said it with a military salute that allowed him to move again to get Russell back in the shot.

"Also, I am leaving the SUV and keys here, with you. If you are needed, you have to switch the 911 calls to central dispatch and then head out. I don't want to have to call in for assistance from those pricks so if I need a body I will call you instead, OK?"

Russell wanted to drive the SUV but the radio was busted still and he could not afford to be out of touch and needed to be mobile.

Jamie nodded enthusiastically, then he remembered he needed to be heard on the tape. "Of course, sir. I know the protocol. I hope you do need me!"

"Help us all if we do, Lord," said Russell, who was not in the video but the audio picked it up.

Chapter 50

As Dottie was filling the dishwasher, she heard the doorbell ring and DH was barking up a storm before she could get to the door. She had just finished cleaning up when her good friend and co-worker Sally had come by to help Dottie take some of the goodies over to the game. Dottie knew there was going to be a huge crowd tonight so she had baked twice as much as normal. She called Sally to help save her from having to make two trips.

They hugged hello. They truly liked each other and enjoyed working the hockey games together. Dottie was the baker and Sally sold the raffle tickets like a pro, working the stands and hitting up the fans right up until the drawing at every game. Tonight the 50/50 raffle would probably make a few thousand dollars so Sally had on her sneakers knowing she was going to have to be on her toes with so many people at The Fish Tank. They liked to arrive at the game just as it began so they would not run out of goodies before the game ended.

As they greeted each other Dottie's phone rang. Dottie hurriedly pointed Sally to the table where the baked goods sat and told her she would be quick. She ran off to speak on the phone and immediately indicated it was an important call to let Sally know she may be a while. Sally started running all the goodies out to the car while she spoke on the phone.

How did Dottie do all this? There were cookies, cakes, muffins, whoopie pies and many different kinds of brownies. After the seventh trip to her car, Sally grabbed the last plate of brownies labeled "Special brownies" and put them in her back seat – her trunk

182

was full. She threw her coat over them in the back and drove off. She let Dottie know she would just see her at the game and ran along.

A few minutes later Dottie hung up the phone and came back to the kitchen to write down some reminders. She was looking for a pen so she could write the note to herself and was now feeling rushed to get over to The Fish Tank.

The phone call was from the woman in Florida from whom she would be renting a condo for a week in April, when hockey season would be done. It was her first vacation since Dear Harry had passed away. She was so excited about her trip and seeing her sister that she just grabbed the keys and headed out to the car. She had the signs and banners they used for the raffle table in her hands and her keys in her teeth and was thinking about umbrella drinks in Florida as she left for the game.

She never noticed Sally had taken her special brownies to the game.

Chapter 51

Warden Davis had seen Rat's car pull in and rushed to see Rat, catching him before he could put the lug bag into his locker. Davis knew he was not popular among the guards so he really went out of his way to see the few who did not hate him openly.

"There is my Captain-to-be! Got a minute?" bellowed Davis as he motioned Rat to follow him to his office.

Because Davis had been an important backer in Rat's promotion, Rat had to play the game now with this idiot. Davis had seen something in Rat, a leadership quality that nobody else saw – mainly because it did not exist. Warden Davis was not a good judge of character. Because Davis thought so highly of him Rat was often put in charge of the facility during his shifts, even over other officers who had worked there much longer.

Rat was suddenly aware he had been careless again. He had not even zipped up his lug bag and the cigarettes were sticking out a bit. Davis did not notice, he was too busy studying Rat's gun.

Another gun nut, phew.

Rat composed himself but he was noticing some miscues on his part today as he smiled and said, "Sure, Warden."

They sat down in the dark, cramped office. The Warden's office was in a trailer that was attached to the jail through a door that was cut into the granite. It was so pathetic, thought Rat, but it also fit Davis. Rat, like most other COs, found Davis to be an idiot but he knew he had to kiss his ass.

Davis had never been a jail guard. He got his job the way the Valley always worked – through connections. He was not fit for the job, though. He abhorred violence, a weird thing for a jail warden. He rarely entered the jail itself out of fear. If anybody competent had been in charge, Bald Boy would not be in this jail but Davis liked to brag to his wife and friends about the dangerous Cuban in his jail.

Rat sat on the other side of the desk and threw the bag at his feet and zipped it as he made it look like he was fixing his boot. "What is on your mind, Warden?"

"Rat, I am relieved that you are going to work tonight. We need you badly. Captain Fritz and I have been invited to the Principal's box for the hockey game tonight plus I have four guys down in DC for that very important terrorist training. And with the game tonight and February vacation all hitting at once, it is the perfect storm for being shorthanded. And that is not even counting the storm, hahaha!"

Rat forced a laugh. Go on, sir, he thought to himself.

"Therefore, I am letting you know that I need you to work the whole weekend as the officer in charge, unless you have plans? No? Good, you can take the temporary bunk in the office and sleep when you need to, I will make sure you earn two times pay for stepping up when needed, also."

Rat could not believe his ears. This was fantastic. He quietly bent a bit lower and felt for his lug bag. He could take his time and pick some jailbait for his fight tomorrow night.

Too easy.

"Officer Wilson is the only veteran who was available all weekend. I am giving him the same deal as you. The other officers who are able to work the whole weekend are fairly new, but you are officially in charge. I let Wilson and the others know it. I need to lean on you here, Rat. All decisions are yours. Just do the same things you have done since you got here. You will be severely shorthanded but you will have full autonomy, Rat."

Oh, Warden, I sure will.

Chapter 52

As Principal Thompson sat in his red line luxury box at The Fish Tank, one of the perks of his position, he nodded and shook hands with other Valley High faculty and important players in Valley politics he had personally invited. He observed the Valley High student body arriving in droves just as the players emerged from their locker rooms.

They were lively, filling the arena with chants and cheers.

He knew why the students were late and agitated. They wanted to get every last drop from those kegs at the Quarry before coming down for the game, typical kids. There was an obvious buzz to the student body mass moving to their assigned sections.

Through his student connection, Thompson had known there was a "kegger" going on up the hill today. He did not want to have such a big day in the school's history marred by a mass incident or arrests behind the school. He had kept that information to himself. They were walking from the Quarry to the game, after all. Nobody was driving. Plus, they added to this festive atmosphere.

All part of this wonderful machine I am an important part of.

Besides, let that prick cop Russell deal with it. Thompson was ready to see Marcus keep St. Mary's out of the tournament.

Go Bulldogs! Drop the puck!

Thompson had just been down on the ice handing out the flowers to the parents of the Senior players as they escorted their sons to center ice to be cheered and recognized. It was a nice tribute and he was shocked at

187

how big Marcus was on skates. Glad he is not hitting me, he thought.

Thompson looked around for Irene Poulin. He could not see her among the mass of people filling every seat. He would wave her up to the suite if he saw her.

He liked what he had seen down her shirt today.

Chapter 53

After his conversation with Warden Davis, Rat was in the jail control room looking at the chart on the wall showing the layout of the jail and the inmates in each cell. He was checking the admittance log to see who arrived today and also reading the most recent incident reports to get up to speed for the weekend. Say what you want about Rat, he knew almost everything going on in this jail. He paid attention. It may have all been to serve his own warped purposes but he did his homework here, unlike at St. Mary's.

He also was still attempting to find the perfect name to serve up as his bait tomorrow night in the gym – fight night. The Show.

Hmmmm.

He then checked the shotguns and saw that all seven were locked in the cabinet. He checked the ammo cabinet and saw that they had fourteen shells total.

If the inmates only knew.

Because their budget was so tight they rarely had ammo paid for by the County. Any ammo that did get delivered was almost immediately stolen by the guards for target practice with their own guns at home.

Rat had found that fascinating – steal ammo from the jail so that you can practice and improve your aim but when you get to the jail you have no ammo so if anything happens what difference does it make if you have a good aim if you have an empty shotgun?

As a county jail Valley Jail had many different levels of inmates among its population. The convicted guys, the convicts, were guys who were already sentenced to a jail term and whose sentences ran two and a half years or less. Any more time than that on a sentence and they'd be sent to State Prison.

But Valley Jail also housed those accused of a crime and either had no bail or could not pay their bail. They were the aforementioned new meat. They were awaiting sentencing on anything from robbery to assault to murder.

There was supposed to be segregation between convicts and those awaiting trial, but since they were housing three times as many guys as this place was supposed to hold all bets were off. You put them where you could fit them.

Rat also put them where it made sense for him to have them. He punished guys who had pissed him off by assigning them to the bottom of Block 4 where it flooded often and was overrun with rats. He had the power.

He could also shake down a cell on a whim. When a cell was shaken down the guards would cuff the inmates to the pole outside the cell so they could watch and make the search legal for the ACLU pussies. The guards would then ransack the cell and look for contraband and weapons. Depending on why the cell was being shaken down would determine how much of the contraband would be taken and what reports would be written up. This was all part of the game that went on within the walls of the jail.

The consequence of possession of contraband, or any rules infraction, was time locked up in solitary confinement. Those notorious cells were in the cellar and the ACLU did not get to see them when they got their bi-annual tour of the jail. These were the torture chambers of the bygone eras during which the jail existed.

Inmates did not like the process of being put in solitary because the "trials" for punishment always got contentious – but the inmates never won. The hearings were held in front of three guards and they rarely if ever ruled against one of their own who had written up a disciplinary report. The typical sentence was called a forty-eight. That meant two days in solitary.

That was more than enough.

The solitary cells at the jail were legendary for the rats that inhabited them. The inmates all had learned that to survive down there they had to tie themselves to the bars when they slept and not lie down at all to rest. The rats were that bad.

To see a visibly shaken inmate emerge from just a few days of solitary made it difficult to remember the enraged man who had entered it. It was a very effective way to maintain order in an environment where the threat of being eaten by rats was a great deterrent to help the guards maintain control.

Another weapon in the guards' arsenal was using a "cooling off" period for an overheated inmate. This was only used in the winter. When an inmate was being unruly and disruptive the guards would hog-tie him with cuffs and shackles. The inmate would be carried to the solitary area, shackled to the bars of the open exterior door, hosed down and left exposed to the winter cold for however long it took for him to cool off.

The inmate would often have icicles formed on his chin and hair when unhooked.

Rat used the shakedowns as another weapon in his quiver. He had many options after a successful shakedown. He could let the guy keep the stuff and the guy now owed Rat a favor. He could take the stuff but not write the guy up – again, for a favor. He could take the contraband and write the guy up to bust his balls or get revenge. Lastly, he could just plant the contraband and use that as leverage.

He knew that the inmates hated him but he also knew that none of them would ever lay a hand on him. Most of these guys were in jail for less than two years. Assaulting a guard was at least two years and it was "on and after" your current sentence, meaning they could not be served concurrently. That was a big sentence to these guys and Rat knew it. He of course used that to his advantage, too. He acted more bravely than he really was because he knew these guys had to take shit from him.

Stir the pot.

He grabbed his lug bag and locked it in his locker. He'd have plenty of time to deal with that delivery later. He needed to think about that.

Chapter 54

Marcus circled the ice pre-game and was amazed because he had never seen so many people stuffed into the Tank. It was like a scene from a European soccer match. The Valley High supporters were screaming their familiar "Vall-ay, Vall-ay" chant to the tune of the Oh-Lay chants in Europe. And the Bostonian accented "Mah-kiss" chant coming from the student section seemed to be enhanced by the contents from the now empty four kegs up at the quarry.

The maroon-and-gold clad St. Mary's crowd, loud but vastly outnumbered and much more sober, mostly sat and waited for the game to start.

The Valley High cheerleaders could not be heard over the crazy crowd noise, but they sure were seen, especially by those same young boys who worshipped Marcus and had asked him for an autograph when he got to the Tank tonight. And some Dads were gawking, of course. These jackasses were the perverts Nicole's Dad hated so much.

He was home drinking and worrying about Nicole.

The cheerleaders had their section roped off, the best seats in the house. Nicole was so happy to be a part of all of this. Kaleigh was a party girl but she was a great cheerleader and really got into it and the squad followed her lead. They had some unique cheers and moves and really added to the atmosphere of the games. They had incorporated the Herald's "Mr. Superstar" into a routine that ended with them all holding up a copy of the paper.

Goat even admitted they were helpful if his team was lazy on some nights – the gals were able to cheer them on and wake them up. He was also quick to blame

193

them when his players would miss a pass – "stop staring at da cheerleaders!"

Aaron and Claire were antsy, wanting to see a great, quick game so they could be on the move and on their flight on time. They had declined an invitation from Principal Thompson to sit in his luxury box. Aaron liked to pace around a bit during the game and Claire felt like Thompson was the kind of guy they should keep at arm's length. The luxury box was a den of ass-kissing and she wanted to watch hockey, not listen to some city councilor tell her about how great he is and what public office he will be gracing next as he hit on her and stared at her boobs.

She was proud of her still-firm rack but those assholes made her feel uncomfortable.

Boots was on the bench and as stoned as the goalie on his team. This shit was good and The Boyz were selling him the best stuff they had. He was too consumed with the game to think about those assholes now, though. He loved this gig. What a rush. When was Goat retiring? I can do this on my own now.

Goat and Murphy shook hands at the red line per their own little ritual, pausing to pose for a picture that would run in the Herald tomorrow.

Marcus was ready. He was ringing shots off the glass with a smack, much to the delight of his many fans watching his every move, including the scouts. And Nicole. The other players were not actually invisible out there, but even their own parents were all awed by the Valley High superstar and could not take their eyes off him as he gracefully warmed up.

Marcus saw the chubby EMT guy at his usual spot near the Zamboni door and caught him not looking when he zinged a puck off the glass right behind his head. The EMT guy swung his head around and was already smiling because having had the same thing happen many times before he knew it was Marcus being Marcus. He turned and Marcus winked at him as he skated by.

Dottie was setting up at the bake sale table and the students sure were hungry. There was a mad scene at her table as the Valley High kids were grabbing anything they could as quickly as she put them on the table. Money was pouring in.

She thanked Sally for running all the treats in and explained the good news about her Florida vacation. Sally was hoping Dottie would begin to socialize a bit and maybe this trip would help.

The sweets were going to run out quickly. The hammered kids were stuffing whatever they could find into their mouths and Dottie was taking money in hand over fist. Much of what was consumed would be regurgitated in the rest rooms before game's end.

Sally ran in with the last of the baked goods for the table. She had emptied out her trunk and run in quickly. She left her coat in the car, still covering the "special brownies" and she forgot all about them even being in the car. She did not need her coat once she got inside so she left it behind. It was only a short run to the car after the game.

Joey Rat was ready, too, as he watched Marcus take his impressive shots at the glass. Coach Murphy had told him what his assignment was and Joey was eager to please. He was much more confident he could neutralize Marcus thinking about it on the bus before he got on the ice and he began watching Marcus shoot the puck about a hundred miles an hour. And Marcus was huge on skates. Joey decided his stick was going to be his weapon tonight. There was no way he could match Marcus physically.

Joey did the sign of the cross after the hot chick sang the anthem and skated by where Mama Rat was always sitting and winked. Mama gave him the fist in the air as a salute. Mama Rat was nuts but she knew, and loved, her hockey.

Mama Rat was going to text Jimmy Rat at the jail to keep him updated. She was losing her marbles and her texts were slowly getting less and less lucid.

Chapter 55

Rat took a longer route to Bald Boy's cell because he did not want the rookie guards to see where he was headed. He knew the hidden routes and secret tunnels of this building better than most. He had decided to wait until Saturday to bring the lugged goods to Bald Boy as a last grasp at showing him who was boss. Bald Boy had been demanding the drugs since last night. Rat was worried at how quickly this thing could unravel. He needed every advantage he could get.

All the contraband was out of sight because he was smartly cautious inside the jail, unlike his blunders at Gordon's Market and with the Warden yesterday. He unlocked the door to Block 3 and walked through a maze of Hispanic men who did not budge but alerted the block of Rat's presence with a series of sounds and signals. Rat stopped at the entrance of Bald Boy's cell.

It had everything that they were allowed – radio, TV, only one roommate, rugs on the floor and blankets strung over their bunks that slid back and forth for privacy, which was not officially allowed. Rat figured they just wanted to jerk off in private and rarely enforced that rule. Unless he hated the piece of shit inmate, then he wrote that up and tore it down.

Bald Boy saw but ignored Rat as he was playing dominos with three other guys and speaking animatedly in Spanish. It never made sense to Rat how seriously these guys took their dominos games. Bald Boy was currently explaining his strategy and they all listened as if he were telling them where to find a million dollars. They were all smoking dark little cigars that smelled like plastic burning to Rat. Nobody else spoke, almost like a king holding court. The air was thickly polluted with the smoke from the cigars adding to the feeling of danger that overcame Rat.

The Cuban nodded and shooed all The Boyz out. Rat unloaded the goods that he had lugged onto the bed beside Bald Boy. He then clapped his hands as if that was it and Bald Boy took inventory of what was on the bed.

The ounce of ganja, rolling papers for joints, a mixed bag of hundreds of pills, two very used cellphones, a dozen prepaid phone cards and some pepperoni for the Mob guys. And the cigarettes, which Rat had to stuff into his socks and walk like he had to take a big shit so they would not fall out.

Bald Boy said, without looking up, "The marijuana baggie looks light again."

Rat was dumbfounded. He had just broken laws to get this shit inside and this fucking commie Cuban was going to say that? In Rat's fucking jail? Jamie was such an idiot. Rat warned him to not be heavy-handed when dipping into the baggie of ganja.

"It's all there, I don't even smoke that shit," Rat lied.

"You calling me a liar, Officer Rat?" Bald Boy stood up as he said this, towering over Rat in the tiny cell. Rat was not prepared for this.

This was new from him, thought Rat. Why this aggression? Rat could not take the bait because he was on the Cuban's turf.

That and he knew Bald Boy would crush him in a fight. He reflexively reached for where his gun would have been on his right hip.

Like the opportunistic man that Bald Boy was, he knew beating up this kid for Rat tonight was a big favor. Rat had dropped off the big kid in Jake's cell knowing Bald Boy was there. Rat told Bald Boy what he wanted done and Bald Boy told Rat how expensive that was going to be for him. Rat did not like hearing that at all. Bald Boy had demanded the goods be brought to him last night and Rat had held out until now just to fuck with Bald Boy.

The more he thought about it the more pissed off Bald Boy was to be used as Rat's muscle in the jail. Sure, it behooved Bald Boy to exert his will upon these victims publicly, but he wanted to fight who he wanted to fight, not some big kid Rat had set up. Bald Boy was leveraging this into asserting himself right here and showing Rat that he, Bald Boy, was the man in charge here. You bring me what I want when I want it.

Rat sensed this was a time for him to take it up a notch and act much more macho than he felt. He was losing his grip and it was a long fall.

Chess match time, my move.

Rat took a deep breath and took a provocative step forward as he pointed to the bed, "And no more fucking cigarettes. They are too big to get in here and I am not buying fucking Virginia Slims for that fucking girlfriend of yours!" He was spraying spit as he spoke. He was fired up.

Rat recalled Gordon's lecture at the store and Darlene's insults at Dunkin Donuts yesterday and he did not have to pretend to be mad. He was now pissed.

He played on his momentum as he blurted out, "And you better do your fucking job in this fight tonight. This kid gets a severe beating or your days of being king inmate are over!"

Bald Boy took this all in and sat back down, shaking his head. Unthreatened by this false bravado, he slowly unwrapped a pack of butts, smacked it on his wrist to pack the tobacco for a slower burn and lit a menthol cigarette. He liked menthols every now and then because of the taste and because he still got buzzed from them, that was true. Gordon knew his shit.

Bald Boy stared at the floor and was flexing his fingers in and out of a fist. It was a show of force. He kept doing it as he spoke, never lifting his eyes off the floor. He spoke quietly and slowly to himself in Spanish, blowing smoke rings and admiring them as Rat slowly calmed down.

Rat hated this fucking inmate but he had painted himself into a corner. He waited for Bald Boy to speak as he saw him making his hands slowly into menacing fists.

When he did address Rat it was with his eyes on the floor still. Through much practice he had no perceivable accent when he spoke English.

"Rat, you bring in what I tell you to bring in, remember? You get paid good money, in cash, to just walk in and drop stuff on my bed. Requires no skill, no brains – perfect for you. Keep that in mind. Also, I fight because I like to and no other reason. You need to remember that, Officer. You want a puppet? Go buy one with all this money I am giving you."

Rat was thinking about how to reply to this arrogant prick when Bald Boy suddenly looked up at him with a dark look in his eye and spoke very directly to Rat.

"Plus, I know you live at home, officer. I know that. Remember that."

He looked right into Rat's eyes when he said the last sentence. He did not blink and stood up and blew smoke at Rat in a very disrespectful way. It was said with sincerity – as if he was intimating that he would hate to have to visit Mama Rat so don't make him do it.

Rat was trying to get his hands around this threat. This game has been taken to a new level. Rat was happy he did not have Marcus jumped earlier that day. He wanted Marcus to do a number on this Cuban motherfucker now. Rat's brain was buzzing with thought.

He stared blankly at Bald Boy as he digested this last threat.

This fight had a few different ways for Rat to savor a victory. He was going through the good possible outcomes and how he would manipulate each to his benefit. He was thinking quickly as he wanted to get out of there but he had to make sure he did not leave with his tail between his legs. He was in his zone right now trying to defend his domain. He had worked too hard to get here to relinquish his status, squashed by an inmate.

Because of his focus on all the great things that would come of this fight, he never really considered the costly outcome if, for some unforeseen reason, this fight went against Rat's best interests. He was in this right up to his man-boobs.

Bald Boy paused and looked at Rat, letting that last sentence sink in. The power had officially shifted. Rat was trapped but for this fight later today. He backed up the step he had just taken and then another.

Bald Boy again blew menthol smoke into Rat's face as he moved close enough to Rat that his personal space most definitely had been invaded.

"The list for next week is ready." He actually winked at him as he handed the new list to Rat, whose mind was scrambling. How was this unwinding so quickly?

Rat suddenly realized Gordon had been right. Bald Boy was in charge. He had been from the start, it was just getting worse as time progressed.

Rat had to change this equation quickly. As he thought of this he looked up to see the same three domino players looking at him through the cell door. Their tattooed faces definitely did not give off a happy look. They all looked at Rat with a scowl knowing that if Bald Boy had just simply nodded to them they would have attacked Rat right there. These guys were showing Rat they, too, had the power over him. It was coordinated and effective. Rat was thinking about nothing but getting out of this block alive. He wondered if they had seen or heard about his visit to Conti today.

Trying in vain to save face at this point, Rat gave a dismissive wave with his hand as he said, "I don't need this shit," and pointed at Bald Boy as he added, "Remember who is in charge here, Angel." He quickly walked out of the cell without saying another word to Bald Boy and lowered his shoulder and jostled his way through the group of Boyz assembled outside of the cell in which Rat had just gotten emasculated.

He now needed Marcus Kelly to kick the shit out of this guy. What a weird couple of days.

Chapter 56

Friday Evening • The Fish Tank

Marcus had told his two wings, Taylor and Hogan, what Goat had told him about the scouts leaving after the first period. He wanted to play all out, not for his personal records, though that would be nice – he had finally admitted to himself. Hogan and Taylor were both good players themselves so the scouts might notice them, too.

He also wanted to win this game very badly. Marcus had gotten Goat to agree to put him out there every time Marcus nodded to Goat on the bench in the first period. Goat never said he could not play the whole first period.

After his first shift, Marcus quickly figured out that Joey was assigned to cover him. By the third shift he knew he was being shadowed and hacked and whacked every chance Joey got. But by that time Marcus had already scored a goal on a slap shot and assisted on Hogan's sweet breakaway goal. He ignored Joey's hacks but the refs did, too. Marcus wanted the puck. He was feeling it. Valley was up 2-0 just like that and Fowler had not seen a puck come near him.

When Marcus had a jump in his stride, like he did so far tonight, it was almost unfair to the other team. Marcus was now typically three or four inches taller and forty pounds heavier than most of the other kids on the ice. He was also faster, quicker, stronger and smarter hockey-wise than all the players on the other team. Oh, and he had the best shot on the ice and had just scored with it.

The student section was a sea of mostly shit-faced kids having a blast and chanting up a storm. The Fish Tank was blowing up. There was no violence in the stands, just gleeful and boisterous fans. It was like a big party and Marcus was the host.

Joey was only slightly effective as a pest at best. He was slashing hard at Marcus, trying to goad him to retaliate, but Marcus did not oblige.

Hack, whack. Ankles and arms. Marcus ignored him and lit him up. Joey had finally gotten a slashing penalty called on him by the oblivious refs and protested loudly to them. He skated by Marcus and lowered his shoulder. Marcus met him with his own shoulder and landed the better shot as Joey was off balance and staggered as he was led to the penalty box.

Marcus scored on the power play and it was 3-0 Valley. He assisted on two others and it was 5-0 Valley after one period. Marcus now only needed one more goal to break the record. Fowler had an easy period with only two shots on net. He was watching the cheerleaders and jealously watching fans eat cupcakes. He suddenly had the munchies and was craving the Cheetos the little girl behind the net was eating.

Goat had waved to a few scouts as they were departing. They all gave him a sign that they were impressed and would give him a call. A couple of them did stay for the rest of the game but not many. Goat now had to make a decision that would not be popular, both in the locker room and in the stands.

Goat was not happy with the officiating. Marcus was constantly being slashed by St. Mary's, mostly by that Joey kid. Marcus also took a very cheap shot that caused him to go dangerously head first into the glass that resulted in no penalty.

Marcus had come back to the bench after one particularly nasty hack to his right hand and was shaking the hand as if he had hurt it. He shook it off eventually. His ankles and feet were also targets of the slashing sticks. Goat had seen enough. He knew

Marcus was tough but Goat knew that any injury to the hand, especially the right hand for righties, meant you could not play hockey. If you cannot grip your stick you are useless out there, even the slightest broken bone. He was not going to let that happen.

They had the tournament coming up and Marcus was the key for Valley; Goat could not risk his getting hurt tonight.

He pulled Marcus aside and told him he was benched for maybe the rest of the game. Goat did not like the way St. Mary's was playing him and Valley was up 5-0. Goat explained about the risks of the slashing game they were playing. Also, the scouts did indeed depart and they had seen all they wanted.

Marcus wanted to tell him to relax and let him play but he also wanted his teammates to get their time in the sun in front of such a big crowd. He grudgingly nodded and headed off.

Coach stayed true to his word, benching Marcus for the second period. Being the knowledgeable fans they were, the Valley High crowd knew why Goat was keeping Marcus on the bench and safe for the tournament. But that did not stop them from screaming bloody murder for his doing so. The drunken student body was throwing things on the ice. "WE WANT MAH-KISS" chants bounced off the walls of The Fish Tank.

The game turned even more aggressive during the second period, as Goat predicted. The teams seemed to feed off the now frenzied crowd. The game was fast-paced and the tone was nasty. St. Mary's had scored twice in a minute and then scored another on a misplay by Fowler to make it 5-3. He had been caught staring at the Cheetos eater and missed a shot from the other end of the rink.

Fowler looked shaky and nervous after that stupid mistake. The St. Mary's goalie, Joseph, was under heavy attack but was playing like an all-star after letting in a few bad goals in the first period. The slap shot that Marcus had scored with was going over ninety miles per hour, there was not a thing he could have done about that one.

The refs eventually warned both coaches to keep their players in line. Goat told them they created the monster by not calling enough penalties in the first period, they can deal with it now.

The roar of the crowd continued to swell and the chants became vulgar and hilarious. The St. Mary's crowd was now boisterous, too, as their team was carrying the day. Claire and Aaron got caught up in the moment and they were chanting, too. They wanted to leave but they also wanted to see if Goat would let Marcus get the one point he needed. Aaron also wanted to give him the nod to crush Joey 13.

The second period ended and Marcus did not play one shift. He skated off the ice but as he neared the gate where Valley's locker room was, Joey skated by and asked Marcus if he was scared to play again that night and called him a fucking pussy. Marcus ignored the punk and turned to the glass where Nicole was lined up with her squad. They were cheering the Valley players as they passed by on their way to the locker room.

Joey motioned to Nicole and said to Marcus, "She blew me the other night."

Marcus turned and told Joey to go fuck himself. Marcus made a note of the 13 on his back as Coach Murphy was screaming Joey's name over and over to skate that way and head to the locker room on their side of the rink.

Finally he screamed, "Rat! Joey Ratkowski, let's go!" and Joey skated to the gate on the other side.

Marcus watched Joey Rat 13 skate away. Fucking punk. Keep your head up. I'm playing the third period.

Chapter 57

The rain was coming down in sheets and visibility was zero. Had he been watching the weather radar Russell would have known that was just a taste of what this storm had in store for the region. Act Two of this storm was not going to be fun.

He checked in with his guys and all was good. He risked a call to Jamie at dispatch and the kid sounded like he was handling the job. He got the score from The Fish Tank and smiled.

Attaboy, Marcus.

Russell was driving around on the streets near The Fish Tank area. Had he looked at the drains along the road where this rain should have been draining off he would have noticed that they were covered with leaves and debris, leaving the road dangerously filled with massive puddles from the rain.

The Valley High hockey team was supposed to have cleared the drains in that area of the city during a money-raising event last fall that the city's businesses all contributed to. It was for Civic Pride Week and the hockey team wanted to do their part.

The only problem was they had paid Boots to buy them a keg and they had a keg party at the Quarry instead of doing any work.

The drains were ineffective and clogged against this onslaught of rain that was just starting.

Chapter 58

Goat did not say a word to the boys between periods. He was hoping his silence would do enough to motivate the troops. He could tell his players were not happy with how they played. Marcus or no Marcus they put some shots on net but they did not play aggressively and that sucked. So did Fowler, he looked distracted and slow.

Cheetos.

Marcus motioned for Goat to stay behind as they trudged back out for the third period.

"Goat, I gotta play. No way can we lose and have me sitting. I want St. Mary's sitting at home when this tournament starts. You do, too."

Goat nodded, "OK, if they get within a goal you go again. But only if it's one goal."

Marcus did not want to argue. Fine. Fowler sucked tonight, Marcus was pretty sure St. Mary's would get the next goal. He did not care about the scoring record for himself but he wanted to keep St. Mary's and Joey out of the tournament.

Aaron and Claire were anxiously looking at their watches as Marcus came out and nodded to them, letting them know he was going to play in the third period. Aaron made eye contact and nodded to Marcus. Marcus nodded as he skated away, message received. Good to know.

Heads up, Joey. It's official. All that hacking is going to get you lit up. And Dad did not even know about the shit the guy said about Nicole.

Claire got Aaron to agree to leave if Marcus scored to break the record. Aaron was lying. There would be other flights, if not other cruises. This was too good. He also badly wanted to go to Fish's party; he had forgotten about that when he had agreed to the cruise.

Dottie was helping Sally sell the raffle tickets because she was too nervous to just stand there. The students had bought everything she had baked. Some of them were licking the plates on her table.

Mama Rat had seen Joey talking to Marcus on the ice and texted to Rat at the jail:

<joey and marcus fighting on ice>

Mama Rat was eating a slice of pizza and had sauce all over her face. The high school kids walking by were openly laughing at her. She was oblivious.

Nicole was nervous but having a blast. She looked for Marcus and screamed with delight when she saw him skate by. She decided right then and there she would go to a big time college and be a cheerleader. This was incredible.

Principal Thompson was hoping Goat would play Marcus again. This was getting too close. And the way that clown Fowler was playing he should have let him fail French class, for fuck's sake. The kid could not stop a puck to save his life.

Sure enough, three minutes into the third period St. Mary's scored a fluke goal that Fowler had somehow let go under his glove.

5-4 Valley now.

Goat nodded to Marcus. As he was strapping his helmet on Joey skated by and gave Marcus the blowjob sign. Marcus calmly assured himself that he was going to find this guy one time. He did not need his Dad's nod for this one but he was glad his Dad agreed. This kid has one coming.

Marcus and Joey battled for the rest of the game. Because Marcus was trying to crush Joey he ended up only landing decent checks on him. He was frustrated. Marcus was winning the skirmishes but not scoring and still getting hacked every time he got near the puck. The refs were letting the boys play hockey again, calling no penalties. The pace was crisp, the action nonstop, the hits mostly clean. After a shaky start, the St. Mary's goalie, Joseph, was now stopping everything. Marcus was snake-bitten and got robbed by Joseph twice late in the third period on point blank chances. Valley also hit two posts. Fowler was spacing out, the puck was in the other end most of the period.

The Cheetos eater was now eating a big pretzel that looked even better.

It was right around this point that a parade of mostly female Valley students, many of whom were freshmen, made their way to the ladies' room to vomit the keg beer that had been fermenting in their bellies. The frenzy they had worked up to while cheering for their team had their hearts pounding, bringing the alcohol through their young bodies with alarming speed. One gal made it to the bottom of the stands, puked, then slipped and fell in her own puddle of vomit and began bawling. The game was so good very few fans even noticed.

Unfortunately for her a classmate did video the whole thing and it went viral among the student body the next day. She would become known as Puddles for the rest of her high school career.

The score remained 5-4, the crowd was bonkers and the pace of the game again matched the crowd's emotions. St. Mary's was showing why it should be a tournament team and Valley was getting frustrated by its lack of goals despite getting so many good shots on net.

Joey was hacking the hell out of Marcus and Marcus was pissed and frustrated now but did not yet have a chance to crush him with a hit. He rarely complained to the refs but he gave them an exasperated look a few times. He got shrugs in return from the incompetent zebras.

There was less than a minute left now and Marcus was on the bench, breathing hard and recovering from his last shift. Goat signaled for Marcus to go finish the game on the ice to receive the recognition from the crowd, and keep them from scoring while doing so. The crowd went nuts when his skates hit the ice and Valley kept the puck harmlessly along the boards and killed time. There were now twenty seconds left and the faceoff was in the St. Mary's end of the rink after an icing. They could not pull their goalie.

Joey jumped on the ice. He was having a great, effective game and Murphy wanted to reward him. He also wanted to win.

As Joey got to the faceoff dot across from Marcus he looked over and saw Mama Rat in her seat near the glass. She took her finger and cut across her throat and pointed to Marcus – the same thing she had seen Rat do this morning. Joey was the only one on the ice who had seen this, but he now knew from where his brother got that crazy look in his eye.

The ref dropped the puck. Marcus won the faceoff as Joey distractedly missed the puck but hacked the thinly protected instep of Marcus's left foot with his stick.

No socks.

Bad toes.

Marcus went to one knee, the pain shooting up his leg.

Ouch. This guy Joey was good at this shit, he had to give him that much.

He limped back up and the pain dissipated as quickly as it came on. He saw the puck eventually get cleared out of the Valley zone by a teammate but the St. Mary's goalie sprinted out of his crease and made a good play. He handled the puck skillfully, looking for a teammate to pass to.

Fifteen seconds left, 5-4 Valley.

Joey skated for the puck and toward his goalie. He looped back inside his own blue line toward the Valley net as the goalie handled the puck in their zone. Joey's body was headed to the Valley end of the rink but he had his head turned to face the puck. He tapped his stick on the ice to call for the pass and saw the puck spinning to him as he neared the red line at full speed, his head turned to accept the nice pass. The goalie then turned to skate to the bench for the extra attacker.

As the puck neared Joey's skates it hit some snow that typically built up at the end of the period and the puck slowed ever so slightly.

Just enough.

It made Joey slow down and turn his head even more to the puck, but he kept his body going forward knowing they had very little time to score. He was going full speed. Marcus saw that he did not have to move to absolutely crush Joey. He was standing right where Joey was blindly headed. Joey's head was fully turned behind him and the puck arrived on his stick as he turned his head quickly in the direction he was headed. He had a jump in his step.

Eleven seconds left.

Marcus had choices here. He could just poke the puck away from Joey or he could let this guy know not to speak like that about Nicole and teach him a fucking lesson.

The lesson won out. He pictured his Dad nodding. He made it official – this kid had it coming.

Marcus braced his whole body. He took one stride forward and lowered his shoulder. He kept his stick and elbows down because this had to be clean. He had time to plan this hit.

He was grinning.

Joey finally had the puck on his stick. He snapped his head forward. He was excited. This could be it. He could be the one to score the goal that put St. Mary's into the tournament; they only needed to tie. He could be the hero. Jimmy would look at him differently. Maybe Dad will come to the tournament games. He did a fancy hop-step to add some flavor to his moment.

You could almost hear the ESPN "da na na na" sound in the background. What was about to happen would have made Top Ten Plays of any day. The clip of the hit did make it to some local sports/entertainment websites around Boston and quickly spread nationwide.

Marcus braced for impact and saw that this poor kid had turned his head forward at the exact wrong time. Baker had taught Marcus all about leverage and force in their many wrestling and boxing lessons. That education was about to pay off.

Joey's forehead caught Marcus's shoulder at full speed and in between strides. Marcus had done nothing illegal. He stood his ground and fucking crushed Joey 13.

Dad did nod.

It was like hitting the sweet spot on a bat, golf club or hockey stick. Marcus felt nothing but pure contact.

The whole crowd sensed what was going to happen, it was painfully obvious from three strides away.

That pest number 13 was going to get hammered finally, thought Dan Baker. He screamed, "Kill him, Marcus!" but with the crowd noise nobody else heard him.

Right before impact there was a hush in the Tank. That allowed the crack of helmet meeting shoulder pad to echo before being drowned out by the gasp of the fans.

The first thing that Joey's head hit after Marcus's shoulder was the ice. Hard. He was bleeding slightly from the nose and was knocked out ever so briefly. His arms were straight up in the air as he lay prone on the ice. His stick almost hit the scoreboard hanging fifty feet above the ice. He was motionless, but for less than a few seconds.

Neither ref blew his whistle. They were astonished by the violence of the hit but neither could move to blow their whistle and they were as stunned as the crowd.

And it was a clean hit.

The puck was now on the St. Mary's blue line and Marcus was all alone and skating to the puck, his powerful strides could be heard cutting through the ice as the anxious crowd sat stunned as Joey got to his knees.

Seven seconds left.

Marcus swooped in alone on Chris Joseph, who was shitting in his pants. He had turned on a dime to just get back near his net after having sprinted to the bench to get pulled. Marcus had a cannon of a shot and had also bruised Joseph a few times already tonight. Joseph zeroed in on the puck. Make the save.

Marcus had many tricks and moves he had practiced over and over, but this move had to be memorable and it had to work, too. He knew he did not have much time.

He was skating at top speed and was at the faceoff dot on the left side of the goalie, the puck on his stick but bouncing from the snow-covered ice.

Three seconds left.

Marcus faked a shot as Joseph pushed out to meet him and cut off his angle. Joseph only slightly bought the fake but that was enough as he slid to his left about a foot too far away from his net. Marcus brought the puck just inches away from Joseph's outstretched stick and slid it past him with his backhand into the now empty net as the buzzer sounded.

Marcus Kelly became the all-time leading scorer his conference had ever produced as he kept St. Mary's out of the tournament.

As he put his stick up to celebrate his goal, Marcus saw the EMT guy running to the Zamboni door area just to the left of the net so he suddenly veered off toward the doors opening to get the EMT guy out to Joey.

Marcus headed to the gate to help skate the chubby EMT guy and his big box of meds over to where Joey was standing. He held his arm and slid him across the ice. They almost tripped over a few of the hats that had been thrown on the ice to celebrate the hat-trick Marcus had just completed. The EMT guy said, "Nice goal," as he held on for dear life.

Marcus hustled him over to Joey and then skated away and let the EMT guy and the trainers go to work on Joey. He was coherent and smiling at something the EMT guy had said. He seemed fine. Just pissed they lost. He got lucky.

As a precaution they put Joey on the stretcher to bring him to the hospital for concussion tests as they were mandated to do when there was a loss of consciousness.

The crowd was going nuts and screaming "MAH-KISSSSSSSSS" as the St. Mary's crowd shuffled out. His proud parents were choked up as they sprinted from the Tank to get to the airport.

Mama Rat saw the hit and left when Joey was put on the stretcher; she sent a text to Rat:

<marcus crushed joey, dirty hit, Dr on ice now, going to hospital>

She never looked up to see if he was OK before she hit send. She left The Tank and went home to knit. Her phone battery died on the way home. She had forgotten about the game when she went to bed.

The crowd was delirious. Valley High had won, St. Mary's did not qualify for the tournament and Marcus Kelly had gotten the record nobody thought would ever be broken on a game-winning goal. The atmosphere in The Fish Tank was at its peak as the players gathered at center ice and thanked the crowd for the support. Nicole was in tears, she had never been happier to be part of something. Kaleigh had even hugged her as they celebrated the win.

The party was now the talk among most of the fans. Let's go Bulldogs!! Civic pride – and civic thirst – were at all-time highs.

It was time to head to Fish's and celebrate. The storm had just intensified but they had just witnessed something special and the mood was festive. Whoever had been considering not going to the party because of the storm now changed their minds after seeing that game. Everybody wanted to continue the great atmosphere this game had created.

Fish was happy he ordered extra booze.

Boots was happy he had made a visit to The Boyz, too.

Party time.

Chapter 59

Bald Boy was sitting in his cell with a few of The Boyz, although nobody was talking. He was smoking a Cuban cigar laced with the marijuana Rat had just lugged. Rat had lugged the cigar last week. Bald Boy wanted to take it easy, though. Not too stoned. He had a fight tonight. But he loved to fight stoned, it allowed the animal in him to really come to the surface. He was an uncaring man in every way and ever since childhood he was known as being a savage. His brother was right to have put him in jail in Cuba – Bald Boy was coming for him and he would have sold his mother to a brothel to do it.

As a kid in Cuba he was sent to a low level boxing academy as punishment for the mayhem he was causing in school. He was doing well there until he got caught stealing from the academy's petty cash box for the third time in one week. Although the other students at the academy feared him, back then he was considered more ruthless than skilled in the ring. He once resorted to stabbing a kid who had beaten him up in the ring during a sparring session.

After being kicked out of the academy he entered his brother's gang at age fifteen and instantly took to it like a duck to water. He was a big boy and a big bully. He beat up who he was told to beat up, broke limbs, sold drugs, stole and raped. His signature move was snapping guys' thumbs. He had a savagely ruthless streak that allowed him to torture and maim indifferently.

He was a natural leader, too. He organized well. They became known as The Boyz secretly – the gang within the gang. Hardcore criminals. Bald Boy was

218

their guy, he got them organized and they were all secretly making money with their hidden schemes and deals. They would kill for him.

His older brother realized how vicious his kid brother was and he feared his little brother Angel was trying to mount a coup and take over from him. His older brother wanted to retain his title and power. He needed to have Angel out of the way so he set him up in an elaborate scheme and got Angel arrested on a Federal charge, a big deal in Cuba, and thrown in the worst jail on the island.

Angel knew what really happened – he would get his revenge.

Although he entered the jail as a feared thug, Angel really learned the art of how to fight and kill in there. He rose to the top spot of the biggest gang in the Cuban jail, too. He fought and raped and ran the drug trade inside the blocks. He began to shave his head and eyebrows. It became his calling card and he became known as Chico Calvo – Bald Boy – head of The Boyz.

He loved the new name and decided to get the tattoo on his forehead inked in English. Bald Boy and his crew all longed to get to the USA and planned and plotted to get there someday as they passed the days in jail. He knew the Bald Boy tattoo would scare the fuck out of Americans.

He laughed in his bunk as he thought back to those days in the Cuban jail.

After being held in jail for seven years, he got his lucky break when a Captain from the Cuban Army was sent to the jail that housed Bald Boy. This Captain had been having an affair with the wife of a member of Castro's inner circle and had been caught in bed with her. He was sent to the jail and a contract was put on his head. Angel got assurances about getting out of jail if the act was done correctly and he took the job.

219

One week after the Captain arrived in jail he was found dead in his cell. His throat was cut ear-to-ear and his balls had been cut off and stuffed in his mouth, as requested.

And his thumbs were broken. Bald Boy threw that in for free.

He was released from jail but had to maintain a low profile and hide in the slums for almost a year. He could not risk being found by his brother or his gang while he was at his weakest.

Eventually Bald Boy was able to re-connect with his main guys and get them aligned with him. They knew that if they could remove Bald Boy's brother they could take over and really expand, as they had plotted to do before and during their jail terms.

They seized upon a chance to blow up his brother's car by planting explosives in it as he dined at their mother's house. The explosion ripped the car, and his brother, into a thousand pieces and blew a huge hole in their mother's house.

After the blast, Bald Boy walked through the hole in the house and informed his family that he was the new boss. His family had not seen him since he was thrown in jail and they recoiled at the grotesque monster that stood in front of them. The tattoo on his forehead was a shock to his mother. She made the sign of the cross as she whispered "el Diablo" over and over. Her Angel had come back as the Devil.

Bald Boy took control of the gang immediately. Nobody argued. They thrived and made money and bribed the right government people and police as they expanded. Bald Boy was a good businessman but he did not delegate the physical part of running the gang to others. He mostly took care of the tortures and beatings himself. He was thriving.

However, he grew bored of Cuba, he had bigger plans, so he schemed to get to the U.S. He had prepared for this his whole criminal career. Bald Boy and The Boyz bribed their way onto a boat headed to Canada and they got smuggled into the States to begin working with his associates in Massachusetts and New York. Their operation was expanding. The Boyz needed Angel "Bald Boy" Hernandez to help with things on the East Coast of the U.S. Bald Boy took the promotion, but he did not come up here to take orders from anybody. He had eyes on taking over the whole U.S. operation and he was not going to ask politely.

As he pursued his goals he mostly wore a cap to cover up his tattoo but he made sure whoever he beat up or punished saw it. Remember me. I am BALD BOY. Victims recoiled at the sight of his scarred face, violent eyes, horribly stained, crooked teeth and menacing tattoo. Bald Boy loved the look of terror it produced from those he beat and tortured.

A cruel man in a cruel business.

He eventually took over the drug operations and used his connections to expand the import of drugs to New England in mass quantity – especially marijuana. They used the ports along the Eastern Seaboard, paying cash to fishermen to meet their boats out at sea. He was showing his skills as a moneymaker and leader. He was moving up the ladder here, too. His Cuban Boyz were a formidable squad and they ruled savagely. They got noticed.

Bald Boy was quickly gaining power and status within the gang, making money and expanding their operations from Maine to Florida. However, he was caught onboard a local fishing boat that was intercepted by the U.S. Coast Guard for a routine check while out at sea. They had just taken on a large marijuana shipment. There was nowhere for Bald Boy to hide. He could not swim.

He had been set up. Again.

They busted him for the pot but also got him on an immigration charge and dumped him directly into Valley Jail without a court appearance.

Angel was not pleased but he had been in worse places. He had learned patience the hard way and was sure in time he could figure out a way to be released to get his revenge. For now he could get what he needed in jail as long as he had that Rat idiot bringing it to him. He had loyal Boyz on the outside that would provide for him and he still was involved in important decisions for the operation of the gang's drug distribution business.

He had gained all of the power inside the jail – that was what gave him the buzz he craved. He was in no hurry to escape or hire a lawyer. If he lost his case and went back to Cuba he'd be put back in prison or worse. This jail was the Four Seasons compared with Cuban prison. He had made peace with his most recent incarceration and was instead focused on clinging to the top spot for which he had viciously fought.

Bald Boy knew that his hold on power was tenuous and needed constant attention. He had to adapt and keep an ear to the ground. Valley Jail held many capable Hispanic guys who had their eyes on running things while they were in jail. And that fucking Gringo Conti was stirring the pot a bit too often lately. What the fuck was that big act in the cafeteria today? Was that supposed to make Bald Boy back off?

The inmates in this jail came and went often, turnover here was rapid and power could change quickly if even one guy got transferred out or a new inmate showed up. There were feuds and alliances emerging daily, along with departures and arrivals. The jail's population was in constant flux.

Bald Boy often felt like the male lion in that show he and Jake watched the other night. All these other male lions would come over to this lion's pride and try to fuck the females or fight the lion and take his pride and become the King.

But the big lion fought them all off and stayed on top. He was the King, motherfucker!

Bald Boy was that lion now. After he had defeated the other males the King lion was vicious in his sexual attacks on the lionesses and Bald Boy was a bit overly aggressive in his assault on Jake that night because of it. He was stoned and hyped up. And he was getting Jake his cigarettes in return.

Rat had a real hair across his ass for this big kid he wanted Bald Boy to take care of for him. He said something about his brother being put in the hospital or something. Rather than have The Boyz gang up on Marcus in the blocks, Rat wanted to have one of his special jail fights in the gym featuring Bald Boy. Rat thought he could hide his real intent behind that phony fight, Bald Boy knew this was about Rat showing the inmates Rat's power over him.

We'll see about that.

Bald Boy had told Rat it would be expensive to take care of this problem for him. Rat had argued that he had already earned this by bringing in all the shit he had risked his career for. Bald Boy laughed. Career? This fucking place? Come on. Like everybody else, he hated the Rat, but he also needed him. It was one thing to be the toughest guy in here. The true power came from having the connection to bring in all the contraband and control it, plus the ability to collect any debts owed to you.

Bald Boy had that now but he needed the Rat to keep it going. His hatred of the need for Rat manifested into the disgusted hostility he had just displayed towards him. The threat against Rat's family was a trump card and he needed to let Rat know the list would be longer in the coming weeks.

The jail power was all that Bald Boy had in his life – at least Rat got to leave and live a normal life. This lugging relationship was the world to Bald Boy so he had to scare the absolute shit out of him to make sure Rat continued to comply. He felt as if this was accomplished today. He hoped so.

His thoughts returned to the fight. This new kid he was going to fight was a big kid and looked very young but strong, too. Bald Boy was a vicious fighter and just as big as Marcus, probably not as strong though. He would have to fight dirty, which was actually the only way he knew.

There was an unusual fear in his mind as he awaited going to the gym. One ability inmates had was lie on their bed and wait. Bald Boy had, for most of his life, abused drugs and smoked cigarettes, cigars and joints in the jail. Sure, he lifted in the gym and played basketball, but he was far from fit. That is why he went for quick knockouts in all of his fights. This kid would not anticipate that so he would try to end this quickly. He would scare the fight out of him and then beat the piss out of him.

He estimated he had been in over two hundred fights in his life, so he had experience that nobody else could compare to. That gave him huge confidence. He had fought every type of fighter and prevailed in most of them. He'd have to rely on being a savage brawler and attack this kid and end it quickly.

Assault and overwhelm. Valley Jail was his jungle and the lion in him wanted it to stay that way. This kid will never have a chance.

Bald Boy planned to keep his shank in his jumpsuit's hidden pocket just in case.

Chapter 60

Friday Night • The Fish Tank

The celebration after the game in the Bulldogs' locker room was quick and subdued. They all knew this win was nice but they had bigger goals than keeping St. Mary's out of the tournament. Goat gave a quick speech and acknowledged the record set by Marcus.

The players all busted his balls but they seemed to get the sentiment.

Goat told them to get their butts to Fish's house for "da big party" before the weather got really bad. Boots was already in his car. This was going to be a big night for him so he loaded his pockets with merchandise for the party.

Nicole took a ride to Fish's from some other gals on the squad. She did not want to go with Kaleigh. She was drinking beers and a shot with these gals on the way to the party and in the driveway. She was feeling good again.

She was going to go after Marcus tonight, screw it.

With each sip she took she got bolder. She was hot and she knew it, time to use it. She saw how he was looking at her today and he had never looked at her like that before. She had changed into tight jeans and boots and kept her Valley High cheerleader sweater on.

She knew how good she looked in it.

And out of it.

Chapter 61

Rat was saying, "Ya ya, get the fuck out before I lock you in!" jokingly to the guards who had already worked that previous shift and were leaving for the night. He assured them he'd be fine working the weekend with so few guards. Many of the departing guards half-heartedly offered to stick around for a while to make sure Rat and his mostly rookie staff could handle the jail. They had already reluctantly been persuaded by the Warden to stay until after dinner was served.

One of the guys who had stayed through dinner shift on Friday was Steve "Stinky" Deveau. Stinky earned his nickname the hard way. Twice, actually.

Valley Jail's cells did not have plumbing until ten years ago. Up until then each cell had a bucket with a lid into which they shat and pissed. At the end of each day they would bring the bucket to the sewer and dump it. However, on occasion the inmates would dump the contents of the bucket from their cell as a sign of protest over treatment or conditions. Stinky Deveau had the misfortune of being in the line of fire from those buckets on two separate occasions. Shit and piss hit him from one hundred feet above. Twice.

After the few who stayed from the day shift had gone there were now only five officers in total remaining at the jail for the weekend and there were four hundred sixty-seven inmates.

Rat was in charge for two full days. He was happy to see them all go but he still did not have Bald Boy's jailbait chosen.

Rat looked at his cell phone, two messages from "mamarat" were indicated.

He saw the two texts telling him Marcus and Joey were fighting and going to the hospital? What the fuck? The game had ended a while ago so he tried but he could not reach Mama or Joey. He kept trying. Nothing.

Marcus Kelly.

His forehead vein was throbbing again. He hated that guy. Someday I will get him and I will get him good. Rat prayed for the day he could get him in his domain – the jail. He dismissed that dream quickly. Marcus was too beloved to ever go to jail.

Rat was pissed and frustrated. He had to go supervise the inmate count with the other guys. He left his phone in the office and went to do the little work that was required of the guy in charge of the jail.

First it was Mr. Gordon, then Darlene and now this. This day sucked.

Chapter 62

Sally and Dottie finished clearing their tables and chairs from the rink and were counting the money. The bake sale had raised $532 and they had sold every single item they had. The raffle had raised $3,983. The winner of the raffle had only taken $500 and given the rest back to the school.

They agreed to meet at Fish's and hugged each other joyously, they were so happy with tonight's results. And Valley High won!

Sally opened the rink door and wished she had taken her jacket into the game. It was windy and chilly and raining harder now. She ran to the car and grabbed her coat and saw the plate of brownies. Oh, Sally! Dottie could have made even more money if she had not forgotten about these. She reminded herself to bring the brownies into the party. She did not need them at home. She was doing Jenny Craig and did not have the willpower to have Dottie's special brownies within her reach.

What made them so special?

Chapter 63

Fish and his wife had built their house for the purpose of throwing parties like the one they were throwing tonight. Their living space was separated from their entertaining space, attached by a long walkway through the pool area.

The entertainment area was perfectly designed. It felt like a nightclub with two separate floors of partying. The top floor was occupied by the adults along with the occasional students sent up to see if the food was out yet.

The adults' section was hopping. Eighties music filled the room and Journey was currently playing. The festive atmosphere from the game remained among the crowd and they were all re-living the game and talking anxiously about the tournament.

And drinking, of course. Hard. Celebratory shots!

The bars were all professionally tended and it was open bar all night. Valley High hockey supporters were, like usual, a thirsty lot. The caterer was putting the final touches on the many carving stations and food carts set up along the perimeter of the huge room. The dance floor was empty right now but soon would be full of drunks dancing badly but having the time of their lives.

Go Bulldogs!!

Down below the kids had taken over and Kaleigh had plugged in her iPod so that their music would drown out the oldies' music blaring from up above. The sound system was making the walls shake.

The kids were psyched that they had their own area to themselves. Because the food was upstairs the adults just waited up there to congratulate the team and the cheering squad. The kids slowly had the guts to bring their booze from their car trunks as they bravely ran through the downpour to retrieve it. The lower area also had a covered deck where the kids were smoking. Some were even smoking cigarettes.

Boots was the only adult in the lower kids' section at the moment. He was doing a lively business on both levels – the adults were not saints. It was his joint he and Kaleigh were smoking with a few other students. He wanted Kaleigh badly but she was looking for Marcus.

Boots could wait.

The hockey team had gotten used to being allowed to drink at these parties. Although Fish always hosted this huge party after the last game, there was usually a post-game gathering at a designated house after each weekend game all season, too. The hockey parents rotated being hosts and usually had beer, wine and pizza or take out from somewhere. After a win everybody went, so this year the parties were packed and the attendees all liquored up. The more the team won the less the parents seemed to care that the kids were drinking one floor beneath them. The kids usually ended up in the cellar, the backyard or in the driveway. They'd sneak beers out from the party and some guys would have their own so they usually had enough to catch a buzz. Boots often ran out for them and left his trunk open so they could get the booze he had bought for them, too.

The players were sure the parents knew they were drinking but the parents seemed to be OK with it, especially after a win. Just be careful, guys.

Don't get in the way of the machine. Winning let them overlook the law.

Fish was out on the deck above the kids' smoking area moving some chairs under the canopy and smelled

231

the familiar scent of marijuana. Fish had smoked pot in high school and college, too. It was harmless and they were celebrating tonight. He knew they were drinking, too.

It was a big win tonight; he was going to get hammered, too. Maybe he should go talk to Boots about something to keep his energy up?

The caterer indicated the food was ready and everybody grabbed a plate and headed for the wonderful feast Fish had paid over the top to provide.

Marcus had arrived with Taylor. Fowler had come over with Boots. Marcus had guzzled two beers on the way over. He left his car at the rink because his folks left the Lexus at the party and Fish's house was on the way to the airport. Marcus was going to drive that car home. He loved driving the Lexus and he was psyched to maybe drive Nicole in it. His folks had texted him that they were almost at Logan earlier. He was happy for them but he'd miss them.

Marcus went upstairs to eat and could not take one step without somebody shaking his hand to congratulate him and tell him how great it was that he scored his fiftieth goal – blah blah blah. He was impatient with the adulation tonight as he only wanted food and Nicole.

Thank you. Thank you so much. Oh, thank you. A picture? Sure. Sign your purse? Really?

After being in line for five minutes, Marcus was sick of being stopped every three seconds upstairs so he dropped his empty plate and ran back down the stairs to drink with the boys and find Nicole.

He saw Nicole when he came back down, she was soaking wet and looked so hot. Marcus made a beeline to her.

"Nice game, fella," said the dripping wet Nicole.

"Thanks, your cheering led the way, as usual."

"Ha ha. Seriously, that was a great game you had. And you crushed Joey at the end, wow. I hate that guy – he hits on me every time I see him anywhere. And his older brother is creepy."

Nicole saw Kaleigh looking at them so she hugged Marcus and held him tight against her chest. She stared right back at Kaleigh as she did so. Bring it on, sister! Marcus smiled and he was now even more pumped that he had walloped Joey and stood up for Nicole.

And her tits felt great pressed against him.

She had a beer in her hand. He needed one. Fowler read his mind and put one in his hand as he walked by, smiling and nodding at Nicole knowingly.

Busch can.

It was obvious to anybody watching these two – Marcus was smitten and so was she.

Kaleigh was painfully aware of this and went out on the patio to get high with Boots again. She was pissed at Marcus and Nicole but also very stoned so she had forgotten all about them after Boots passed her the joint a few more times. She'd just find somebody else to be with tonight. She was hot, drunk and easy and she and Boots had hooked up once before, maybe they would again tonight. Kaleigh's parents were on a weekend trip to Foxwoods and not home until Sunday night – per usual. They could go back to her parents' house. Let that little slut Nicole have her fun with Marcus. Hiccup. Fuck them. I am hungry.

Marcus and Nicole found a corner that nobody was walking near and stood and talked for an hour – two beers each. Marcus found this girl fascinating. She was smart, funny and so pretty. Seriously, how did he miss this all year?

She was asking him questions and not just talking about herself. Kaleigh never asked Marcus about hockey, she just talked about herself before she took her shirt off to indicate to him that time for talk was over. She always made the first move with Marcus.

Nicole knew her hockey, too. She was telling Marcus the list of teams she hoped would draft him – basically she wanted the Bruins to pick him but after that any team but Montreal. It was the typical Boston reply Marcus heard when the draft was brought up to him. They laughed and they touched each other's arms when making a point. The party raged around them while they chatted the night away, oblivious to the world and nobody but Kaleigh really paid them any attention. There were so many very buzzed students that the party downstairs seemed to be rocking much earlier than the geezers' bash upstairs. They were dancing, screaming and Santorelli was shirtless as he was sandwiched between two cheerleaders grinding away on the dance floor.

Outside, the rain began to pelt the Valley mercilessly. It was a few degrees over freezing but the wind was whipping. It was getting just a bit colder as the night progressed.

Chapter 64

Dottie was upstairs on the covered deck still talking with Mr. Gordon from the convenience store. The music was loud inside and Fish had propane heaters on the deck making it pleasantly warm while listening to the rainfall nearby. There were a few other couples on the deck enjoying the more quiet setting. Dottie had always liked Mr. Gordon but hated his wife, she was happy for him when they divorced a few years ago. He and Harry had been acquaintances. They had always been friendly to each other, but tonight felt different. He had touched her shoulder a few times. She did not move away.

Sally came by as they were talking and winked at Dottie. Sally had left the brownies and plate by the stairs on a small table when she came in. She figured they'd go unnoticed because the caterer had brought so many amazing desserts. She was going to tell Dottie where her plate was but Dottie was flirting with Mr. Gordon so she figured she'd tell her later. Good for you, Dottie! It's about time, girl!

Sally realized she had given Harry and Dottie that plate as an anniversary gift so she was sure Dottie would really want it back because it was so nice. Sally thought of herself as a Martha Stewart of the Valley. It bugged Dottie.

Dottie was on her third glass of champagne and enjoying the interest she was getting from Mr. Gordon. Doug, call me Doug, Dottie. They were looking across the valley and Doug told Dottie that if the night had been clearer they would have been able to see the jail's lights in the distance.

"That horrible place? I'd never last a day in a place like that," said Dottie as she shuddered.

Doug put his arm around Dottie. Dottie leaned on his shoulder, lost in the moment.

Downstairs, Marcus wanted to get Nicole alone. He was ready to leave. Kaleigh was acting weird and staring at them and she was really fucked up. Boots was helping them a bit by hitting on her and taking her outside to get high, thankfully.

Marcus asked Nicole if she wanted a ride home and she eagerly accepted. Marcus ran upstairs to retrieve the Lexus keys from Fish. His parents had left them with Mrs. Fisher after parking there to meet their friends.

He wanted to remain low profile so he could exit quickly, but when he walked upstairs the whole room hushed and suddenly his many adult fans all at once rushed to him to shake his hand and wish him well. Many were now really drunk and slurring and spraying spittle at Marcus as they groveled and flattered him. Marcus was not in the mood for the well wishes. He had an agenda. After posing for a few group photos, he abruptly thanked everybody and pointed to Fish as he hastily walked to him.

He shook hands with Fish, thanked him for a great party and then found himself in a huge bear hug as Fish was drunkenly telling him how special Marcus was and how privileged Fish felt to have Marcus skate at his rink – more blah blah blah.

OK, Fish, I get it. Can I go now? Marcus reached for the keys in Fish's hand once he got out of the uncomfortable, drunken hug. This was the bad part about being a superstar.

He assured Fish he was fine to drive and put his head down and walked out.

Geez.

He had the keys but he was famished. He did not want to get in line for food and risk getting into another drunken hug from one of his adult fans. Marcus bolted for the stairs and miraculously saw a wrapped plate of brownies on a ceramic plate on a table. Untouched. His empty stomach grumbled.

Special brownies?

He grabbed them and put his coat over them as he ran down the stairs – he did not want to share them. The sticky note said they were special.

He grabbed a few beers and found Nicole. They playfully ran through the rain laughing as they got in the Lexus and caught their breath. It was colder than when they first got to Fish's. The car was parked away from the house so it would not be blocked in. There was nobody around.

Marcus turned the key to warm it up and then Nicole was sitting on his lap. They kissed in the Lexus for the first time and for a long time.

Chapter 65

Jamie was playing a video game on his phone when Russell's voice snapped him out of it. Despite the storm it had been a boring night so far.

"Jamie, any issues?"

"Negative, Captain. Or is it Chief now?" Jamie could sense Russell turning beet red. Jamie was mimicking a laugh as he mocked his superior. Jamie was coming down a bit from earlier but still very much stoned as he manned the dispatch and 911 lines alone.

"Jamie, I am driving near the school, it's deserted mostly now. But it is getting icy around here, do you know if the sand trucks are out yet?"

"Yes sir, about an hour ago." Jamie looked at his window and it was icing over.

Russell was thankful that most of the fans went from The Tank to Fish's house before the roads began to freeze. And most of the local roads were deserted. Russell was nervously grateful for a quiet night, but something told him that would not last.

"All quiet otherwise?"

"Yes Chief Russell." Hee hee.

Russell shook his head in disgust as he signed off and Jamie went back to his video game.

Chapter 66

After they fooled around for a while, Marcus opened one of the beers he had smuggled out of the party. They shared that as he ate four big brownies very quickly. "I am fucking stah-vin," he said as he sprayed brownie crumbs and snickered. They were not as good as his Mom's and left his mouth really dry, but at this point he would have eaten anything. Nicole was playfully taking bites of a big corner brownie, her favorite part. She was pretty drunk already.

He had been careful to limit his drinking tonight to buzz level knowing he had to drive the Lexus home. He knew where to draw the line. He hoped the brownies would absorb some of the alcohol but they were hard to eat quickly, they were dry and not that special tasting at all, but he was stah-vin'.

He ate four more brownies and guzzled another beer to quench his mounting thirst. That was eight brownies in total, the health nut in him justified it by saying it was his dinner and post-game meal all in one.

He smacked his lips a few times. He wished he had Santorelli's gallon of milk right now. He drank the beers as a thirst quencher, but they were not really sating his rapidly growing thirst.

God, his mouth was dry. He smacked his lips and giggled as he did so. At what he was giggling he did not know. Nicole picked up on it and soon they were both giggling and then just all-out laughing at nothing in particular. He noticed Nicole was smacking and licking her lips like he was but she looked so hot doing it.

Dottie would eat a half of one brownie and feel wildly buzzed. Marcus had eaten eight brownies and

239

Nicole had eaten two and they each had been drinking. With little other food in their stomachs, and their lustful hearts pounding, the marijuana was being quickly distributed through their bodies.

As they were about to find out, marijuana consumed as food had a much more potent effect than if smoked, especially with Dottie tripling the amount of really good Green Mountain Special marijuana in her brownie recipe. That name was written in black magic marker on the large freezer bag in which it was delivered. That is why she called them "special brownies."

These two unsuspecting kids were about to find out just how special they were.

Nicole had smoked pot occasionally so her system knew what was entering. Marcus had never smoked pot so he was in for a treat.

The car had been running the whole time they were fooling around to defrost and warm up but Marcus noticed ice forming on the cars next to them so he told Nicole to put on her seat belt so they could get going. He wanted to beat the storm. He felt so fucking good right now.

I am driving a fucking Lexus! How you doing?

His heart was racing and Nicole was a great kisser. She had the same first move of taking her shirt off as Kaleigh but she did it in a much more seductive way. Kaleigh was more saying, "Shut up and take off my bra, we got work to do."

Nicole had an amazing body. Marcus wanted more. She was eating her brownies topless in the car. She had a great rack and Marcus was staring at them and motorboating with his lips as he giggled and drank more beer. She was rubbing his extremely erect penis through his jeans.

He could take Nicole back to his house. Nobody was home and she lived nearby to his house ... Whoa.

He felt like he got punched in the jaw and had his eggs scrambled like in a boxing session. This was no beer buzz. He shook his head vigorously and it did nothing to help. The rain hitting the windshield was mesmerizing him.

He was hoping she'd leave her cheering sweater where it was – in a ball in the backseat. But she grabbed it and put it on very slowly as Marcus got one last good look at the goods.

He shook his head vigorously and put the car in drive. As he drove he was forced to constantly straighten the car as he veered a bit off to the right and hit one of the many puddles on Rink Road.

What the fuck? He slowed down but this road was curvy and had a lot of hills. He really wanted to get home and explore that body next to him some more.

Focus.

He was trying to act cool but his mind was racing and he was trying to sneak looks at Nicole – she was so hot! She was stuffing her bra into her bag.

He neared the corner that led to the incline that took them over Turner Hill where the road was unlit and tricky. He somehow got through that part of the ride – the Lexus was a dream to drive. Marcus began to foolishly feel cool and confident and chanced a look over at Nicole who was smiling at him and eating another brownie. She took that as a sign to do something crazy.

She was out of her fucking mind right now.

That they did not know what they had eaten was a big part of the buzz. They did not expect it and it was kicking their ass.

His head swam again. He shook out the cobwebs and focused. The car's wipers were on high and struggling to keep up with the rain. If he had been straight it would have been a hellish ride. In his present condition he was tempting fate. He drove on.

Relax, Marcus, you are just buzzed. You got this.

All of a sudden Nicole reached over to his side of the car and put her hand on his leg. He smiled. She was working on undoing his belt. He did not stop her.

By now the waves of a serious buzz were too much to dismiss. Dottie's special brownies were having their way with Marcus. Full on. The THC from the ganja was being rushed around his body as his heart hammered in his chest – from both fear and the hot chick next to him. He had never experienced anything close to this mystery buzz he was now on. What else could he do but drive on and hope he got home?

Nicole was feeling really good herself. The THC was having the same effect on her, so she undid her seat belt and knelt on the middle armrest. She stuck her tongue in Marcus's ear, nibbling his ear lobe and talking a bit dirty. It was exactly what Marcus did not need at that point, but he was so turned on by Nicole that he could not say no to her. He adjusted in his seat and smiled.

She unzipped his pants.

As she did this to him Marcus hit the gas slowly but steadily and repeatedly shifted in his seat. His heart rate was insanely high thus helping the marijuana to continue to flood his system.

He wanted to tell her to wait but then again – he was a nineteen year old boy about to get a blowjob from a hot chick. Hello?

Captain Russell was at the rink now making sure no students had hung around after the game. He was relieved that it had been a quiet night despite the weather. He changed the station on the car radio and began to pull out from the school's parking lot. His attention was on the radio dial.

Marcus was really fucked up and the lower part of his body, his penis, was in total control now. She had his shaft in her hand as she continued to clean his ear. He was oblivious to the police car about to pull into his lane.

They passed the rink going seventy-two in a thirty-five mph zone. Captain Russell was just pulling out and had to jam on his brakes to avoid being sideswiped by Marcus. Marcus never saw him.

Russell flipped on his lights and siren and pursued.

He was fucking pissed.

Chapter 67

Friday Night • Fish's House

Dottie had drunk way more than she should have and she was getting too comfortable with Doug. He had just kissed her.

With tongue!

She had a sudden flash of guilt and felt ashamed. Her Dear Harry had only been dead for fifteen months and here she was acting like a common whore. She had to leave right this instant. She pulled away from his hug.

She lied about having to go to the bathroom to Doug, umm Mr. Gordon again, and grabbed her keys and coat and ran to Harry's car. She slipped a few times on the now icy driveway. She just wanted to get home to DH and maybe have a special brownie while she watched Leno.

She would be driving the same roads Marcus had a few minutes before her.

Just a little faster.

Chapter 68

Friday Night • The Lexus

Marcus was enjoying having his ear cleaned by Nicole's tongue, but he was swerving a bit and sliding on the somewhat icy surface. The few cars that were coming the other way were beeping and narrowly missing the Lexus when it swerved left. The massive puddles were not helping him keep it straight, but the hot girl was the far bigger distraction. He could smell the brownie on her hot breath. He could not bring himself to ask her to stop giving him a hand job as he drove. His heart was pounding in his chest, he felt like he was driving in a video game. The Lexus had an awesome stereo and the music playing loudly added to his bewilderment.

Ludacris.

Russell was in hot pursuit but he had to go slowly because there were huge puddles near every storm drain. He could see the dark sedan ahead of him swerving through the rain, but he could not catch them.

As Nicole dipped her head to begin to blow him, Marcus looked in the rearview mirror and finally saw the blue lights.

Uh oh.

He pulled over immediately on pure instinct and Nicole sat back down quickly and struggled to put on her seat belt as he tried in vain to help her find the buckle. He was zipping up his pants and almost caught his dick in his zipper.

She was singing while they waited for the cop to come to their car. Marcus pulled his shirt over his unzipped pants. He began to search for his license but forgot why he had grabbed his wallet and instead of his license he pulled out the small wad of bills in his billfold. He held a small wad of cash up as he lowered his window. His head was bobbing and he was mumbling.

Russell got out of his car and was careful not to slip. As he was pursuing Marcus he heard over the radio that there had just been a major pileup on the state highway that cut through the Valley. He had the guys who had been working the hockey game already out that way so there was enough manpower for now. He heard them call for the ambulance and fire department.

And so it begins, he thought. This asshole is going to pay for almost hitting me. They had better pray they are not drunk.

He approached the Lexus. The driver had lowered the window and was holding money up as if to say, "Let's make this go away."

Russell could not believe his eyes. It was Marcus Kelly and he was really out of it. His head was bobbing and he was incoherent. He had a cheerleader in the passenger seat. Wonderful.

Mr. Superstar.

Russell looked in the back seat and saw a tipped plate with a bunch of brownies scattered around it. He told Marcus to sit tight, to which Marcus had said "Okee dokee artichokee," and Russell went back to his car.

Think like a Chief.

He had just met with Goat and Principal Thompson and talked this big game about how seriously DUIs were going to be handled going forward. Today. Tonight. He had said that just hours ago.

Hypocrite?

Now he had the dilemma of arresting the superstar and risk ruining his career or letting him go and being the soft cop that he abhorred.

Fuck this. I am arresting him for DUI. He could have killed somebody. I am a good cop. This is the right thing. Change starts with me.

The officers out at the highway were calling desperately for help and they wanted Russell to get out there. There was a fatality and the Chief was needed. Jamie was calling over the radio for help from other towns to get out to the highway. The Chief was needed at the crash site to coordinate.

Pressure.

Russell acted quickly. They were somewhat near the PD building right now and Jamie had the SUV. He called Jamie on the radio and told him where he was and who he had in custody and to get out there as soon as possible. He reminded Jamie to switch the 911 calls out of town for the short time he was off the desk. He'd be there and back in half an hour if Jamie hurried.

Russell would use this time to write this incident up and stay on the radio with the guys at the crash as he waited for Jamie to arrive. He called the EMT, tow truck and Fire Department to make sure they were on their way to the highway. He radioed the guys out at the highway and got updated on the situation there. He formulated his plan quickly. He would have Jamie drive Marcus and Nicole back to the PD in the SUV as he sped off for the highway crash. Jamie would lock Marcus and Nicole in the holding cell for the night – she was as drunk as Marcus was. She was singing when Russell walked away from their car a moment ago. He would have the Lexus towed to the Police Lot.

As he thought this through Russell began to have regrets about not just giving Marcus a ride home. It would have been easy. Too late now, he had gone over the radio and run his name over the system to check for warrants.

The shit was going to hit the fan tomorrow for sure. Goat might have a heart attack. Marcus might be lost for the tournament now and Valley really could not win without him.

Russell now felt bad but at the same time this could be a teaching moment for the whole city. This was done for the greater good and maybe Marcus will be the incident that smartens this town up. They all look the other way and enable these kids. They are going to kill somebody soon enough. As he was thinking this through Jamie pulled up in the SUV. The idiot was on time. Jamie opened the door and adjusted his pen camera, soaking Russell.

Thankfully the road was mostly deserted as the storm was keeping people inside. These kids had pulled over in a tough section of road and the traffic coming in their direction had little time to react as they came over the rise. There was a huge puddle to avoid near the cruiser. He could not risk asking Marcus to move his car given his condition.

Make this quick. Russell kept his blues on.

Jamie remembered his camera and said, "Marcus Kelly, huh? Wow." Russell said nothing, nodded and opened his door and walked to Marcus's car and cuffed him before leading Marcus back to the SUV. Marcus was swaying as he was dumped into the back seat. Jamie hopped back into the SUV and put his blues on, too. That felt good, he had never gotten to do that until tonight. Russell slammed the door shut and turned to go back to the Lexus to get Nicole and bring her to the SUV.

He opened the passenger door of the Lexus and led her through the freezing rain past his squad car to the SUV behind it. His own squad car was close to the guardrail and in between the Lexus and SUV so they

248

had to walk around the car and slightly into the street to reach the SUV.

Russell chivalrously kept Nicole behind him and close to the squad car as they hurried past his car.

Suddenly over the hill there was a car flying at them. Russell guided Nicole behind him and more to the outside now, but as he did so he slipped and had to stick his butt out a bit to catch his balance. He held her hand so they could walk single file back to the SUV. She was still singing.

Fucking drunks.

As he was thinking this, Dottie was coming toward them like a drunken bat out of hell in Dear Harry's old car. She had driven this instead of her smaller car because it was heavy and better in the bad weather.

They had used this car to pull a small RV around on vacations. Harry had put really big rearview mirrors on each side of the car so that he would be able to see behind the RV when he was driving. They stuck out about fifteen inches from each side. Dottie rarely drove this car but did not dare sell it. It would be like selling a part of Harry. He had loved this car.

Dottie was ashamed she had let herself drink way too much and for getting caught up in the moment. I let that man kiss me! She felt like a cheap slut. She just wanted to eat a brownie and cuddle with DH.

She was speeding and never slowed down as she neared the suddenly bright blue lights that appeared quickly on the right. As she gunned it through the puddle her passenger-side oversized mirror clipped Russell's right hip hard as he slipped while protecting Nicole.

Russell never saw her coming as his head was lowered to keep the rain out of his eyes. Dottie hit him going fifty-five mph. Her mirror caught him square on the hip and he went flying. As he flew by Nicole his arm swung around and broke her nose. Nothing serious, but it was bleeding badly, making it look worse than it really was. She went down like she had been shot.

Dottie never stopped and never felt the heavy car hit Russell. The champagne, rain and her tears had been sufficient to blur her vision and she could see very little. The oversized mirror was ripped off on contact and flew over the guardrail and down an embankment. She wouldn't have to worry about hitting the garage with it in the future.

Jamie had been in the SUV with an incoherent Marcus in the back and had seen the whole thing right in front of him. So had his camera.

Oh my fucking head! Video gold! He tapped his pocket and felt the pen. Yes.

What do I do now? Uncharacteristically he jumped quickly from the SUV without thought. He was about to come through in a tough spot. He went for Nicole and got her into the SUV. She was bleeding badly from her nose so he gave her some gauze from the medical kit to hold to her nose. He had the feeling she did not feel a thing since she was still singing.

Journey?

He found Russell in the breakdown lane. He was alive but twisted up grotesquely. He picked him up by the shoulders and dragged him to the SUV. He dumped him in the passenger seat and struggled to get his lower half inside so he could shut the door.

He got in the driver's side and was suddenly in the state of paralysis by analysis. The gravity of the situation had hit him hard. He had used up his ability to think clearly. He sat there in semi-shock. The panic had set in and he was now freaked out. The multiple bong hits from earlier today were not helping. He was in over his head.

Think!

Just as he was about to call for help on the radio he remembered he had no radio in the SUV to call out what had happened. He eyed Russell's squad car and hoped that radio worked.

At that precise moment Rat called Jamie on his cell. The ring startled him back to reality.

"I heard you got a DUI over the radio." Rat had been in the office when he heard Russell radio to Jamie about Marcus. He called Jamie as soon as he could. He was going to ask Jamie to fuck with Marcus while he had him in their holding cell at Valley PD.

Then Jamie told him what had just happened.

Jamie explained the whole thing about Russell getting hit and Marcus and a hot cheerleader passed out in the back of his car. The tone Rat heard was that Jamie was obviously panicked and not thinking straight. Jamie was in way over his head now. Rat perked up again when he realized the obvious opportunity he might be able to take advantage of here. He just had to get Jamie to go along.

He had an epiphany. He had his jailbait! The Lord did work in mysterious ways.

"Jamie, here's what you do. The jail is on the way to the hospital. I already called for an ambulance (he had not) and they are not available – they are all out at the highway. So here is the plan – drop Kelly off here and then take the chick and the dickhead Captain to the hospital. I can keep Kelly here in a holding cell away from general population until you come back for him. He'll be fine here and we have a cell. If Marcus wakes up in that car he might get physical with you." Jamie looked at Marcus in the rearview mirror and knew he did not want that to happen. Marcus was huge and the SUV did not have the bars separating the back from the front like the sedans had.

251

Rat was playing his hand perfectly. He could picture Jamie looking at Marcus, scared shitless.

Marcus was coming around a bit in the back seat, making funny noises but also saying Nicole's name. He was belching something fierce. Nicole was holding gauze to her nose and appeared to be singing but asleep. Captain Russell looked dead.

Jamie had to move quickly now. He was thankful Rat had such a clear head. He agreed to do what Rat had suggested and told Rat he'd be there soon.

This was a good plan.

Jamie put the SUV in drive and adjusted his pen camera forward, making sure to not have anything block the view. He said "Action" and put on his blinker.

At that precise moment Marcus's stomach said enough is enough, we need to get this foreign matter out. Marcus then projectile vomited all over Jamie from the seat behind him. Eight pot brownies streaming out in liquid form.

Because there was no divider in the SUV the puke was all over Jamie. It smelled like beer, brownies and pot. It was dark and syrupy and had hit the windshield, dashboard and steering wheel. Some dripped from Jamie's right ear, too. He was covered in brown puke. He shook a walnut off his video pen.

So much for Marcus's streak of not puking.

Chapter 69

Marcus climbed up to the top bunk of his new cell, careful to not let the shank in his waistband slide out or cut him. This mattress smelled like garlic cigarettes, a huge improvement from the one he had carried down here.

He knew he was going to have the first real fight of his life coming up soon so he was trying to remember some of the techniques that Baker had taught him to get ready. The problem was they had always trained for a spontaneous fight, one that would erupt during a hockey game in a moment of violence. This was like a fight in the Coliseum and Emperor Rat was bringing Marcus into his den of death. He was exhausted but his brain was going a mile a minute as he lay there with his eyes closed. He was running on fumes.

In a weird way Marcus was relieved he would finally put his training to the test. It was not ideal but there would be no ramifications to his career or future if he beat the piss out of this tattooed motherfucker. He had years of pent-up venom to release.

He was getting cocky and feeling like this fucking guy had no idea what he was up against. But as soon as he had these thoughts there would be flashes of panic and emptiness. He thought of his parents again.

He was calling himself kiddo more and more, too.

Marcus had put two and two together on the Rat angle. He remembered the coach for St. Mary's yelling the name Rat to the kid Joey talking about Nicole. But Marcus had no idea how much Rat hated him, resented his talent and success and believed Marcus had put Joey in the hospital.

OK, he had done that to Joey. No argument there.

He was hoping Nicole was fine, too, but there would be time for that. He could do nothing for her while behind these bars. He did remember her being in the car with the cop he puked on. Jamie something.

Whoops.

He also remembered he was getting jacked off by Nicole as he drove. That made his balls throb and he now had a case of blue balls inside a jail.

The previous evening's events were slowly coming back to him now. He was convinced something was in those brownies that he had eaten and then puked up. What else could it have been? Nicole was wasted too, he remembered them giggling in the car. The sound of his cellmates got his attention back to the fight upcoming.

Marcus opened his eyes and observed his two new cellmates. They were in their sixties and quietly talking in the corner and gesturing to yesterday's Herald on the stool in front of them. Marcus saw his picture in the upper corner of the back page. He had never felt less like a Mr. Superstar than he did lying there in jail. He still worried he had hurt somebody with the car. Why else would he be here?

Did somebody have a paper route in here?

As usual with sanctioned fights, there were bets being placed within the jail and the two older Italian guys that Marcus was bunked with were the ones setting the odds and taking the action. They were talking about Marcus in Italian.

Wilson had done Marcus a favor by putting him in here. Rat had been distracted so Wilson took the initiative and moved Marcus in with the Mob guys before Rat could move him himself, probably to the soaking wet Block 4. Wilson would just lie as to where Marcus was if asked by Rat.

When he first arrived at his new cell with Wilson, Marcus had waited for the door to open and shuffled in with his new mattress. The old guys told him to keep that fucking dirty thing out of their cell, they had a mattress already on the top bunk.

This cell was three times bigger than any other cell in this block. There was a "jail kitchen" set up near the sink – a few hot plates smartly hooked up to batteries and working despite the power outage. Ingenious idea. They had used this set up before, but that time the battery was hooked up to a deadbeat's testicles.

There were milk crates full of food and bowls, dishes and a bunch of plastic sporks from the cafeteria. There was a TV, radio and small bookshelves on the near wall to the left. Tony Bennett quietly played on the battery-powered radio. This was the Hilton compared with Jake's cell.

These two guys had been in Valley Jail for over twenty years, they were fixtures there. They were ex-Mob guys who got blindsided when their fingerprints were found on duct tape around the ankles of a body found at the bottom of a quarry.

How did that get there?

At the time it was a new technique to get prints from bodies long buried or underwater. These two guys were the first ones to be convicted with it. They were part of the Boston Mob but they were also on their way out as their younger peers saw them as unnecessary. They often wondered if maybe they had been ratted out. They were quickly found guilty and the state was thrilled with their newest technique.

Once they got sentenced they used their dwindling Mob influence and had gotten the state to allow them to remain housed at Valley Jail for their life sentences to be near family. They knew the risks of being at Valley Jail but they also knew they would be respected and their stays at the jail were far different than the average convict. They were two of the very few inmates to have a parade of visitors almost daily – it was a tight-knit familia.

They were known in the jail as the Mob guys. They were older but far from harmless. Luc and Dom were their names and the two old-time made men were the bookies at the jail for all sorts of bets. Sports on TV, dominos tournaments and basketball games in the gym were popular things to bet on. The action kept the Mob guys alive, thinking.

But a sanctioned fight in the gym was the event that just about everybody bet on. There was usually one a month now that Rat was using Bald Boy as his thug. The currency, per usual, was money, drugs or cigarettes. No sex bets for these guys.

Most of the inmates paid up on time, but when needed Luc and Dom would rely on their good relationships with Conti and Bald Boy if they needed help with collecting. They shared a portion of their take with them as a sort of pre-payment for future need.

The Italians had a long history of being the bookies in Valley Jail. They had started taking bets when they first got sentenced. But there had been a Dominican guy already taking the Hispanics' action. He was politely asked to step aside and allow Luc and Dom to take over – for a price, of course. He said no defiantly and disrespectfully. The Italians nodded and shuffled away. They were not physically imposing at all.

A few days passed and one day while the Hispanic bookie was napping Dom put a sharp shank through his right hand as he held another one a centimeter above his eye, ready to plunge it in if they could not come to an agreement.

The Italians had been the sole bookies in Valley Jail ever since.

These two mobsters were like the Vatican inside the walls because unlike the other inmates, they did not really have to "belong" to The Gringos or anybody else. They stood together but apart from all others. They operated on their own, required little protection and had Bald Boy and Conti on their payrolls. Nobody bugged them but they were always careful to have at least one guy guarding their cell. Their whole lives in the jail were in that cell. Like all other long-time convicts, they did not have much in jail so what they did have was important and fiercely protected.

They indirectly relied on the lugging guards to bring in ingredients for their meals that they could not buy from the inmate trustees working in the kitchen. They always went through Conti or Bald Boy to get their contraband because they knew how the machine worked.

Luc was stirring a wonderfully smelling tomato sauce while skillfully probing Marcus with questions about his fighting ability and history. Marcus was amused slightly by the questions and the situation in which he now found himself.

Although he was still on edge, this was the first time he could somewhat relax since he had gotten there. Wilson assured him nobody knew where he was and the Italians would be fine with his being there.

Wilson was actually paying the Italians back a favor by bringing Marcus to them. He knew these guys were setting the betting lines on the fight and would probably like to know who Bald Boy's next victim was so they could set a line.

As usual, word of the fight had spread fast. Rat had been the source, he wanted it spread through the jail so the other fucking convicts would know that Bald Boy did Rat's bidding. Power may corrupt but getting it was such a rush to Rat. He had a cocky strut to his stride, he was feeling good.

What could go wrong?

This was the first time a guy was going to be in this type of fight on his first day in jail. Usually they would have been in for a while and the Mob guys could make a betting line based on having seen them and heard about them. So they were grateful to Wilson for having the forethought to bring Marcus to them so they could avoid a mistake. These guys took this very seriously and did whatever homework they could. It was all they had in jail to keep them from going insane.

They peppered Marcus with questions about his fighting ability, background, and experience.

He answered honestly. These guys seemed OK and he wanted to help them out. He was going to fight, that was happening. To not confront that would be foolish. It also helped time go by. They knew what to ask, too. Marcus guessed they had trained boxers in the past.

Luc had opened with, "OK, kid. Don't want to scare ya but if you can help me out then maybe I can help you out. You ever fight before? You look plenty big, tough." Then he and Dom sat and soaked up the stories that Marcus told them.

They both were won over by Marcus and his stories. They were each hoping this kid would survive what he was about to do. What a waste of a good kid if not.

Marcus told them about Baker's gym and his training. He held nothing back. It was basically a chronology of his athletic life with the three major components all talked about – hockey, lifting, fight training. The Italians liked what they were hearing.

"Since you were ten years old?" asked Luc about his fight training. They knew Dan Baker, too. Boxing was a small world around Boston. He was impressed and nodding at Dom who was scribbling notes as they spoke. Dom was reading parts of the Herald articles aloud to confirm some of what Marcus was telling them.

Dom asked Marcus to hop down and throw a few punches into a pillow propped up on the bookcase. Marcus did as asked and fell into the familiar routine of shadow boxing quickly. He shredded the pillow with a vicious left hook that had power on it that even surprised Marcus. Evil unleashed, kiddo?

For most of Bald Boy's fights the odds were around twenty-to-one or greater. The Mob guys would have gotten some action on that line today. But after what they had just seen and heard they wanted the jail to bet heavy on the Cuban. They had seen Marcus rip into that pillow and they knew this kid was powerful and trained well. He was no sure bet, but the guys adjusted the line to get more wagers.

They put Marcus as a ten-to-one shot and had their runners spread the word. As the hours passed they took a lot of action on Bald Boy from the blocks. They had devised simple systems to spread the odds and attract attention and bets. They had runners in each block to relay the odds and they would run back with the lists of who was betting what on whom. Marcus was amazed at how efficiently this machine operated. He dozed off here and there but for the most part he was attentive and fascinated by the proceedings.

Luc stirred the sauce and said, "If you can't make a sauce or make book then what good are you as an Italian?"

Dom laughed at his cellmate, they loved that line and used it often.

Because the jail was so shorthanded the inmates were brought boxed meals in their cells for lunch and then dinner later that afternoon. The guards could not risk letting the inmates into the kitchen in that big of a group again, especially ahead of the fight with so few guards working. The kitchen trustees were passing out the boxes and also were able to distribute stolen food items to their buddies for cigarettes. Sandwich? Five cigarettes. Half-a-loaf of bread? Pack of butts. There was a guard standing not ten feet away, oblivious to the black market action occurring right under his nose.

Because they had a sauce going, Luc and Dom let Marcus eat their hot dogs and chips and a thankful Marcus ate everything in sight, he was starving and needed the energy. He was back to feeling close to a hundred percent when he finished eating.

Luc and Dom were having a sauce with smuggled pepperoni later on and they had a small bottle of fermented sugar vino to wash it down. The sugar wine was delivered by the trustees with lunch – it had cost them two packs of butts.

Jake Pinkham had been the only one who had bet on Marcus so far. Then Conti put up a big number on Marcus. He had also sent one of his own guys and not a runner to relay the bet.

Keep that one low, fellas. Dom and Luc understood discretion better than most.

They were up to their eyeballs in bets on Bald Boy. They had trouble on their hands now if Marcus did not win. They had reserves but this would cut into them deeply. Marijuana, money, cigarettes, food and drugs were waged and the Mob guys had all that and more hidden throughout their cell. It was an unwritten agreement, with payment to Rat, to not have their cell shaken down. The Italians could cover just about any type of bet. It was almost like a currency exchange being operated.

Marcus began pacing the cell as the bookies counted and re-counted the wagers. He had to admit that if it were not the fight for his life this would have been pretty exciting to watch it and see how this betting machine worked so well.

He lay down and told the guys to wake him up when it was time.

Luc and Dom nodded and then went back to their sauce and their betting sheet. Dom had remembered reading about Tom Brady having a nap before the first Super Bowl he had ever played in. That went pretty well for the Patriots.

Chapter 70

Jamie was still soaked with puke when they got to the covered bridge that would take them to the jail. The river beneath it was almost touching the bridge, ten feet higher than normal. The rain was slower now but there was ice everywhere. The trees were swaying from the increasing burden of the weight of the ice and many were going down. Jamie raced across the bridge. Since the SUV had no radio he was using his cell phone to tell Rat where he was.

Rat was waiting for them at the back gate and saw the headlights approaching. He was anxious to process this all-star as he playfully mimicked a fishing reel in his hands, reeling in his bait.

Right about this time Joey was finding out from the doctors that he was going to be OK, no concussion. The only reason he was being held overnight was because nobody had come to pick him up.

He was fine from the hit. Not knowing that, Rat only had revenge on his mind as he pictured his brother hooked up to tubes and machines. It had blinded him to the possible trouble he was getting himself into by bringing Marcus into the jail in this manner. Rat only cared about the fight that had fallen into his lap. He'd deal with the other stuff later.

He was in charge, no worries.

Jamie opened the back door of the SUV because he wanted Marcus out of his car quickly. He was coming around a bit and he was way too big for Jamie to control. Rat snuck a peek at Nicole, he could immediately tell she had no bra on. He was just about to lift up her sweater to have a look at her perfect tits when Jamie told him they had no time for that and told him to come look at Russell.

Rat cursed the half-a-cop, laughed at the story about his getting puked on and slammed the back door shut. He opened the passenger door and saw Russell and noticed his lower half was weirdly contorted.

Yuck.

Jamie reminded Rat to keep Marcus in the holding cell, away from the other prisoners, like they had agreed upon. Rat told Jamie not to worry about it. He knew exactly where he was bringing Marcus. Go the fuck away now!

Did Jamie really think he could tell Rat what to do in his own jail?

Jamie was so happy Rat was his buddy because he would have been lost without him tonight. He got back in the SUV and sped off. The wind was whipping the trees and he saw the covered bridge in the distance. He could see the swollen river hitting it with force. He closed his eyes and floored it and got across. He took the right to the hospital and heard a big crack but never looked back. The crack was a huge tree being blown over and hitting the bridge and slicing through it, washing it away down the river and breaking the old bridge into hundreds of pieces.

The jail was now officially cut off from the world.

So was Marcus.

Chapter 71

Rat was again trying in vain to text either his Mom or his brother but cell service was still iffy from the downed trees and Mama was not the most reliable cell phone user. Joey was napping and his phone was turned off.

Suddenly the jail's radio blared to life and Rat cursed as he heard the Warden's voice crackling over the air. The Warden informed Rat that the bridge had washed away last night and there was no way they could get out to the jail until Sunday. They had the National Guard coming up to set up one of their temporary bridges.

Rat stifled a guffaw and he was smiling ear to ear. He had forgotten all about Darlene and Mr. Gordon from yesterday. This was too good.

Rat had not minded being cut off from communicating with the outside world. He was happy to hear about not having to worry about any outside interference in the fight he had planned. The Warden had no idea these fights occurred and Rat did not want him here poking around.

Rat assured him there was no need to rush, he had everything in control and he foresaw no reason that would change.

The Warden was relieved and stopped just short of calling Rat a hero. Then the radio went dead again.

Rat resisted the urge to hit it with a club to complete the isolation.

Chapter 72

Jamie pulled into the hospital parking lot and let out a huge breath. The ride from the jail was one of the worst experiences of his life. He was still semi-stoned and the smell of puke had him on the verge of puking the whole way to the hospital. He was dry heaving and trying to pay attention to the worst road conditions he had ever driven in. There were trees down everywhere and no streetlights to help him see the debris in the roads.

It did not help that he could not stop staring at Russell's grotesquely twisted lower half and at Nicole's cheering sweater in the rearview mirror. It had blood all over it, but Jamie was not looking at the blood.

He pulled up to the emergency room doors and the attendants were there immediately upon seeing the Police SUV. Jamie hopped out and explained what had happened to Russell as they opened the door to get him.

Jamie knew it was bad when they both recoiled at seeing how he had been positioned in the car.

"Dude, it smells like a chocolate puke pie in here."

"Damn, it does," echoed the second guy.

A third guy came out for Nicole and Jamie explained her injuries, too. Nicole was wildly out of it still because she still had the brownies in her stomach and not puked them all over the car.

He wished he had a gun belt right now. He loved how Rat used his power move to pull up the gun belt and make sure the gun was seen. That was so cool.

They wheeled Nicole away into the hospital as Jamie looked down to get a piece of puked up walnut off his shirt. Russell was semi-conscious and in pain. He saw Nicole and asked Jamie about Marcus. Jamie proudly told him where he had dropped Marcus, figuring Russell would want to give him an award for his quick thinking.

Russell had a jolt of pain as they moved him to the stretcher. "You did what?" He was incensed but in shock, too. The attendants waved Jamie off and rushed Russell inside.

Jamie saw his camera and thought, "It had been a good night of filming so far."

Jamie went inside to make a call to the PD to let them know about Marcus and the Captain but half-fainted and was caught by a hefty nurse. She led him into an empty room, took off his shoes and dirty shirt and pants and laid him on the bed. She gave him a sedative which would knock him out for the next sixteen hours.

He was the only person outside the jail who knew where Marcus was.

Chapter 73

Luc nudged Marcus awake and told him he had a half an hour before his block would get called for gym. Marcus hopped down and started stretching out his legs and back. He had incredible flexibility from all those years of training.

Luc and Dom nodded and looked at each other as Marcus started to shadow box and throw kicks, knees and elbows. He was working himself into a pre-fight lather as Baker had taught him to do before sparring sessions.

Luc and Dom were betting that a young, well-trained guy like Marcus should win over an aged drug abuser who smoked, drank and had been eating jail food for years.

Truth being told, the Italians were a bit leery of Bald Boy and would not mind seeing him get knocked out. They knew what that would do to his jail credibility. They also knew that the Cuban was a vicious fighter and this kid had never been in a real fight despite a decade of sparring in the gym.

Marcus was ready and Dom had given him two Advils after lunch and before his nap. The food, although not great, had helped give him some energy. Luc handed him a perfectly ripe banana for quick energy as fight time approached.

Marcus felt ready and still oddly eager to finally pull the trigger. As ready as he'd ever feel before a fight in a jail as a nineteen-year old going up against a thirty four year old Cuban murderer with a large tattoo on his forehead. His mind was alternating between confidence and panic still.

He made a deal with himself. He would follow Baker's advice – make sure there are no other options before engaging in a fight. Marcus laughed to himself – I think that is a yes. Therefore, he planned to fight all out and even if he lost his knuckles would be bloody. There would be no surrender, tap-out or throwing in the towel from Marcus Kelly tonight. This guy had better be ready to fight.

Then he pictured Bald Boy in his mind and he sure looked ready to fight. Marcus almost wished he could fight Mike Tyson instead.

As his cell door opened he thought of his folks and promised himself he would see them again.

Luc and Dom hugged him and kissed him on each cheek while they said something in Italian and did the sign of the cross. They did not go to the gym because their interests were right where they were. They lived by an old Jewish saying, "A man who cannot protect his property owns nothing." These guys had shanks in their cells that had been used before and would be used again. They wanted to protect this kid but they were also confident he could do that himself. They were not going up, they rarely went to the gym.

Luc reached up and grabbed the back of Marcus's neck and pulled him to his face, "Kid, listen to me good here. You are about to get in a jail fight. This guy is vicious as hell, you gotta match that and more. He has killed before, you have to be ready to do the same up there tonight if you need to."

He released his neck and did the sign of the cross.

Marcus was ready now. This motherfucker was not going to forget fighting Marcus Kelly. He was ready to kill with his bare hands, had to be. The jail's evil had brought this mindset out in Marcus. He had been pure, innocent upon arrival. What a weapon.

He kept the shank in his pocket, too. Never know.

Chapter 74

Rat was still amazed at his luck about Marcus, especially on a weekend when he could pull something like this off. He had sanctioned a fight that would help Rat no matter who won. He had warned the new, young COs about keeping quiet about this fight. He had his fellow lugger Wilson watching the gym's door during the fight so he could keep an eye on him, too.

What could go wrong? He was getting revenge for Joey, putting Marcus Kelly in a bad place and gaining power within the jail while hopefully putting the Cuban in the infirmary.

He was rooting for Marcus since his scary trip earlier to Bald Boy's cell. He highly doubted Marcus could win but he was a big kid and he looked like he could handle himself. Who was he kidding? He was fighting Bald Boy. Duh. This big kid was going to get fucked up. He deserved it, too.

If Bald Boy won it would be further known that Bald Boy had done this for Rat and gotten Rat even more respect among the inmate population. That was hugely important to Rat. This power struggle between the two of them ended today.

But that threat against Mama and Joey had shaken Rat.

If Marcus could somehow win, Bald Boy would lose his grip on the power over The Boyz and somebody new would take over. Rat would then have Bald Boy moved to a shitty cell in a shitty block and be done with him. Any new relationships in the lugging of contraband would be on Rat's terms and he would be in charge. He had made mistakes with Bald Boy and that would not happen again.

Rat opened the cells. It was fight night and many guys who had not been to the gym since the last sanctioned fight in January found their way back up, Jake Pinkham among them.

There was a buzz in the air. They all knew who Bald Boy was one way or another. Many of the convicts had been victimized by The Boyz in some way, therefore there was always an undercurrent of hoping he got his ass kicked mixed into the buzz. They had, however, seen him mercilessly beat everybody that Rat put in front of him so far.

They loved to watch him fight because he was violent and aggressive. He wanted to put on a show, give the jail something to talk about for a few days. And he did, that was part of this whole thing for him. He ended most within a few minutes.

The emergency lighting in the gym was perfect for a fight. It gave the large room a spooky, muted light like candlelight. It was plenty of light for the combatants to throw down, too. It was as if mankind was going to step back into caveman times.

Bald Boy was pensive during his walk to the gym. Like everything else in Valley Jail, these fights had more meaning than met the eye. Sure, it was a fight. Everybody could see that. But to Bald Boy this jail was his world, all he had, and he knew that he had to work hard to remain on top. He had aggressive guys in his crew who would slice him up if they could get away with it. That was the nature of the people he was dealing with. He had to be the most vicious animal in here that he could be.

His power over Jake served that purpose, too. When Jake arrived he was sought after for sexual purposes by many of the guys because of his looks and mannerisms. He brought out depraved feelings in many inmates. Many would-be suitors ended up with ferocious claw marks all over their body from Jake's tiger claws. But eventually somebody overcame Jake's defenses and violently had his way with him.

Bald Boy had also noticed Jake and was attracted to him. He had learned in Cuba that sex in jail had nothing to do with being gay or straight. The physical act fell under the "it don't count in jail" motto. The message was one of power and submission. You are my bitch. But Bald Boy wanted to send a message to the whole jail. He had claimed Jake for himself.

Bald Boy got Rat to sanction a fight and Bald Boy destroyed the guy who had beaten and aggressively and repeatedly raped Jake. Bald Boy beat this guy severely and Rat let it go on until the guy could take no more. It was Bald Boy's crowning moment, actually. It left no doubt who was the boss of the inmates in Valley Jail. Bald Boy had sent a message. Jake is mine, hands off or what happened to that guy will happen to you.

Chapter 75

Dottie got home and parked the car carefully in the garage in Harold's spot, never spotting the missing passenger side mirror. She was crying and hyperventilating. She felt horrible and the ride had taken a long time. Trees were down everywhere once she got past the rink and she thought she might have hit one near the rink. Her section of town still had power.

She saw the big picture of her Dear Harry in the kitchen and broke down sobbing. How could I have let that man kiss me?

She greeted DH and took him out to pee. Then she went to the kitchen and turned on the coffee pot. She turned the TV on and went to get the brownies where she had left them. They were gone. She did not panic, figuring she had absentmindedly put them somewhere else.

She searched the whole house and the only reason she did not think DH had eaten them was because the plate was gone too. Oh no.

The lights went out in her house.

Chapter 76

Saturday Afternoon • Atlantic Ocean

Aaron and Claire were frantically calling home from the ship trying to get any news from Marcus and the storm that they had just missed. They were getting Marcus's voice mail and could reach nobody else. They had heard that cell towers, phone lines and power lines were decimated by the storm in New England. At first they were sure he'd call back, but as time passed they became worried.

They were hopeful that the storm was the reason they could not reach their son. They were frantic and not enjoying their cruise. There was a stomach bug going around the ship.

Aaron caught it.

Chapter 77

Marcus walked up to the gym with the rest of the block. There was a direct staircase from the block to the gym, all enclosed by granite on one side and chain link on the other. It was a claustrophobic's nightmare as the chain link continued overhead to completely encase the staircase to form a tunnel. His mind was frantically switching from ready to fight to absolute fear.

He was used to people noticing him in the real world but this felt more like being recognized as the guy who was going to be fed to the lions. The other inmates gave Marcus a comfortable distance, almost as if what he had was contagious. Marcus was relying on his training to get him through this. He threw slow, deliberate punches to keep loose.

Sparring match, kiddo.

Then he walked into the gym and the terror overcame him again. Those who had walked up the stairs with him immediately scattered as if to say, "I am not with him."

The roof of the gym was also the peak at the very top of the jail, fifty feet above the gym floor. It was loud and the atmosphere was electric, like a Vegas arena before a boxing match. There was excited chatter and jostling for best viewing positions.

Marcus was truly on an island. How can I do this? The crying urge hit him hard. I am sure Bald Boy would love to see that. The voice in his head was keeping him strong, and he was hearing Baker's calm voice, too. He was going to hug Baker and give him a big kiss if he ever saw him again.

Officer Wilson locked the gym door and nodded to Rat, who was in the middle of the basketball court and was indicating to the inmates with an impatient wave of his hand to make the circle in which they would fight. The inmates slowly did so.

They made a circle that was about forty feet in diameter. The inmates were three deep with many pulling benches and other things over to stand on. The tension in the gym was mounting and Bald Boy was in the circle and waving his arms and imploring his fans to cheer for him. The circle began closing in with excitement.

They were bloodthirsty. Whose? Don't care. Just bleed, baby.

Marcus was on the outside of the circle and nobody had noticed. They were in such a fury that they had forgotten that it takes two to tango.

Rat realized the problem and screamed for the dumb animals to move aside to allow Marcus to enter the ring. As the circle parted and all eyes turned to him, Marcus looked surprisingly confident. He was bouncing on his toes and glaring at Bald Boy. Many inmates elbowed each other and pointed as they noticed it. His shadow boxing was impressive. Marcus knew how to intimidate, too. His fists cut through the air and he stared at Bald Boy menacingly, his hockey hair obscuring his eyes.

Crying was no longer an option with the evil of this jail driving the car called Marcus. The jail loved its new toy. There would be no more waves of panic for the time being, kiddo. We got this.

He spat on the floor. Fuck you. He had seen that in a movie and had always wanted to do it.

It was a stunning difference from the past opponents of Bald Boy. Most of them had shit their pants at this point and were literally pushed into the ring by the crowd of rowdy inmates to get their brains beaten in.

Rat had not expected this bravado and was suddenly less confident in a Bald Boy victory as he could literally hear the fists whipping by his head as Marcus neared him. He was staring right at Rat now with a scowl. Why was this kid not pissing his pants?

When Marcus was fully visible to the crowd of inmates there was a hush. The circle closed and tightened again. Bald Boy sensed he had lost his momentum so he stripped of his shirt to reveal his impressive physique and to intimidate Marcus. His muscular upper body was covered in scars and tattoos. There were so many tattoos on his torso that it looked to Marcus like he gave crayons to a first grade class and told them to draw something on him. Was that a dolphin or a shark on his arm?

Bald Boy flexed and screamed and spat on the ground in front of him. Marcus thought he looked way better than Marcus had when he spat.

Bald Boy had on Nike high tops and the bottom half of his orange jump suit held up with a shoelace for a belt. The shank was in the pocket near his hip and out of sight.

All eyes now shifted to Marcus. Fuck it, he did not have his orange jumpsuit cut in top and bottom like Bald Boy did, so he just took it off and was in his black compression shorts, no shirt. No shoes. He did not flex or yell. He did not have to. Marcus was jacked, rivers of veins visible and throbbing over his sinewy muscles. He had not a hint of a tattoo or a scar. No, wait. He had the vaccination scar on his left shoulder and it looked bad-ass in this light.

Marcus was way more physically impressive than Bald Boy. He was chiseled and in top condition. Jake Pinkham let out a gasp when he saw Marcus.

Oh my goodnesssss …

Rat screamed, "Let's go," which was barely audible over the frenzied crowd. Bald Boy sprinted across the ring at his rookie opponent, using the opening move that always worked for him and ended some fights right there. The inmates had seen the move and they all readied for the poor kid to get smacked.

However, Bald Boy badly miscalculated what he had waded into. Sure, Bald Boy was a brutal, sadistic man whose victims were often restrained or far inferior physically. It is one thing to beat the piss out of a guy who is tied to a chair or has a hood over his face while his arms were held behind him or cuffed.

It is totally different to enter a ring of combat against a young, highly trained, healthy, strong opponent who is not bound or blindfolded and has something to prove to himself.

And with evil intent running through his brain.

Chapter 78

Nicole was sleeping and had an IV in her arm. She had two black eyes and her nose was just slightly broken. She'd be fine.

Russell was not so lucky. He had a badly broken pelvis and his hip needed immediate surgery. He would have a long recovery and likely need a cane to walk.

Jamie was in deep, drug-induced REM sleep and was dreaming about life in California.

The hospital was able to reach Nicole's Dad to let him know what happened and that she was going to be just fine.

Tony cried himself to sleep, vowing he would make more of an effort to be a Dad going forward.

Chapter 79

Bald Boy wanted to get the crowd going early so he was going to try his favorite opening move – land a huge, flying overhand right and surprise this young newbie. If Marcus ducked this punch Bald Boy had alternative moves to unleash. The moves had all worked in the past. Tonight would be no different. He practiced this one move over and over.

Bald Boy fed off the crowd's approval. They had seen him fight many times and knew he started off aggressively every time. They sensed he was going to land this flying straight right as usual. He roared and pointed at Marcus, marking the official start of this fight. Marcus put his fists up in a classic fighter's position. It was obvious that he knew what he was doing.

Bald Boy charged at him at full speed and jumped up for the attack and cocked his right hand by his ear. He was going to use gravity pulling him down as leverage when he landed the punch. If it landed flush it would knock Marcus out as it had to many others before him.

He was in mid-air when Marcus stepped to his left with surprising alacrity for a guy his size and ducked out of the way, forcing Bald Boy to miss just barely and to land off balance slightly. Because he was off balance he then missed with his patented follow-up kick as he spun by Marcus and landed clumsily in the front row of inmates. They were lustily cheering for blood. The inmates held Bald Boy up as if he had done a leap into the stands after a touchdown.

279

Rat could not believe his eyes. He had never seen that move not work and he was blown away by how quickly Marcus moved.

Bald Boy could also not believe he had missed with both moves. It was his patented combo, his power moves. It had worked in every previous gym fight he had been in and many more in the streets.

Marcus sensed the doubt and grinned at Bald Boy confidently. The evil that had awakened within him was pushing the buttons of this ath-a-lete it had just recently introduced itself to. It was providing the ingredient missing from the arsenal Marcus possessed – maliciousness.

Marcus knew that he had to be aggressive. His mind was racing but he was able to channel the energy and get his brain to rely on the instincts he had developed with Baker over the years. He could not help but look around at the ring of inmates who were cheering for blood to be spilled.

There were some ugly motherfuckers in jail.

He could also hear Baker's voice in his ear telling him what to do, calming him down. To the dismay of Bald Boy, this scenario was now almost identical to an NHL fight. There was a bloodthirsty crowd screaming for blood and two big, tough guys going one on one.

It was what Marcus had trained to do for the last nine years while Bald Boy was drugging, drinking and smoking butts while beating up smaller guys who were scared of him.

Marcus danced in, hopping on his bare feet, maintaining a right handed boxer's stance and closing the distance between himself and Bald Boy. Bald Boy was standing flatfooted and still trying to figure out how his opening move had missed so badly. It was like a chess match where one guy had an opening set of moves that always resulted in checkmate only this one time it had not. There seemed to be no plan B for the guy with two Bs tattooed onto his forehead, ironically.

Marcus did not want to get this guy too close and wrestle him. He knew there were no rules so Bald Boy, being the savage that he was, would probably bite and eye gouge more readily than Marcus would. He'd have to box him to win. Stay outside and strike, he could practically hear Baker coaching him.

Bald Boy shook his head, screamed again and assumed a fighter's stance, trying to regain his machismo. Marcus saw that he would have opportunities to strike big but only if he did it correctly and did not get distracted by the surroundings. The crowd was screaming in anticipation as the two combatants circled each other a few more times cautiously. The ring was getting smaller as the crowd inched closer and closer. Marcus did too, his circles becoming smaller and smaller, Bald Boy slowly coming into range.

Down below the inmates still in their cells or blocks heard the commotion and excitement from the gym above and they, too, began to stir and awaken. The young guards patrolling the main floor and blocks sensed the excitement among the inmates and headed toward the control room to safety.

Bald Boy had recovered from his earlier miss and was smiling and talking in Spanish to Marcus. Marcus was trying figure out what he was saying to him – "you want to fuck my hot mother's toaster?" Marcus sucked in Spanish.

He was looking for a way to pop this motherfucker in the nose to shut him up. Bald Boy was a big boy with long arms, no time to be careless. They circled a few more times. The crowd was officially berserk. It was male bonding at its finest, but they wanted some action.

Fuck it, thought Marcus, enough dancing. It was time to do something. He pictured his Dad nodding.

Marcus bounced forward twice and faked a left hook, getting Bald Boy to react just enough for Marcus to come over the top with a straight right that landed crisply over Bald Boy's left eye and opened a nasty cut that ripped the tattooed Y in Boy on his forehead into two pieces.

"The bald Cuban fucker is officially in deep shit," Baker would have said.

Bald Boy stumbled backwards and was held up and pushed back toward his opponent by a few stunned inmates. He was already bleeding badly and his left eye was swollen and blood was flowing into both eyes, slightly blinding him. He was now softened up and Marcus could teach him a formal lesson in the finer arts of kicking ass.

Bald Boy was about to pay for many, many past sins.

Rat had climbed a small ladder and was now standing on the guard's platform with a perfect view of the fight. He was still shocked that Bald Boy's first move was so easily defended by Marcus and he was saying "No fucking way" over and over when Marcus landed the huge right hand to that bald skull. It was a beautifully thrown punch and the CRACK it made on impact was like a wooden bat hitting a ball. This was so fucking good. Rat was already figuring out which shitty cell he'd be sending the bald asshole to.

Marcus recovered from throwing that bomb of a punch and was shaking his right hand as if he may have hurt it. The crowd picked up on it and urged Bald Boy to make a move. Bald Boy sensed this and immediately attacked, moving right in on Marcus's apparently hurt hand instinctively.

Baker had taught Marcus this move and they practiced it often. It would be effective against an aggressive guy like Bald Boy – like a shark smelling blood he would go to it. Baker had nailed Marcus a few times with it even after Marcus knew the move. The key was to really sell it and let the hand hang limp and look useless.

Baker would've been proud of Marcus. He was earning an Academy Award and this bloodied monster was buying it. Bald Boy made a move as if Marcus did not even have a right hand and Marcus suddenly brought the right back and came up with an upper cut as Bald Boy was diving in to tackle him. The timing was impeccable as Marcus caught him perfectly in the solar plexus and knocked every bit of air from his body. It sounded like a belly flop into a pool. A smack and a thud occurred at the same time. The smack was from ribs cracking. The thud was from the donkey kick power Marcus had.

Marcus was enjoying this. Bald Boy's ruptured spleen was not.

Marcus made eye contact with Jake and smiled. Jake smiled back admiringly.

Bald Boy hit the ground with a grunt and the blood from the cut on his forehead made a colorful impression on the floor. After lying on the floor for ten seconds, he got up and warily scanned the crowd. They were joyous and not afraid to show it in front of Bald Boy any more. The fear factor was gone and these guys were thrilled to see that the lion was losing his pride to a kid.

A big kid.

Marcus was now playing to the crowd, waving his arms to get them to acknowledge the show he was giving them. He even put his hand to his ear to show he wanted more noise. The crowd of misfits was loving this young buck and Marcus had the evil pulsing through him and pushing him forward to continue this thumping in a mean-spirited, torturous manner.

Bald Boy's leadership of The Boyz was getting sucked out of the room with each punch Marcus punished him with. That left jab that Baker had loved so much was cracking into Bald Boy's unprotected face with sickening force. The front row of inmates was being sprayed with his blood.

Marcus was fucking with Bald Boy now. Marcus was the jail's puppet and the puppet-master was a mean son of a bitch.

Conti tried to hide his emotions but he was as happy as he had ever been while in jail. The kid was doing his dirty work. This was Conti's inauguration as the new king of Valley Jail. He savored every punch that landed. The kid was destroying Conti's enemy for him.

Bald Boy was now fighting on rage and embarrassment and he was throwing punches and kicks wildly. Marcus simply moved to avoid the slow and obvious attempted punches and kicks and countered with power shot after power shot. Give Bald Boy credit because he took some blows that would've put lesser men down. Rat was witnessing something he thought might happen, but not like this. This was a mismatch and a beating like nothing he had ever expected.

Marcus continued to toy with the bloody mess in front of him that would not go down. It felt good to be using what he had trained for half his life and doing it really well. He was so alive and alert yet he felt like somebody had turned off his morals. He was attacking cruelly, picking spots that maximized the damage to Bald Boy.

He was sure he had broken Bald Boy's nose, some ribs and his orbital bones around his eyes. But the Cuban would not go down. Marcus was ready to end this fight. It was dangerous to let a guy like this to keep fighting. This guy was a killer.

Bald Boy was having trouble seeing. The blood was still flowing into his grotesquely swollen eyes and his head was woozy. He was hurt badly. He could see through the blood that Rat was clapping and jumping on his platform with delight at his demise. He then saw The Boyz talking among themselves quietly, seemingly making plans for after this fight. He saw inmates who once feared him now cheering for Marcus to kick his ass and pointing at Bald Boy with taunts and slurs.

He knew what he had to do. He had to save his top spot. He had worked too hard. He had to show these weak lions that he was still in charge.

He whipped out the shank from his shorts and the whole gym went silent. He was waving it menacingly and telling Marcus to come get some. Marcus was trying to translate the Spanish but having no luck. He wants ice cream on a boat? What?

The crowd instinctively moved back a few steps. The shank was a four-inch metal rod that had been sharpened to a deadly point and had a taped up handle. It was a good shank and had been used a few times before. It could be thrown or used to stab.

Marcus was not moving and waiting for the next move by anybody to stop this. Officer Wilson had said no weapons. He looked to Rat on the platform. Rat smiled sheepishly and shrugged as if to say, "What can I do?"

Marcus looked for Wilson but he was at the door and unable to see any of what was going on.

Initially the inmates were screaming that the shank was a violation and booing Bald Boy for having one. Then they sensed this was the only way Bald Boy had a chance so they started clapping and telling Marcus to fight. They just wanted to see more fighting. And more blood. This was not a group that followed rules all that often and would cheer for any type of violence to continue.

Marcus looked to his jumpsuit and the shank in it. He could go get it and make it a fair fight.

Fuck it, I don't need it. Time to end this.

He was bullshit. He calmed himself with deep breaths but his adrenaline was firing on all pistons. Bald Boy was wiping blood out of his eyes with his left hand while waving the blade at Marcus with his right. Marcus was plotting the takedown. He and Baker had trained with weapon removal a bit but it was not a focus of their training. Still, he was supremely confident.

He had kicked the shit out of his self-doubt as he had been doing the same to the bloody guy in front of him.

Bald Boy surprised Marcus by suddenly charging him and slashing from left to right at his chest. Marcus timed it and ducked the closest swipe of the blade and came back up and threw a left uppercut into Bald Boy's jaw.

CRACK!

The crowd gasped and waited for Bald Boy to finally hit the floor and not get up.

Nope.

A dark-colored blood was now streaming from Bald Boy's mouth. He was almost ready to throw the knife like a dagger but he never got the chance. As he shifted the shank into a throwing position he made the mistake of looking down for a second. That was all Marcus needed. He took the fight to him and ran at Bald Boy like a bull. Bald Boy swung at the approaching teenager but Marcus disappeared into a foot first slide below the wild swoosh of the blade going over his head and missing badly.

Bald Boy was badly off balance and Marcus had slid like a baseball player stealing a base, leading with his cleats. He hopped up quickly behind Bald Boy and got to his feet as Bald Boy clumsily tried to turn back around but he was too slow and when he finally did turn Marcus snapped Bald Boy's head back with a vicious elbow to the chin. An Israeli military move. His jaws snapped together quickly on impact and part of his tongue fell to the floor, as did the shank.

Marcus then kicked him in the balls as hard as he could. The thud it made sounded like a melon being dropped from the top of the block onto the granite floor. Marcus danced back, maintaining his fighter's stance. How much more could this guy take?

The gym erupted in laughter as they joyously savored seeing the bully among them get his ass handed to him. And who didn't laugh at a good kick in the balls – as long as they were somebody else's balls, of course.

The thud the kick had made reminded Marcus of hitting his father in the nuts with a street hockey ball a long time ago. He had done that on purpose that day. He needed a new hockey stick.

Sorry, Dad.

Bald Boy had that same look of pain on his face. He then fell face first onto the hard floor, breaking his fall with his battered face.

It was over. He ain't getting up, kiddo.

Marcus did not have a scratch on him but his hands were covered in Bald Boy's blood. His right hand started to hurt just a little. He was flying so high right now on the buzz he got from fighting he barely felt it.

The jail had done its part in bringing the violence out of Marcus. It was the component Marcus needed to pull the trigger and unleash his pent-up rage and frustration. He now knew he could use his training. He had scratched that itch. Any future fight would trigger

287

the remnants of the jail that Marcus would be taking home with him.

Nobody made a move to help Bald Boy. He was blowing blood bubbles through his badly broken nose as he lay on the floor. He was alive, that was good enough.

Wilson flicked the lights and that indicated to the frenzied crowd to head back to their cells. The inmates were all talking about the fight as they left the gym to return to their blocks. There was an elevated agitation to this crowd that was quickly picked up by the remaining blocks. All of the inmates were out of their cells but locked in their individual blocks. There was hooting and hollering coming from every corner of the jail as word spread about the fight. They were getting worked up collectively.

Wilson had seen this before. He was smiling and shaking his head as he quickened his pace. Fucking kid can fight. Wow, can he fight. He sprinted from the gym ahead of everybody else. He closed off certain doors so the inmates could only go from the gym back to their blocks. He sensed something might happen as a result of this fight so he did not want them to have access to the main floor if something erupted. He then ran to the office's safety.

Chapter 80

Marcus was hustled out of the gym and back to Dom and Luc's cell by an escort of The Gringos led by Conti. It was Conti's way of saying there was a new power in the jail. Plus, he had no idea if Marcus was lying to him about the DUI or not. What if Marcus was really an inmate and sentenced to be in the jail for a while? Conti wanted this motherfucker on his side because this kid was an asset in a place where brute force ruled. This march was an obvious sign to all that Bald Boy's reign was done.

Marcus was ushered back into the cell and the inmates now guarded the cell door. A dozen or so Gringos and Conti stood outside the cell and made sure nobody tried to get Marcus.

Luc and Dom were armed with their shanks and they handed Marcus one of theirs after they laughed at his pink toothbrush, although Marcus did notice Dom then put the pink shank into his milk crate. Marcus was holding a serious weapon. It was a paint roller that had been straightened into a six-inch ice pick and sharpened to a deadly point.

They were all on edge and the jail around them was exploding. Thick, black smoke was quickly filling the blocks. This cell was at the end of the block and on the bottom tier so The Gringos were able to keep the crazed, rioting inmates from getting anywhere near them.

Inside the cell the Mob guys made Marcus tell them about the fight and Conti excitedly filled in details from his perspective. Upon finishing the story Marcus puked into the toilet of the cell. He was pissed. He had gone ten years since puking and now he had puked twice within twenty four hours? It had also felt like he had exorcised something from his body when he regurgitated into the jail's plumbing system. He suddenly felt like himself again and was trembling with fear where just seconds before he was feeling jubilant and cocky. He also sensed the jail erupting into a riot around him. He noticed his right hand was slightly swollen.

While all other inmates had already left the gym to return to their cells, a few of The Boyz were seeing if Bald Boy was alive. He was sitting up and his formerly shiny head was now stained red and ripped apart. Marcus had done damage to this man.

As Rat tried to quietly climb down the rickety ladder to the floor, the last rung squeaked and caught their attention. They signaled for him to come over to Bald Boy.

The guy who would be taking the place of Bald Boy was Hector Sanchez. He was facing a murder charge and had been in the jail for over a year. He was feared and had been Bald Boy's right hand man.

He spoke rapidly in Spanish to the one member of the gang who spoke some English. Rat looked around nervously while impatiently waiting for him to stop talking.

Miguel the interpreter began, "Hector says you bring the goods to him now. No change other than that."

"Jesus, that was a lot of words to just say that," said Rat.

Miguel scowled at Rat and said, "There is much more, Officer Rat. Hector says you set Bald Boy up by having him fight this young white boxer. Therefore there is a price to be paid for this act."

Time to be brave. "Any-fucking-thing else, Hector?" he asked sarcastically and with false bravado.

Nobody looked up so Rat left.

For the first time ever he was scared to be in the jail. He made for the door and did not look back. He had to get back to the office now. He was shocked to emerge from the gym to see the jail erupting into a riot so quickly.

As word spread through the jail that Bald Boy had gotten his ass kicked there were sporadic fires started in the blocks, like the weird ritual of starting fires when your team won the World Series.

The main area was vacant of inmates but the jail was dissolving into a riot in each block quickly. The fires were getting bigger and more numerous and the thick black smoke of mattresses being burned overtook the jail and gave the air a light fog from floor to unvented ceiling. The stone structure was not going to burn down but it was not letting any smoke out, either. It quickly became mayhem and there were no guards in sight.

Rat had snuck out of the gym and taken a back staircase. He ran through the control room and the rookie guards were huddled in there and in shock at the lack of ammo they had to defend themselves. Wilson was trying to make a phone call. They were thrilled to see Rat and have somebody in charge. Rat ran through without saying a word or even looking at the terrified guards. He went and hid in his bunk with his gun locked and loaded. The ramifications of what he had done to Marcus and how it was causing this riot had finally dawned on him. He was fucked. His thirst for revenge on Marcus was going to be his undoing. Survival was now the only thing he was concerned with. His survival. He cocked the gun.

Had he not known the bridge had been washed away he would have run to his car to flee this fiasco. How did this go from a no-lose fight to a riot that Rat had caused so quickly?

Wilson kept radioing and had the other guards calling out using any radio or cell phones. They were unable to contact anybody that could help them. They kept trying and there was a sense of urgency as they all knew that there were a total of three doors between them and hundreds of rioting inmates. Time was not on their side and they had nowhere to hide.

An hour had passed since the gym fight and the inmates were in frenzy. Those who were higher in the food chain were preying upon the weakest inmates within each block mercilessly. Their cells were being ransacked, anything of value taken and the rest set on fire. There were gang beatings and gang rapes.

They were trying to pick the locks to get out of the blocks and into the main area where they could do some real destruction but these doors were heavily armored and so far holding them back. They continued to hack at the locks with steel pipes.

Wilson finally got in touch with Warden Davis. Davis was overwhelmed and useless so Wilson told him exactly who to call and how to say what needed to be said. Wilson was amazed at the incompetence on the other end of the line.

However, Davis asked Wilson a chilling question that Wilson had completely forgotten about.

"Wilson, what about the inmates in the Protective Custody Unit?"

All Wilson could say in reply was, "Oh my God I forgot about that. If they get in there they will kill them all! We cannot get to the PC unit, sir. There are twenty-one guys in there. God help them. Make the calls, sir!"

Davis stammered a good bye and started calling the State Officials who would put out the emergency call to the State Riot Team. They were always on call. They lived for this shit.

Chapter 81

Jimmy MacAdam was one of twenty one inmates being held within the Protective Custody Unit at Valley Jail. They were there for assorted reasons, but it all came down to one thing – they would get raped, beaten or killed if they went into general population.

Many were either accused or convicted of indecent sexual child assault. These were sexual predators of children and called "diddlers" in the jail. Others in the PC Unit were rapists. Some were just meek and seeking a safer haven after getting assaulted in one way or another in general population.

In jail there exists a type of frontier justice toward sexual criminals. Most of the inmates had family on the outside and they felt as if they had left them unprotected while they were incarcerated. So they felt a strange need to hunt these diddlers down – to protect their families.

Therefore, when a diddler or rapist entered the jail the officers would encourage them to "take a PC," to avoid getting beaten due to the nature of their crimes. Most of these guys followed that advice. Most were weak sickos who preyed on women and children.

The diddlers were in a tough spot. The inmates wanted to kill them and the guards treated them with their worst contempt and disrespect. The vitriol and projectiles hurled at them were ignored and almost encouraged by the guards. They had family, too. They thought of the diddlers as the biggest pieces of shit they had in the whole jail. So the PC inmates existed in jail in a very tight vice of possible violence. Like birds at a feeder they were on alert, eyes darting left and right constantly.

Jimmy MacAdam was in PC for a much different reason than being a diddler. He had been attending Valley State College as a partial scholarship student and needed to work to fully afford his tuition and room and board. That still was not enough money for the high cost of being a student near Boston, so he became an entrepreneur. He dealt cocaine to fellow students.

It was going great until he got busted selling drugs in an elementary school zone for the second time in a few months. He really needed money to pay for the drugs the cops took from him during his first arrest. He got sentenced to the jail for four months. The judge from his first arrest was lenient with a fine and community service the first time he had seen MacAdam in his court. He was not so easy going the second time he saw Jimmy for the same offense within a month.

Jimmy's pro bono lawyer put up a feeble defense. The gavel struck, the judge gave Jimmy four months of jail time to serve. Want a lesson, kid? We call this the jail. The judge thought he was doing Jimmy a favor.

"Scared Straight" was not a concept for which the evil of the jail made an exception. He was thrown into the mix with the rest of the new meat. He became an instant target with his longish blonde hair. Even in jail blondes got noticed.

Jimmy did not thrive in the jail; he was docile and did not belong there. He was very out of place. He had been in one fight his whole life – in third grade. He got the shit kicked out of him by the biggest girl in the class.

The Boyz preyed him upon without mercy the moment he arrived. They told him to put money into their canteen fund. They stole his food in the cafeteria. They took his cigarettes, which he had just started smoking in jail. Three weeks into his sentence he was forced at knifepoint to perform oral sex on three guys in the shower. This continued for a month – the same three guys would appear out of nowhere and push him to his knees.

He was crying himself to sleep and contemplating suicide.

Then one night they beat the shit out of him in the shower. For no reason, they just felt like it. The officers who responded told Jimmy to take a PC if he wanted to survive his sentence. They were blaming Jimmy for not having taken one to begin with. Jimmy was desperate and did not fully understand that once he took the PC he was no different than the diddlers and rapists.

He was one of them now.

Jimmy was now among the weirdest lot of perverts on earth. The sex criminals were extremely bizarre and being stuck in with twenty of them in a small cell for twenty-three hours a day was getting unbearable. But he felt safer than he had in general population.

They played chess, watched TV and read books. There was only one toilet so there were some squabbles over that but other than that it was fairly non-violent in the PC Unit. And he did not have to blow anybody.

Their cell was at the end of Block 2, tucked into one of the nooks of the jail. The Warden had knocked down two walls to make it one larger cell. It was sealed off from the rest of the block behind two armored doors. They were mostly out of sight and out of mind. Mostly.

When the PC Unit was let out of their cell for their daily showers they were pelted with cups of urine and horrible insults and threats from the inmates who could see them from their cells. Rat loved to loudly announce that the diddlers had their hour out of their cells as he opened their doors, thus alerting the inmates to grab their cups of piss to hurl at them.

Although the PC Unit was currently safely locked behind the two doors, Jimmy could hear the loud commotion and smell the thick, black smoke from the riot seeping into their cell. He was filled with dread.

Just then the first perimeter door separating PC from the block violently opened and the smoke poured in behind the crazed gang of inmates who had beaten their way through one of the doors and were now just one door away from wreaking the mayhem for which they lusted.

This last door was not solid steel but it was made of thick bars with an enclosed locking mechanism. It allowed the attackers to see into the PC cell. The inmates were hacking at the lock with steel bars as they graphically screamed what they were going to do with the diddlers.

One guy pointed to Jimmy and told him the steel pipe in his hand was going to be shoved up Jimmy's ass in a very painful manner. Many of Jimmy's cellmates were praying while others openly panicked and screamed in terror. It was a horrifying scene. Jimmy could not move – he could barely breathe.

Every inmate held in PC was now one door away from being tortured, raped and beaten to death slowly. Jimmy sat on his bunk wondering why he had chosen to go to such an expensive city to go to college.

There were no shanks or weapons in PC. They were helpless. Pieces were flying off the last door between them and painful death as the inmates kept hammering at the door with their steel pipes.

Chapter 82

The riot was currently still contained to the blocks in the jail, but the brutality was rampant and getting worse. The fires were subsiding because the geniuses finally figured out that they needed to breathe. The previous fires smoldered and did nothing to help the air quality or visibility. A thin layer of black soot was painted onto the granite, which contained and absorbed the mayhem like a vampire drinking blood. The jail was happy to be hosting yet another inmate riot.

Jake Pinkham was safely locked inside his cell alone during the riot. He was hiding under his mattress. Bald Boy had left a large padlock, which Rat had smuggled in for him, under the mattress in Jake's cell. Bald Boy feared a coup against him so he wanted a place where he could lock himself in and not get jumped by a gang, should the need arise. When Jake sensed the mayhem was about to begin after the fight he ran back to his cell. He had shifted the cell door back to its closed position manually and then locked the door to a steel post just in time. Jake was relieved he was locked in but still felt far from safe. These monsters were relentless. He was praying for the first time he could remember.

When the rioting started, and with Bald Boy not protecting him any more, Jake was an immediate target of the rioters. When they found him locked in his cell they threw things at him but his mattress protected Jake. The rioters lost interest and moved on to more accessible victims. There were plenty.

Chapter 83

The jail had been in full riot for over three hours. The National Guard finally was able to put in a very shaky three-foot wide walking bridge over the river to get The State Riot Team into the jail. The Guard soldiers were amazed at how well trained, strong and coordinated the Riot Team was as they crossed the river skillfully.

They did indeed live for this shit.

When the call went out to respond to a riot, the Riot Team members who could get to the jail got to the jail. They had made a commitment when they joined this team and they were serious about their mission. There was never a convenient time for a riot, nor was it ever scheduled. There would be quick exits from dinners, abrupt departures from parties and peaceful sleep interrupted.

Amazingly, even in this storm, there were fifty Riot Team members already assembled in the parking lot. They were in full uniform, black from head to toe. Their helmets were painted with SRT on one side. They wore motorcycle helmets and had shields protecting their faces with black ski masks hiding their identities. There was nothing to identify them individually.

They had body armor on their torsos, hockey shin pads and football thigh pads, huge elbow pads and very bad attitudes toward rioting inmates.

They were trained for one thing – quell the riot by whatever means necessary. The building was at risk of serious damage. There were lives at risk.

They trained often and took this role very seriously. They reviewed and refined techniques and maneuvers. There were no camera guys on the SRT team.

What happened in Vegas stayed in Vegas.

The team also had seven highly-trained German Shepherds under their command tonight. Most of the SRT guys carried three-foot long clubs that they called Long Shanks – it was their preferred weapon. They were made of hard wood and painted black. They were lethal. All Riot Team members were experts at using the club to both attack and defend.

Within the team there was a squad of guys who carried thick Plexiglas shields that were five-feet in height. The shields had handles that allowed them to be used as battering rams. They led the attack. The Shield Team members were the biggest guys and they called themselves "300" after the movie by that title. Like the soldiers in the movie these guys did the work of many men. They were the key in moving rioting inmates to an area the Riot Team wanted them and could best control them. The Shield Team looked formidable and angry.

The SRT formed into their training groups and entered the front door of the jail slapping their clubs into the palms of their gloves in unison with their march. The gloves were black leather and filled with lead particles in the knuckles – totally illegal for a civilian to have but for these guys they were near and dear to them. If you landed a punch wearing these it was a knockout every time.

They moved in highly coordinated fashion. They oozed dominance as soon as they assembled on the main floor.

Even the jail itself seemed to take notice of the approaching thunder headed its way. The jail's evil seemed to shrink back at this sight, choosing to live to terrorize another day. However, the Riot Team was being transformed from being Dads, coaches and buddies into cold-blooded thugs. Being inside the jail brought out the animal within them, too, plus they had the cloak of anonymity behind which to hide. And they had orders to follow – take back Valley Jail from the rioting inmates.

They were anxious to get started.

The "thwack" that the Long Shanks made slapping against the leather of gloves was a powerful sign of what was to come. These guys did not mess around. There were no verbal commands among the men, just hand gestures.

The inmates of this jail had become accustomed to lazy, out of shape guards. They were about to meet the exact opposite of that head on. Initially they were taunting the SRT members to come in the blocks as they held up their crude weapons and projectiles to throw at them. As the SRT guys ignored them and continued to smack their palms, the inmates grew less animated and most of them stopped rioting and just stared in awe of the SRT's precision.

The SRT guys were lined up and faced Block 2, still smacking their clubs into their palms, louder and more quickly than before. They knew where the PC Unit was; Wilson had instructed them upon arrival and handed them the keys to open the two doors. Block 2 inmates were all now standing still and wondering what was next as the inmates in the other blocks lined up at the front bars to watch. The taunts and threats were replaced by whimpers and retreat.

One SRT guy opened the door as a bar of soap thrown by an inmate harmlessly whizzed by his helmet. The door was opened and the inmates shrunk back even more. The first group of SRT guys had the Plexiglas shields and stormed in and formed a straight line across the width of the block. They stepped forward in unison, allowing no gaps in their line. Using the shields they backed all the inmates into the common outdoor area where recreation was held.

Ten SRT members peeled off toward the PC Unit. They found a dozen unlucky inmates about three hacks of the pipe away from busting down the last door and getting into the PC unit to do their damage. They were preoccupied with getting the diddlers and never noticed the danger approaching them from behind.

The SRT team went in with Long Shanks cracking bones. The rioters who were trying to get into the PC Unit were cut down quickly and then forced out with the rest of their block. They had welts all over their heads and bodies. They had taken a beating. Most were crying. The SRT was far more aggressive with this group than they had been with the rest of the block's inmates.

Many of the inmates had been beaten during the riot by fellow inmates. They were now all being beaten by the Riot Team.

Double whammy.

The PC Unit's inmates were rushed out to an adjacent outside area separated by a fence and barbed wire from the general population. Many were still crying and terrified. Jimmy MacAdam was forming his plans to get the hell out of Boston as soon as he got out of the jail.

If he got out of the jail.

The SRT then proceeded to clear the remaining blocks in a similarly vicious manner until all inmates were standing outside, packed like rats into the rec area and not saying a word. There was a sense of panic among them initially. The very few inmates that had put up a fight with the SRT guys in the blocks were badly beaten up and many were screaming about a lawsuit at the top of their lungs. It was cold outside, they were packed in like cattle on a train. But they were slowly regaining their riot machismo and chanting and pumping their fists in the air as time passed. Then they all got really cold and nobody said much. The SRT's plan was to freeze the fight out of the rioters. They'd be much more easily handled in the next phase if they were mellowed. The weather did that for them.

As the cells were being cleared Jake was found in his cell and the lock was cut off. He was led to where the PC Unit was being held by the SRT after seeing Jake sashay toward the rec area. He was grateful and blew the SRT guy who brought him there a kiss. The SRT guy laughed and winked at Jake. They were human after all.

The SRT Commander had a picture of Marcus, given to them by Wilson and taken by Rat the previous night, so they pulled him aside. He was given a helmet and black overalls so he did not look like he was an inmate. To be safe he was told to stand with one of the K9 SRT members who happened to be the commander of the K9 officers. He was gruff and in charge, no doubt.

Marcus had requested that Dom and Luc be treated well and explained quickly how they had helped him survive. The SRT guys grudgingly led the Mob guys to a holding cell away from the rioters. Their cell was locked and kept safe. They had been rewarded for their kindness toward Marcus. They were saying something in Italian to Marcus as he was led away, their hands gesturing the sign of the cross as they thanked him over and over.

As the inmates continued to be calmed by the cold temperature and rain, the SRT guys swept the blocks again to be sure there were no remaining rioters hiding inside. When they were sure they had all of them outside the SRT Commander took a bullhorn and cleared his throat. He loved this part of the job.

Above the freezing inmates a window opened and the Commander began his usual address to rioting inmates.

He announced, with very little emotion, "Inmates, listen up – this jail is now under my command. You had your fun, now is the time to pay for that fun. You boys fucked up and now you get fucked up. Every one of you is to take your clothes off and leave everything right where you are standing. If we see one thing in anybody's hands as you re-enter this jail you will be dealt with severely. You have one minute to comply." He abruptly shut the window and after a minute the doors to the cafeteria were thrown open by the SRT guys with the huge shields.

There was a murmuring among the confused inmates but they all did as they were told and quickly there were many naked rioters wishing they had behaved and freezing their asses off in the cold rain.

Too late.

You could have heard a pin drop as the first inmates were pushed inside the now opening doors.

The inmates closest to the door were shoved inside by the guys with big shields – ten at a time. Then the shield group re-formed a barrier keeping the inmates outside until the next ten were shoved through. It was well orchestrated and beautifully executed by the shield guys. They were kicking the absolute shit out of the inmates and winking at each other and screaming encouragement as they knocked guys down with force. And that was just a taste of what was to come for the rioters. The SRT always wanted to let the inmates know not to do this again; this is what you get.

Riot prevention.

Marcus was standing with the K9 Commander in the cafeteria and watching this all go down. It was the

304

wildest thing he had ever seen. What a night. He was forever changed.

His right hand was throbbing with pain.

He caught the K9 Commander smiling under his shield as he said to Marcus, "Here we go."

Inside the jail the Riot Team had formed an oft-practiced gauntlet. Seven big guys were positioned on each side of the door through which the Shield Team was shoving the inmates. As the naked inmates were run through the gauntlet they slapped at their shins with their clubs, tripping them and causing other inmates to trip over them. They were then pushed and shoved and told to kneel and face the wall of the cafeteria, hands folded on the back of their heads in a line against the wall. Many were crying.

When all ten inmates were kneeling the K9 guys brought their dogs to within three feet of the backs of their heads. The dogs were ferociously barking and growling just behind the kneeling inmates' heads, filling the large, open room with their bloodthirsty snarls.

It was the SRT's signature move. It was humiliating and potent. The dogs owned the moment. They sensed it and provided a very authoritative addition to the SRT. Their handlers were perfectly in sync with the dogs and the other pairings. It was orchestrated, practiced and perfected. Even the commands shouted in German to the dogs were impressive. Marcus could not take his eyes off the dogs as they would, in perfect unison, do the exact same thing when they heard the German commands being screamed at them in the mayhem.

The K9 Team knew that this was the part of the procedure that cut the inmates' balls off completely. Being naked and getting the dog treatment was usually enough to make most inmates cry, tonight was no different. Marcus saw some really tough guys whom he had seen earlier that day now bawling their eyes out and begging to get the dogs away. It was pathetic to watch but the Riot Team was working with precision and brutality perfectly. It was textbook and Marcus saw the K9 Commander nodding and smiling as the dogs stole the show.

Many inmates feared dogs and were wailing and begging for them to get the dogs away. They were a pitiful sight that the SRT guys loved to see. They were laughing and taunting the hysterical inmates.

The scene was repeated over and over. Ten inmates at a time were brought in, given shin shots and the K9 treatment and then run up to the blocks by a different group of SRT guys and moved to any cell available.

As Bald Boy was being pushed through the gauntlet he was tripped and shoved from behind and went sliding on the wet floor. He broke through the SRT gauntlet, gliding right at Marcus on the slippery, wet cement floor.

The K9 Commander had left just enough slack on his leash for his dog, Adolph, to jump forward and bite down on Bald Boy's thigh before he could be pulled away. The dog bit down hard and gave the leg the "death roll" with his head, going back and forth rapidly and ripping flesh with his strong jaws and sharp teeth. The handler then pulled Adolph away as Bald Boy was writhing in pain and looking to Marcus for help. Marcus gave him the middle finger as two guards grabbed him and dragged him to a cell.

Bye-bye, Bald Boy.

As the last group of the inmates was shoved into the cafeteria, one of the more memorable scenes from the gauntlet procedure occurred. The PC Unit was allowed back in after the general population had been locked away. The SRT guys knew the PC Unit was not part of the riot so they did not whack them or make them kneel facing the wall. They just simply walked back in and headed to their cell.

When Jake Pinkham was escorted back in with the PC guys the SRT team just stopped and stared. Jake strutted in like a supermodel on a runway, waving left and right as if he were a politician in a parade. He was naked and his six-inch limp penis swung back and forth like an elephant's trunk, slapping on his thighs. He winked at Marcus as he passed by. The SRT guys had a good laugh but then got right back to the task at hand.

It took the Riot Team a total of two hours after arriving to get all the inmates into cells and put out any fires that were still burning.

They then went cell to cell taking attendance with the sheet of names Wilson had provided. Some of the inmates were still mouthing off during this process so they were removed from their cells and dragged down the stairs to the solitary area. These SRT guys were true pros and the inmates were made painfully aware of their power tonight.

The National Guard had, by this time, set up a bridge over which vehicles could drive and more personnel were brought inside the jail to handle procedure and take over for the Riot Team. They were exhausted but congratulating themselves and patting their K9s. The dogs were invaluable again. It had been a good night for the SRT boys.

The SRT commander debriefed Marcus and the Riot Team loved his story about the fight, making him tell it again and again, more slowly each time. He was then driven home. His right hand began throbbing even more when he got home.

As he unzipped his black overalls the orange jumpsuit was revealed. Marcus thought back to his math class – was that really yesterday? His teacher, Mr.

Burns, had said intersecting circles would bring the color of other circles with it after they had intersected.

You got some orange in you now, kiddo. The jail would be part of his story forever.

Conclusion

Dottie

When the Valley PD investigated the DUI and looked inside the Lexus at the towing area they found Dottie's plate and her special brownies in his back seat. They tested them and found them to be loaded with highly potent marijuana, as they had suspected.

As the investigation ensued over the next few weeks, Dottie Cataldo's name kept popping up from every angle.

The DA's office had gotten their hands on Jamie's pen video. They watched it and were able to identify Dottie's license plate as the car that hit Russell. It was painful to see and hear Russell get hit as they had to watch the video a few dozen times to get the numbers from the plate.

It was video gold, too. Russell went flying and Nicole just disappeared. Jamie was laughing hysterically as it happened on the video being played. They also saw and heard Marcus puking on Jamie and they must have rewound that part fifty times. They called in whomever they could find to show them. It was just too good.

Dottie now faced many serious charges for the marijuana brownies and almost killing Russell. She was looking at fifteen years in jail and her lawyer was expensive. She hated the looks she was getting around town during the trial. She had screwed up Valley's hockey season and was treated like a pariah.

The machine was coming for her.

She had kept the proceeds from Dear Harry's life insurance policy in cash and gold coins in the garden shed. It was wrapped in Saran Wrap and hidden in old barrels. One million dollars completely filled two of them.

She had a feeling she was going to be found guilty and sentenced to a jail term so she decided to make a bold move. She knew Harry's brother had always coveted her so she called him and asked him to bring her back to Vermont quickly. He was thrilled to do it.

They took DH, the money and Dear Harry's old car and took off, never to be seen in Juniper Valley again.

Dottie Cataldo was now a fugitive from justice.

Marcus

Marcus was not charged with DUI given what he endured after his arrest and given the explanation about the brownies.

However, he really had broken a bone in his right hand in the fight with Bald Boy and could not play in the state tournament. It was just a hairline fracture. It would heal quickly but it was his right hand and he could not grip his stick. His hand was in a cast for four weeks.

Valley High lost in the first round of the hockey tournament, at The Fish Tank, to a team whom they had beaten 9-2 earlier that year. They were done for the year. Marcus was ashamed of himself. He had let many people down. Fish was despondent.

Dan Baker made Marcus tell him about beating the shit out of Bald Boy about a hundred times, punch by punch. He was even having Marcus speak to large groups of his students so that they could know how valuable this training could be. It was not just a cardio workout.

He cackled every time he heard the story.

You can't make this shit up.

Aaron and Claire were relieved that despite this incident Marcus was still drafted in the first round of that summer's draft. The word was that the story about jail actually made him an even more attractive candidate.

The only problem was that the hated Montreal Canadiens had drafted him. He should have taken French. Nah, he would have sucked at that, too.

He had learned a lot about himself in those hours he was behind bars. He knew that the reason he had kicked Bald Boy's ass was that he was in peak condition and highly trained so he needed to get even stronger and tougher. That kept him in the gym, at the rink and in the ring, working and learning constantly. Dan Baker noticed a change in Marcus, he was so fucking confident now. He had passed his test and had put the self-doubt in the rearview mirror. Mess with Marcus Kelly at your own risk. The jail's sticky evil stayed with him and would be available if needed again in the future.

He called it his orange aid.

He also learned that his life's goal of the NHL was within reach even though he almost fucked it up badly via bad decisions and bad luck. He gave up beers until he was legal to drink, he would re-visit alcohol then. It had gotten him off track and almost cost him his life. Nicole had made the same pledge so that helped Marcus stick with it. He would wait until he was more mature to see how he handled it in a few years.

He had also learned that he had big, brass balls and any fight in the NHL would pale in comparison with the fight he had in jail.

A fight that had odds set by two Italian Mobsters. A fight that was arranged by a corrupt guard named Rat. A fight versus a Cuban killer named Bald Boy.

Bring it on, NHL.

311

Rat

Rat lost his job when it was learned what he had done with Marcus and what he had been bringing into the jail. Although he tried to blame Jamie for bringing Marcus to the jail it was recorded on Jamie's video and audio that it was his idea. Rat had to spend his lugger money on a lawyer now. He had the prospect of going into the jail as an inmate facing him. He hired a very expensive lawyer.

Doug Gordon had marked the packages of cigarettes with a stamp from his store and taken pictures of them the day Rat bought cigarettes from him. Those cigarettes were found in the jail after the riot, nailing Rat as a lugger on top of all the other charges. Gordon and his son rejoiced at playing a part in the demise of Rat.

Rat was surprised one night a few weeks after the riot when Darlene called him and asked to meet him at a remote bar for a drink.

Rat went to where she had told him she would be and per usual had his pistol with him so he felt safe even out here in the boondocks. He was getting laid tonight, baby. He had a condom, if needed. He was hoping Darlene was a naughty girl.

When he entered the secluded pub to meet her he was rushed from behind and had no time to react. He had a hood thrown over his head and was shoved out of the back door of the bar. His gun was taken from him and he was thrown into the back of a pickup roughly.

He was in the hands of The Boyz and they were getting revenge for Bald Boy being set up in that fight. The Boyz still did not like this piece of shit jail guard setting up one of their leaders. There was a price to be paid for that, a message to be sent.

The Boyz had found out about Rat hitting on Darlene through Darlene's co-worker at Dunkin Donuts. She was dating one of them and scored points by giving them this information. She knew she had put Darlene at risk but Darlene was kind of a bitch to work with and she was helping her boyfriend. So The Boyz visited Darlene and asked her to make a phone call to set Rat up. Darlene was scared shitless but happy to help.

Once they had him in the truck, The Boyz drove Rat out to a field in the middle of nowhere with their van following them. They left Rat and the truck there when they were through with him.

Some hikers had the misfortune the next day to find the truck. Rat was naked in the back of the truck with his arms and legs tied to the corners of the bed of the truck – face down and fat ass up. He was beaten badly and his eyes were swollen shut. He was covered in welts and cigarette burns and his right thumb was broken, Bald Boy's signature.

His gun was also shoved painfully up his ass, Darlene had asked them to do this for her.

Jamie

The prosecutors wanted to go after Jamie when they found out the role that he had played in Marcus's being put into the jail. But he had the video of everything that had happened that night so his lawyer used that leverage and got him a plea deal and a fine. Jamie took the deal and took off for California to become the next Spielberg.

He ran out of money so he got only as far as the Idaho panhandle and now works at a video rental store and grows marijuana. He smokes most of what he grows.

313

Principal Thompson

Principal Thompson was fired when it was learned that he knew of the keg party before the hockey game. The police had questioned many students to try to piece together the details of that fateful night. The student who had told Thompson about the party told the police the story and that Thompson had not done anything to stop it, even though it was in his backyard.

Irene Poulin, sensing an opportunity, told the School Board about the pressure from Thompson to change Fowler's grade. She smiled the same condescending smile he had given her right back at Thompson on her way out of his hearing. She had helped put a nail in his coffin. She gave Thompson the finger as she walked out of the conference room.

Boots/Kaleigh

When the students were interviewed, Boots Balboni was mentioned as the source of drugs and booze by just about all of them.

The cops pulled Boots over on a warrant and he had pot, pills, coke and $763 in small bills on him. Boots was arrested and did not have enough money for his high bail. He was sent to the jail and had already been beaten up twice by The Boyz. The same Boyz he was buying drugs from on the outside. He now owed them money.

Kaleigh got pregnant by Boots the night of Fish's party. She graduated from Valley High with a baby bump and is now waiting for Boots to get out of jail so they can get married. Boots is not on board with that plan. Canada sounds good to Boots. Solo trip.

Nicole

Nicole was fine after healing from her broken nose. She and her Dad went on to become closer after that night. She calmed her partying down after the scare she had with Marcus. She and Marcus got serious and dated exclusively throughout the rest of that school year. They were in love and Nicole's Dad could not have been happier. Marcus treated his daughter with respect and he had a bright future.

Captain Russell

Dottie's mirror had crushed Russell mentally and physically. He never fully recovered and still walks with a cane on good days, with a walker on bad days.

He was vilified by the Valley citizens for having the nerve to have not given Marcus a break that night and thus was blamed for the tournament loss by the hockey team. The machine was not happy and he was basically run out of town.

He would never get appointed Chief even if he could walk without assistance again, which he could not. He was being run over by the machine – Valley High Athletics. He had gotten in the way by trying to make a stand. Like many before him, he was overmatched.

He relocated to Lake Tahoe and retired to a miserable, mainly sedentary life. He was bitter. His wife missed the Valley. He was in the process of suing Dottie's estate. He first had to locate Dottie to do that.

The jail

The jail itself was amazingly unharmed from the riot. Once the burned debris was removed the damage was almost imperceptible. Valley Jail historically shrugged off riots like a horse does a fly. The new layer of soot on the granite was yet another layer of evil added to a building that needed no more but never said no. The building consumed the evil that occurred that night and did not bat an eye. It missed Marcus and had enjoyed hosting him.

Bald Boy

Bald Boy's leg injury from the dog bite was severe. The doctor who had fixed him after the beating and the dog bite was taken aback when he first saw him on his surgery table. Where do I start? It looked like he had been beaten with an axe. The leg looked like it was set on fire and put out with a cheese grater.

He needed twenty-seven stitches over his left eye. He had his nose re-broken and set. He had his left eye cut with a scalpel like Rocky Balboa to relieve pressure on his broken orbital bone. He had his tongue stitched with thirteen stitches, which would lead to his speaking with a lisp the rest of his life. He also had four broken ribs and his testicles were swollen to the size of tennis balls. His jaw was slightly dislocated.

When he returned to the jail he became more Angel Hernandez than Bald Boy. His feared tattoo had been badly damaged by Marcus and looked like it said "Bald Box" now. Bald Box was funny, vulgar and somewhat ironic – not intimidating or scary.

His ribs never healed correctly. The nurse at the jail was called "Lady Tylenol" and that was basically all the treatment he got after returning from the hospital. He was barely able to lift his right arm over his head and his left eye was droopy. His lisp was worsening.

The guards would mimic a dog bark whenever they saw him after the riot. If they caught him off guard he would recoil in fear. He had dropped so far so fast that even rookie guards were disrespectfully barking at him. He was a low level flunky for Hector and had to fight off guys looking to make him their bitch. He lost all of his personal contraband and was bumming cigarettes off newbies.

The End

Afterword

I worked as a CO in a jail in Lawrence, MA from 1988 to 1991. Most of the jail characters are based on real inmates and most of the jail anecdotes did occur. I may have embellished them a bit in the hope that it would make a more entertaining read, but for the most part the jail stories did happen as I have written them. We sanctioned fights; there were known luggers; we shook down cells to screw with inmates; I witnessed a riot; I saw the Riot Team in action; we broke up too many fights to count.

The only Cuban inmate whom I ever encountered in the jail was the scariest man I have ever met, even to this day. His eyes were carved from the Devil's pupils. I gave him space but constantly observed him whenever we were locked up together. It was fascinating to watch him operate and rise in power during his brief stay.

I took liberty in painting the jail guards as lazy incompetents because that was needed for the story. Most of the guys I worked with were dedicated and accountable. Society should show appreciation for the job these men do and how well they do it. It is a thankless job and the sad cycle of seeing the same guys commit the same crimes over and over makes the job feel hopeless. I have the utmost respect for any and all jail personnel. It is hard to describe the total feeling of despair that immediately envelops you within the walls to somebody who has never experienced it.

CPSIA information can be obtained at www.ICGtesting.com
Printed in the USA
BVOW04s1432031013

332811BV00002B/28/P

9 781909 878884